THE
FRAT
CHAT

Books by Edward Allen Karr

The Frat Chat (Adult drama, sexy & twisted romance)
The Frat Chat 2 (Adult drama, sexy & twisted romance)
* * * * *
SERIES: Risk and the Killers
(Action/adventure/adult urban fantasy)
Below the Bay – Book One
Dying To Be Widow – Book Two
The Blood Deeper – Book Three
* * * * *
SERIES: Thrills N Kills in the Hills
(Racy, Comical Horror in Beverly Hills)
Dayzee Dazzle and the Kildare Killers – Book One
Dayzee Dazzle and Her Manic Mansion – Book Two
Dayzee Dazzle and the On-Set Onslaught – Book Three
Dayzee Dazzle and the Cadaver Collectors – Book Four
* * * * *
SERIES: Socrates Lewis Stories
(Psychological/Religious Fiction)
Crosswinds – Book One
Crossovers – Book Two
* * * * *
SERIES: Fringes Of Infinity
(Contemporary Fantasy Fiction)
Lin Finity and Her Mayhem Rising – Book One
Lin Finity in Holding On – A Novella
Lin Finity and the Words Unspoken – Book Two
Lin Finity and the Islands of Time – Book Three
Lin Finity and the Flights to Forever – Book Four
Tayo Tersoo and the Hunter of Souls – Book Five
* * * * *
SERIES: A World So Close
(Middle-grade Fantasy Adventure & Coming of Age)
Jayden Blue and the Gift to Imagine – A Prequel
Jayden Blue and the Sword in His Shadow – Book One
Jayden Blue and the Call of the Wings – Book Two
Jayden Blue and the Lair of the Iron Lions – Book Three
Jayden Blue and the Journey to Val ka'Yoom – Book Four
Jayden Blue and the Forest of Night Fallen – Book Five
Jayden Blue and the Wait of the Sun – Book Six

THE
FRAT
CHAT

Edward Allen Karr

Lakeside Letters, LLC
30628 Detroit Road, #247
Westlake, OH 44145

This is a work of fiction. Names, characters, businesses, events, and incidents are the products of the author's imagination. Any resemblance to actual persons, living or dead, or actual events is purely coincidental. Certain long-standing institutions are mentioned, but the characters are imaginary. The opinions expressed are those of the characters and should not be confused with those of the author.

The Frat Chat

First Edition, 2025
Lakeside Letters, LLC

Cover design by JD Smith Design

ISBN-13: 978-1-950886-72-2

And the voice from the burning darkness called out with zeal: "Let that facet of woman's true nature become known as a vice, a failing, a hunger deserving only of scorn. So, then, shall remain unknown forever her dual glory—as an angel that nourishes hearts and also as a mystery that confounds men's senses. Let part of what is divine about her fall so far as to never again earn any man's admitted favor. And with that falling, so, too, shall vanish forever the full splendor and incontestable power of the feminine."

– A message found in a book.

Excerpt

From Chapter 15 – No Denying the Divine

"Well, class, it seems that our resident, self-appointed substitute professor is compelling us to launch into an impromptu discussion of—"

"Divinity!"

Amos squinted at Emilio's big grin and finger pointing toward the ceiling. His first look anywhere else gave him a view of Lindsey shaking her head slowly and rolling her eyes.

"Divinity?" Amos said. "Is that allowed at this university?"

He looked around, grinning while basking in the sights and sounds of his having scored some comedic victory.

Emilio shook his head, pausing just long enough to have the majority of eyes on him, then said, "Doesn't matter. There's no escaping it."

Table of Contents

Chapter 1 – Me, Sexy and Wild?

Only the reliable ticking of the clock on the living room wall competed with the listless scraping of Lenore's frumpy slippers on the hardwood floor. Amos, exercising his usual unnaturally admirable posture where he sat at his end of the couch, watched the second hand snapping the two of them along toward their future until he could turn mostly just his eyes to watch her walk into the room.

She kept a watch on the TV, which was alive with multi-colored blinking lights but muted, and walked around the coffee table to stand where she usually sat, at the couch's other end. With the remote in her hand, she focused on flipping channels as Amos studied her quietly.

Whatever figure she kept hidden under her long thick robe had first been covered by long flannel pajamas. He couldn't see the slippers from where he sat but if he'd have leaned, he could have confirmed that loose white socks filled the gap between slipper and pant hem.

After scanning quickly along her amorphous shape, he settled his gaze on her blond hair, which she'd woven together, bound up with bands and pins, and piled up on her head, not letting a single strand stray low enough to graze a shoulder.

Satisfied with the channel, she turned.

"What?" she said while sitting, then slouching back and letting the remote rattle onto the end table.

Across the empty expanse of the couch cushions between them, ignoring the flickering light of the quietly obnoxious TV, he rubbed at his short, graying beard and said, "I'm, uh, just wondering if the house is too warm."

He pointed and continued, saying, "For, um . . ."

She smirked and said, while tidying up the robe and smoothing it out over her lap, "Oh. You're thinking these pajamas are too much again?"

"Uh, well, I do wonder. Probably that robe too."

She pulled it tighter across her chest, then tightened up the belt while gazing calmly at him. His eyes dipped just once, giving him only the briefest of glances at where a pair of breasts were suffocating behind layers of thick cloth, making confirmation of their existence unlikely.

"You should be used to it by now," she said. "And be honest—this is what you like."

Neither of them looked when the clock slipped in a few more clicks.

"No, I, uh, didn't even have to get used to it. And yeah, I do like it."

"Amos," she said and checked for any stray wisps of her tied-up, controlled blond clump of thick hair. "It was in my profile."

"That you're modest. Yes, I noticed that right away, and I love that about you."

She tipped her head, her grin not at all eager to expand into an outright smile.

"Yeah. You said in your profile that you liked that. And you must because you didn't waste any time proposing."

She showed him the back of her left hand, then wiggled her fingers around.

"A unique, custom engagement ring too. I didn't waste any time putting it on either."

He laughed once, looked down, then said, "Yes, I still can't believe my good fortune in finding you. I really do think you're perfect for me."

"So, you must love my pajamas, too, then. It's just part of what got your interest, right?"

Looking back up, he shook his head while saying, "Uh, yes. That's part of what attracted me to you."

She was just beginning to comment when he hurried to say, "Not just that, though. But yes, modesty is good."

"Well, it's not just a random lifestyle choice. I do have to maintain some kind of professional appearance."

"You surely do. Especially at your office. One might conclude that altering one's behavior and habits at home could easily spill over into one's life outside of the home."

Nodding, she said, "Yeah. I can see how that could happen."

She sighed, glanced at the TV, and said, "And besides, software's boring, but it's what I do. That persona of being demure and not flashy fits the workplace and the industry."

"And it's best to maintain that persona at home too. I wouldn't change a thing. I admire how professional you are."

"Well, thank you. You too. A very accomplished college professor. You're kind of channeled into being a proper kind of guy, too, even if you don't want to be."

"Well, but I do want to be, and it's all good. It might be the luckiest thing that happened to me—that the woman I fell for just happens to reside in a town with a university."

"With an open position for a professor, no less. In your field too."

"Psychology. Yes, how fortuitous."

"It seems that it was meant to be that I could lure you here."

"Yes, one might say that you sure did lure me. And after moving here, what? Two months ago? Already, my first lecture is tomorrow. Wish me luck."

"You don't need luck. You're good. You've been at it a while."

"Huh. Yes, for a good portion of my forty-five years—I've been slogging through the field for a while. And look at you—forty-five, too, and poised to have the company you built from nothing explode any day now."

"Well, that would be nice. We're working on one big proposal that could really get things moving. We hope to hear good news tomorrow."

He let his eyes drop to her legs, which were bent from placing her slippers against the edge of the coffee table. The clock ticked a few more times as he took in the shape of her calves hidden away under the thick flannel, and he gave her thighs only the briefest of glances before looking up and meeting her steady gaze.

"You're still worried that I'm too warm?" she said and straightened her long robe to cover more.

"Always. It's just a sign of how much I care."

"Hmm. That's nice," she said, and his eyes followed her hand reaching again toward her ankle.

She rubbed her fingertips around on a thin band of smooth skin exposed between the edge of her pant leg and the top of a thick, floppy sock.

"Are you sure that you, uh, really want to wear all that?"

While tugging the pants down, she said, "Well, of course. So, what's your first lecture going to be about tomorrow?"

He looked up, met her gaze, and said, "I'm winging it. I have nothing outlined—just an intro, get to know the students, stuff like that. Sometimes, things need to take a life of their own."

"Yeah, you're so right about that."

Another glance of his toward her ankle, which no longer offered even a sliver of a view of her, prompted another tug on the pajama pants, so he looked back up.

"They're not long enough," she said. "I know."

She scoffed and added, "Quite attractive, though, I'd bet."

"Uh, yes. Quite. They're, um, kind of sexy in their own way."

She laughed and said, "Liar. Nice of you to say that, though. This just suits my level of daring, I'd guess. But this is what you like—unless you've changed your mind?"

"Oh no, I'm not about to change my mind about that. No, Lenore, I truly do love you, so don't feel any pressure to be more daring."

"You mean that?"

"I wouldn't change a thing about you even if I could. Heck, I can't even think of anything I'd change."

"Not even the pajamas?"

He laughed and said, "No, they're quite nice. I like the robe too."

"Hmm. Well, it's all comfortable at least."

"Well, yes. But I do know that you have such an attractive figure."

"So, you're saying you want me to wear more revealing things?"

"What? No."

"If you really wanted, I could—"

"It's not necessary. I already know you look splendid. There's no need to flaunt it."

"I didn't exactly say that I'd—"

"Lenore, there's just no real need, whether one would call that flaunting or use some other descriptor. Pajamas are good. The robe too. You look quite nice."

She sighed, looked toward the bedroom, then said, "Well, I don't wear this much all the time."

Grinning, he pointed at her and said, "You simply cannot. You'd become an unwitting, tangled captive of sheets and blankets."

She didn't smile, but he added, "And pillows. You'd never get any quality sleep with thick pajamas and robes and stuff. So, it's only wise to wear—"

"Just my nightgown. Uh-huh. It would be even more comfortable if it was—"

"Shorter?" he said with his eyebrows raised.

"Um, no. No, I was going to say thinner."

"Oh, thinner. Yes, that would be practical for sleeping."

"Practical, yeah," she said. "Past my knees is practical too."

"Comfortable and modest. I believe it's a fair compromise between comfort and modesty. Wouldn't you say?"

"Uh, yeah. You already know that I value modesty. I'm sure you studied my profile carefully before making contact."

"I did indeed. Yes."

"Of course," she said, "if you were to ever change your mind and think that shorter is good, too, because—"

"No, Lenore, no," he said, chuckling. "Modest is very attractive. And I knew that you were—"

"You read that I was modest before you—"

"Fell in love with you."

She managed a smile and said, "And I love you too. Especially because you'd never think me a prude."

"Lenore, I never would think that. Besides, this,"—he scanned her up and down with a pointing finger—"is part of what I love about you. I could never find you any more attractive than I do right now. You could wear a giant brown paper bag and still be sexy and wild."

"Me, sexy and wild? Have you seen any hint that I could ever be like that?"

"Well, no. But I'll just go ahead and say it: I believe you have the shapely figure and good looks to be as sexy and wild as you want."

"Hmm. But neither of us want that."

"Uh, no, proper is good. Better. Your pajamas are kind of sexy, you know."

"You think so?"

"Mm-hmm. Even your robe."

She stretched her arms out and yawned.

"My thick robe. Yeah. And it's about time for bed. I'll go on ahead."

She stood and stretched again while he said, "I'll, uh, give you a minute, like usual, then I'll be in."

"Okay."

She pulled both sides of the robe tighter across, cinched up the belt, then walked toward the hallway to the bedroom.

As the gentle padding of her slippers faded, the clock's cadence segmented the silence in a room with a quiet, flickering screen.

* * *

Amos sat straight up with his eyes fixed on the silent TV, sometimes wincing at the strobing lights and listening to the clock, and moving only his eyes to the sounds of Lenore shuffling through the quiet house. She'd switched off the bathroom lights and fan, adding two soft clicks to the somber house in the suburbs, then scuffed her slippers along the wood floor of the hallway.

Tipping his head and holding his breath, he smirked at the sound of her flipping on the lights in the bedroom before giving the door a soft clunk to close it.

Sighing and scoffing silently while standing and clicking off the TV, he paused and turned to look toward the bedroom.

But he ambled the other way, off to make his own bedtime preparations, then quietly approached the bedroom door.

He reached out and felt the warm metal of the doorknob, and he tipped himself sideways enough to see light filling the gap below the door's bottom edge.

In a quick series of orderly and well-practiced steps, he turned the knob, swung in the door, then reached for and snapped the light switch, causing the lamps on each nightstand to deny any illumination of the woman buried under layers of blankets.

"Hey, you can leave that on," she said to the silhouette that he'd become in the doorway. "I mean, if you want."

Not moving, he said, "Well, I suppose, I mean, we could if, um—"

"Amos, not if you don't want to."

"I, uh . . . do you want to? Is that what you want?"

After a pause, Lenore cleared her throat and said, "Well, no. I was just thinking, you know, if you wanted to. Off is fine by me."

"Well, good, uh, we don't really need those lamps on."

"No. Of course not."

He closed the door, then turned his eyes to the feeble night light stuck in the wall plug across the room, which had dutifully begun its shift, giving him enough light to not cripple himself en route to his side of the bed.

Unbuttoning his shirt, he said to the vague shape in the dark folds, "Besides, I already saw you. You looked picture-perfect all tucked in."

"Hmm. You saw just part of me, that's all. You must have seen where I left the pajamas and robe, too, if you'd—"

"Looked at the hook behind the door. Yes. So," he said, chuckling, "that must mean you're completely—"

"Wearing my nightie. That's right."

"Well, it's a very nice nightie. I like it."

"Come on to bed. We both have important days tomorrow."

He'd just kicked off his pants, wearing only his boxers and a t-shirt, and he pulled open the covers while saying, "Best suggestion I've heard since the last time you said 'come to bed.'"

"You're silly."

"One might say that I'm honored at such an invitation."

"Hmm. Honored is . . . good."

"Yes, it is."

He climbed in and pulled the covers over both of them, then reached his hands around her waist.

"Oh, may I?"

"Of course," she said.

She held his shoulder with her free hand but kept the other to herself, and he leaned close enough to kiss her.

"Mm, you feel good."

"You too. See? No pajamas."

He rubbed around her waist and said, "Yes. Nice. Just this wonderful nightgown. I must say, your waist is tiny."

"You mean, compared to my . . ."

He reached for one of her breasts, began some gentle squeezing, and said, "Yes, very nice. I had no idea before I met you."

He kissed her and backed away enough that she could say, "Well, that's not something I should advertise to the world, is it? Unless you'd want me to be a little more—"

"No, of course not. It was very prudent of you to not emphasize such aspects of yourself."

While he was fondling her gently, she began folding the blankets down off of them.

He laughed, let go of her, then said, "Oh, Lenore," and fought with her just enough to pull it all back up.

His hand immediately got back to work. Under the blankets, though.

"God, you feel so good," he said as he rubbed all around. "Hmm, I wonder if the other feels good too."

"Oh, you're already busy, so I should get the other strap? I'd be, um—"

"Undressing for me. I know. But that's not at all your style."

"I wouldn't mind, uh, undressing for you."

"Hmm, lights on and now undressing too?"

"Well, we're home alone, Amos, and—"

"I'd like the honor for myself," he said, then let go of her long enough to slide the other strap down, baring the pair of them under the blankets.

Up on one forearm, he kept his other hand from getting bored with either of them.

"Oh, God," he said, keeping his hand moving from one to the other while she made sure that the blankets stayed pulled up high.

"You've been such a perfect fiancé, Amos. I love how you respect me so much and value modesty."

"Mm-hmm. I absolutely love that about you too."

She said, "Amos, it's almost completely dark in here."

"Yes, it is. Just that tiny little light way over there."

While he was busy, she moved the layers of blankets down all in one quick motion, leaving his busy hand and her breasts out in a room not nearly as dark as she'd said.

With a loud gasp, he backed his hand away and stared at her large, perfect breasts. The lacy edging of her nightgown squeezed them from where it had been pulled down just far enough to reveal two prominent features.

"Oh God, Lenore, you're—"

"Mm-hmm, Amos. Yes, it's not so bad for you to—"

He yanked the coverings back up, almost enough to smother her, and he remained propped up and staring into her eyes.

"That wasn't so bad, was it?" she said. "I mean, we're home alone, and it's not like I'm showing them off to the world."

"You never would! Oh, Lenore, I won't say that's terrible, but—"

"No, it wouldn't be terrible."

"Huh. I'll just say it's unnecessary, then. You're quite beautiful, and you don't need to do that."

"I know," she said as he leaned in to kiss her. "Forgive me?"

"Hmm," he said, grinning at her, "I'll think about it."

"Well, while you're thinking . . ."

She rolled onto her back, and she held his shoulder with one hand while the other kept the blankets under control. After giving her breasts a few quick fondles, he reached down for the bottom hem of her nightshirt, way down near her knees.

Kissing her and working the plain material up along her thighs, Amos's moving around almost folded the blankets down again, but Lenore had a solid hold on the thick layer.

He left the nightie near her waist, gave her leg and hip a few hurried rubs up and down, then shifted himself over to lie between her legs.

"Oh, Amos . . ."

"Lenore, you're so perfectly beautiful. Almost too beautiful for such vulgar activities."

He found his place and got into a steady rhythm.

"But I'll dare to take such liberties with you. Don't hate me for that, okay?"

"Hmm, such liberties. No, of course, I don't hate you, Amos. Oh, that feels good."

"Even in the dark," he said.

Looking to the side, she said, "Mm-hmm. Even . . . in the dark."

Chapter 2 – Just Appreciating Contrasts

Standing near a plain wooden lectern in the lowest area of a large lecture hall, Amos looked from side to side at seated students crowding the curving levels and rising like a noisy, distracted wave about to tumble down onto him.

"Class," he said, then exaggerated a look at his watch.

He earned a few snickers and laughs, but the even mix of male and female freshman psychology students mostly abandoned their conversations and at least looked in his direction.

"Welcome to day one of this intro to psychology class. Since it's a freshman course, I'm guessing you're all kind of new. And guess what: I'm new too. I'm professor Riley—Amos Riley. Feel free to call me Professor Amos if you want."

He paused to look around and saw that only a few were fiddling with phones or notebooks or other escapes from class. He glanced down at his work surface and spent more than a few seconds arranging everything before again looking up.

Then, he cleared his throat and continued.

"We'll get into serious coursework with our very next class, I assure you. My only goal for today is to have a conversation with you, maybe get to know each other better. I hope you always feel free to share your thoughts and observations on whatever we're discussing—maybe even on other stuff too. Whatever's on your mind."

A young man in the back row called out, "What's on your mind, then?"

Amos scanned until he found the speaker, a fit fellow with short dark hair and wearing a white t-shirt and ball cap.

"I don't believe we've met."

"I'm Emilio. I'm a, uh, philosophy major. No offense."

"None taken. Happy that you could join us. I hope you can share some of your philosophizing with us from time to time."

"As if I could help myself."

He got elbowed amid soft laughter.

"Okay. Good," said Amos.

Sweeping his eyes across all of them again, Amos said, "I only moved to town a few months ago to take this position. I don't usually like disruptions in my life, but I met someone truly special and decided to take a chance and move here. My hope is that the chaos of the move will subside, and I'll be able soon to settle into a comfortable, more stable life. That, I think, is probably the best path for anyone that—"

"I disagree," said Emilio. "Sir. Professor, sir."

"Uh, Amos is fine. And you're not wasting any time. You disagree how, Emilio?"

"That bit about a comfortable, stable life."

Amos pointed, grinning, and said, "And just like that, Emilio is veering us in the direction of a philosophy class. Very well. Let's drift over from psychology since they share a lot of common ground anyway. So, Emilio, what does your brand of philosophy tell us about living a good life?"

"Roller coaster."

Amos looked around at the quiet students, most looking at Emilio but some glancing briefly at him too.

"That's a bit short of a treatise. Expand on that, please."

"If it's comfortable and stable, it isn't going anywhere. So, it's not exactly a fun ride."

"Oh, I see. Sure. You're saying that life should be more for the thrills?"

"Uh, no. Not exactly."

Amos looked around at the confused faces, then he squinted up at Emilio.

"Alright. Life's not for sitting still but not for thrills either. I'm not sure if this is psychology or philosophy, but—"

Someone else called out, "Or both?"

Amos pointed toward the source of the comment but kept his eyes on Emilio.

"Yes. Likely both. Whatever subject matter we're wading into, it seems to be—"

"He's writing a book," someone else called out.

It took a few seconds for Amos to locate the speaker, a smiling young woman, and she added, "A philosophy book."

"Yes. That I believe," said Amos.

Looking up again, Amos said, "Emilio, you have our attention. What is it about a roller coaster that should serve as a guide to one's life if it isn't the sitting in a motionless seat or in getting the shit scared out of us? Oh, can I swear here? At this university?"

"Probably shouldn't," said a fellow in the front row.

"Uh-uh. Not recommended," said another.

"Stuff," said Amos. "Getting the stuff scared out of us. We don't want to get the university too upset."

He fixed his gaze back up at Emilio and waited. They all waited.

"It's like this: staying in one place is empty. It's kind of dead. What I mean is that just sitting there isn't good, and riding the hill nonstop isn't good either."

"What, then?"

He held both hands out, palm to palm and close together.

"The space in between. You want the hill because you were sitting still. Then, you're relieved to sit still because the hill scared the,"—he paused to look around the room—"stuff out of you. It's that passing between the two that matters. That's where your best life is."

"The contrast?" said Amos. "Like appreciating heat after being cold? Like that?"

"Yep. Not staying all comfortable and stable. Like the lives of, uh, well, most professors."

"Mine's not completely entrenched in stability. I just packed up and moved here."

"All you did was move your boring life somewhere else."

"Who said my life is boring?"

"You did. You said it's comfortable and stable. Sounds kind of dead to me."

"It's really not, Emilio. So, you're saying it should be chaotic? That's your solution to life?"

"Uh-uh. Not chaotic. Just appreciating contrasts. That's Chapter 1."

"Of your book."

"Yep. Chapter 2 will be—"

The buzzer above the door announced the end of the class period.

"Will be what?" Amos said after the alert went silent.

Emilio stood, books in hand, and looked around at everyone else filing out of their rows and toward the exit. He grinned and pointed down at Amos.

"Too late. Just stay bored, if you are bored, until next class."

The chatter and laughter rose up, and Amos didn't argue the point as Emilio and almost all of the rest began streaming out of the hall.

"Professor Amos?"

He looked toward the voice and saw a pretty girl with her hands on a stack of books in the first row.

"Yes?"

"I'm Lindsey. He, um,"—she turned to glance toward the exit, where Emilio had already passed through—"he likes to mess with professors. He should be a junior by now, but he's just a troublemaker."

"Oh, nice to meet you, Lindsey. No trouble. He, um, has some strong opinions, that's all. Will he drop out before the next class?"

"He really might! Then, he'd have to try harder at fitness modeling."

"Oh, he's a philosopher slash model, then. Unique."

"That's funny, professor. But maybe 'troublemaker' is still the best word. You should go find him in the park around lunch time. He's always there. Maybe you're the one that can talk some sense into him."

"I'm not actually a psychologist, you know."
"I know. Okay, never mind. See you next class."

Chapter 3 – A Hot Tub on Ice

Most of the midday sunlight was being choked out by the thick trees where Amos paused to buy coffee from a vendor in the park, a large square area crisscrossed with pathways, surrounded by college buildings, and teeming with students and locals.

"Thanks. Keep the change."

"I surely will. Thank you. You're new."

"Yes. It's my first day teaching at the university. Psychology."

"Oh, that stuff. All Voodoo to me. You go fill those young heads with all that learning, you hear?"

"Uh, sure. Yes. I fully intend to. Have a good afternoon."

Amos took a sip while stepping along the blacktop walkway, scanning ahead at the small groups of students at picnic tables, standing or walking around, almost all carrying or at least close to textbooks.

A second later, his eye caught a white t-shirt, and focusing for another second proved that it was Emilio up ahead, lounging with his back against a weathered table that was in unfiltered sunshine. While walking toward him, the young man he was with, a larger, bulkier, but well-dressed guy without any books or backpacks or any other student gear bumped fists with Emilio, then sauntered off in the opposite direction.

Emilio had just stuffed the last of a sandwich into his mouth when he saw Amos approaching, and he pointed at him.

"Chapter 2. You just can't wait."

"Is it that obvious?"

"No, how could it be? Walking through the park around lunch, coffee in hand, might be the first installment of your new routine, one which will become etched in granite, never to be altered in any way."

"Good one. May I?" he said, tipping his head toward the bench.

"Be my guest."

Amos sat and kept his back straight and barely using the tabletop.

"Hey," said Emilio, "I'm just kind of an asshole. Everyone knows that."

"I didn't know that."

"You do now. I was just guessing about your life being boring from what you said. I really have no clue. You can tell me, though."

"Tell you what?"

"If your life is boring. All comfortable and stable."

Amos looked away and said, "Uh, stable enough, I suppose. I don't really look for chaos."

"I never said chaos. Seriously, though, stable is a killer. Comfort zones kill."

"And you know this . . . how?"

He held Emilio's gaze until he smirked and looked away.

"I don't. Just philosophizing. The theory is sound, though."

"Yes. So, you're writing a book about it. What's Chapter 2 about?"

Emilio scoffed and picked at his teeth, then spit something out into the grass.

"Let's review. Chapter 1 is about going from hot to cold."

"Yes," said Amos, "or going from sitting still to screaming down a hill. It's about that space between, right?"

"Yep. Even better is when you have both at the same time."

"Huh? Like a roller coaster car sitting still and racing downhill at the same time? How exactly are you going to arrange that?"

"Well, no, maybe not that. Bad example. How about this: sitting in a hot tub when the temperature's low enough to freeze your ass solid?"

Amos laughed at the blue sky, then nodded and looked out across the freshly-mowed lawn.

"Alright. Yes, I can see that. That's, what? A peak human experience?"

"Shit, man, I don't know. I'm kind of making it up as I go."

"Maybe all great philosophers do that."

He waited with a grin until Emilio turned toward him, then grinned himself.

"You're alright, professor. Hey, sorry about making a scene in class."

"You didn't mean it?"

"No, I meant it—I think your life is probably boring. I'm just an asshole for saying it out loud."

"Why did you, then?"

"Well, shit, in general, I tend to talk way too much. I lose chicks over that. It seems that not all like to listen to a man babbling at such an intimate time."

"I don't believe I've ever heard anything quite like that. Huh."

"Besides spouting off too much, I think I wanted to feel that crossover moment. You know, sitting there all proper with an esteemed professor. I mean, I'm there to hang on his every word— he's a bona fide font of knowledge. And I slipped right over to being an asshole and, well, kind of tearing that professor down."

Amos waited again until he had Emilio's attention.

"How was it? That crossing over?"

"Damn good. Not only that, it was kind of a Chapter 2 thing too. I was giving you shit and at the same time, I knew you were a decent guy that didn't deserve it. Hot and cold."

"A hot tub on ice."

Emilio pointed and said, "Exactly. Hey, uh, you don't have to admit that your life is boring or anything, but maybe you'd like to get out of your lane a little anyway."

"I kind of like my lane."

"Of course. Everyone's happy buckled in that coaster car for a while. All nice and safe."

Amos scoffed and said, "Funny. Yes. So, what's your idea for my steep race to the bottom?"

"Shit, you make it sound like something self-destructive. No, man, just something fun. Sometimes, just something different, even if it isn't anything special, can give you a boost."

"Well, one might say that a boost isn't a bad thing."

"Doesn't have to be, no. Whatever, professor, I'll try to constrain myself during your class time."

"It's your class time, too, Emilio. Which makes it sound like you plan to keep attending my lectures."

"Yep, of course. You need that drama to keep everyone else awake."

Amos laughed, sipped his coffee, then sighed loudly.

"Yes. I like psychology, but it could easily be a snooze fest if I'm not creative with it."

"Happy to help. Hey, after class tomorrow, coffee's on me, alright?"

"Sure, Emilio. Does letting you treat me to coffee count as getting out of my lane?"

"Not a chance, professor. Uh-uh."

Chapter 4 – I Like Approval

The afternoon sun made a lackluster effort to reach into the quiet house when Amos swept open the front door. He paused, hand on the knob, just long enough to see a dormant TV and two sweeps of a second hand tracing circles on the far wall, but no one was close enough to greet him after his first day on his new job.

Sighing but grinning, too, he closed the door quietly and dumped his keys noisily on the small wood table near the door, then held himself still, his breath, too, and listened. After a few seconds, with no sounds of footsteps or any happy voice calling to him, he smirked and aimed his steps toward the kitchen.

"Lenore," he said, standing in the doorway. "I wasn't sure you were home."

"Oh, just focusing on dinner. Spaghetti sound good?"

She'd only glanced over her shoulder as she faced the stove while stirring things around in a big pot. It took only a second for him to scan her up and down, studying a shape that offered few details and was cloistered away beneath baggy pants and an untucked, oversized long-sleeved shirt. At the very top, her hair was conspiring to conceal its natural luster and appeal by mounding itself into a sloppy knot.

"You're amazing. A productive day at the office, and you still manage to whip up some kind of dinner. It was a productive day, wasn't it? How did things go?"

She turned with one hand on her hip, the other keeping the handle of a long wooden spoon planted in the pot.

Before speaking, she blew out a breath, then shook her head.

"Uh-oh," he said before letting her say any more.

"Right. We didn't get that client. At least not yet. She said she just wanted more time to consider our capabilities, but that's usually just a polite rejection."

"Ooh, a rejection. Not good."

"Never. I like approval—there's nothing better than unmistakable, enthusiastic approval. So, life goes on. How was your day? Do any good professor stuff?"

He pulled out a chair at the kitchen table, sat, then drummed the fingers of both hands and kept his eyes on hers.

"It's like I was still at my old position, just with different faces looking back. It was fine, though, don't get me wrong. It just didn't seem all that new."

"You're bored already?"

"What? No, I'm not saying that. It's just all kind of familiar. Same subject being broadcast to a new crowd of students. I think maybe I can develop more of a connection with the students here, though. Too soon to tell."

"That sounds promising."

"Yes. Hey, you didn't, um, wear that to the office, did you?"

"No, Amos. That would have killed that contract even quicker. No, I changed into more comfortable stuff as soon as I got through the door."

"Comfortable. Yes, that's good. You look comfortable."

Facing her work at the stove, she sighed but didn't comment.

A few seconds later, over her shoulder, she said, "Dinner's ready."

She turned with a loaded, steaming plate, then walked the few steps and set it in front of him.

"Thanks. Mm, it looks good."

"You're welcome. Maybe I can't land the big contracts, but I can slop up dinner well enough."

"Uh, yes, but there will be other big contracts. And no one would call this slop."

She set her plate down and took her seat opposite him, picked up a fork, then paused and held his gaze.

"Thanks. About both contracts and slop. Amos,"—she let her fork rest on the table—"about last night. We—"

"I really didn't mind all that much, uh, you being more of an, um, exhibitionist."

Pointing at him with her fork, she said, "Yes, but you sure don't want that, like you've said in your profile and every message we sent."

"Hey, I never exactly said anything about—"

"Not in so many words, Amos, no. It's just . . . I know how you are, and I shouldn't be doing things with the blankets like that, even if it's just playing around."

"And you don't really want to, you know, be more—"

"I want to keep you happy. That's number one. That's not so bad, is it?"

"Well, I am happy. Yes, I'm trying to, uh, loosen up. It's just that I'm trying to, uh, be—"

"A role model of a professor. I know. All proper. And I love that. It's fine. Really, things are fine."

"So, you don't feel like you'd rather—"

She scoffed and said, "Be an exhibitionist? How have I ever given you that impression? Oh no, that would just feel weird. Besides, I know you like me being more on the modest side."

He laughed and poked at his food.

"Long pajamas."

"And a long robe."

"Huh," he said. "A really long robe. Which is perfectly fine because I already have a good idea what's under all that."

"And you wouldn't want me to parade myself around, would you? I don't think you'd want a woman like that."

"Decidedly not. No. No parades requested."

"So, the pajamas are what you like."

"Yes."

Grinning, she added, "And the robe?"

"The robe is quite attractive and, one might say, adorable."

She looked down at her plate but still didn't make a move for it.

"Oh, the lights," she said. "Really, the dark is fine. It's good."

"Yes, no blaring lights are needed. I'm glad you understand. The night light is plenty."

She looked up, nodded, and said, "Yeah, of course. A little bit of light is enough."

"Yes."

"Okay."

Each took a bite, focusing on the task of twirling spaghetti around their forks.

"I, uh, have some yard work to get to after dinner."

She sighed, gave a glance up and saw him still looking down at his plate, then said, "Oh, the yard. Yeah. Well, I have some project notes to go through, so . . ."

Chapter 5 – Just a Sexy Party Favor

Lenore scoffed at the neat but unremarkable manicured nails on the two fingers that were about to spread open the mini blinds to give her a view of the yard. She saw that her day at the office hadn't scuffed them at all and neither had preparing dinner, and they looked almost as modest as most of her wardrobe.

Prying open a small gap allowed one eye to see Amos many steps away at the edge of the property, fighting with large shears and trying to even out the top of the shrubs.

Glancing down only long enough to tap her phone a few times, she got her eyes back on his progress, and his distance from the house, while the rock-and-roll ringback played.

"Lenore, hey."

"Hi, Laura. Bad time?"

"Never. Well, shit, maybe if I'm doing something perverted."

"You're not?" Lenore said with a laugh.

"Not at this exact moment, no. Give me a minute, though."

"Funny. You always make me kind of jealous."

"Uh-oh. Same old thing, huh?"

"I love Amos, I really do."

"Uh-huh. Yep."

"It's just that he's so . . . proper."

"Huh. You wanted to add some kind of adjective there. Try it again."

Lenore smiled, still watching Amos at work, and said, "He's so . . . damn proper."

"There you go. Feel better?"

"Like that would be enough. Look, I shouldn't be venting to you all the time about the same old—"

"Yeah, you should. Lenore, we've been friends forever. Shit, we could even be twins."

"Yeah, I know. We could probably change lives and it'd be weeks before anyone knew."

"Yep. So, my dear twin girl, go ahead and vent."

"Alright. You know I really do care for Amos."

"You work too much, and I told you that meeting someone online was never going to—"

"Yeah, you warned me. But he's a good guy, and I knew what I was getting into. We chatted and messaged a lot, and I knew he was, uh, kind of—"

"A prude? Gigantic stick up his—"

"Laura! I'm not trying to be mean or anything. It's just making me crazy."

"What, exactly? Come on. Spill it."

"Alright. Since you asked."

"Yep, it's why I called you."

"You're too much. Alright. It's just, I'm not an exhibitionist or anything, but he insists on the lights being off, and we have to keep the blankets pulled up, and he—"

"Oh my God. Lenore, you're too gorgeous for a life like that. Have you tried to, uh, you know, tempt him?"

"Last night, yeah. I pulled the blankets down, which gave him a good view of my breasts, even with just the night light on."

"Well, good. Drove him crazy, right?"

"Huh. No. He covered me back up."

"Well, shit. Oh, Lenore. What did I just tell you he was?"

"You said he's a . . . prude."

"Try that again," Laura said, laughing into her phone.

"Alright. He's a damn prude. And I know, I swear I know, that if I keep pushing that, it wouldn't be long before he'd decide I'm just not . . . oh, shit, not damn proper enough."

"Good for you. You didn't need me poking you to spit that out."

"Oh, Laura, that's another thing."

"What? Something I said?"

"Yeah. Spitting it out," she said with a droll laugh. "When we were just getting to know each other, he made some negative comments about women he knew, ones that would, uh, give . . ."

"Head?"

"Oral. I was going to say oral."

"Such harsh language you're using! He's got you beat down pretty good, Lenore."

"Hmm. Maybe. Anyway, I'm just left wondering how he couldn't want that. I mean, who wouldn't, right?"

"No one would turn that down. Not from you. You're gorgeous."

"Aw, thanks, but it's not like I'm going around offering."

"Hmm."

"What was that? Anyway, if I ever suggested that again, he'd probably think I'm actually a harlot."

"Tell me he never actually used that word."

"Huh. More than once."

"Oh my gosh. Well, Lenore, you should stand there totally naked the next time he walks into the bedroom."

"Oh, he would die."

"Or better yet, get on your hands and knees and get that ass pointing right at him. Give him some dirty talking too."

"Dirty talk? About what?"

"You'll know when you get started. Just say what you want, what you'll do, what he should—"

"Laura, he'd have a heart attack. And if he survived, he wouldn't even pack—he'd just catch the first flight back, and that would be that."

"Which, as I've been saying, is about how it's going to end up anyway."

"God, I don't know. This helps, though—venting to you. But it's not enough—I'm almost sure I'll have to call off this engagement. I don't think there's any way to fix this . . . situation."

Lenore listened to the laughter for few seconds, then said, "Fine, Laura. This goddamn situation."

"The F-bomb would have been better. Hey, I knew there'd come a day. You gave the guy a chance."

"You think I should just end it? I mean, he really is a good guy."

"Yeah, a guy who wants to be a saint or something. Yeah, you should end it. You'll never be happy with all that. Shit, I think you've already made up your mind."

"Uh, almost. Yeah, Laura. It's just not easy."

"Hey, maybe do it like a bandage: just rip the thing off."

"You think?"

"Oh, hey, wait. I got another idea. Oh, it's a good one too."

"What?"

"Well. Remember back in college, how—"

"You weren't there long."

"Uh, no. It wasn't for me. But we did some cheerleading and had some laughs. And you won't admit it, but you were always kind of, uh, envious, maybe? Of how I just had my fun and said the hell with it."

"I'll admit it. Yeah, and I still am jealous."

"Wishing you were having more fun?"

"Hmm. I try not to think about it too much. I might not stop."

"That's my point. I never gave you any steamy details, but you know that I still have some wild times, right?"

"Well, sort of. You're kind of reliving your past with—"

"It isn't past, and it's not about reliving anything. Young guys, Lenore. There's just no comparison. God, they're like animals."

"And you still go to that frat house?"

"Uh-huh. More often than I'll admit. So, here's the thing, sexy blonde that could be my absolute, identical—"

"Uh-oh. No, no, no. Don't even say that I should—"

"Yeah. Oh, yeah. Take my place. Just the one time, and no one will know the difference."

"I couldn't do that."

"Here's the sweet thing: you don't have to do anything. You just let those young studs do it all."

"Laura, that's crazy."

"No crazier than you wearing ten layers of flannel for a guy that's campaigning for sainthood."

"It's not that bad. It's only about . . . two layers. I've always been curious, though. What exactly happens?"

"You want the short version?"

Lenore caught her breath at the sight of Amos dropping the shears, wiping his brow, then looking toward the house.

"Yeah, make it quick—he's coming back inside."

"Alright. You just show up, wait for them in the room that's kind of special just for that, and—"

"What? You said 'them?' You mean, it's not just the class president, or some guy that won a raffle, or maybe—"

"Uh-uh. Oh God, Lenore, it's not just one of them. Tell me you've never thought of doing something so bad like that."

"Oh, Laura, maybe back in the day. But I'm forty-five, and the guy or guys there are what, twenty?"

"Crazy, huh?"

"Yeah. Anything else? Hurry, I need to go."

"Yep. The most important thing: you don't ever say no."

"Because—"

"Because you're just a sexy party favor."

"Oh, seriously?"

"Uh-huh. You're just something to be used for sex."

Giggling nervously, Lenore said, "I bet the lights are on too."

"Enough. Yeah, I'm nothing but a naked party favor for them, and I'm not keeping a damn thing secret."

"Oh my God. Um, I got to go. I'll call you soon."

"Sure. Let me know, sexy party favor that could be my twin."

"Even our hair. Yeah."

"You haven't cut it, then, right?"

"No. Even though Amos wants me to. He bugs me about that a lot, so I tend to keep it all tied up."

"Oh, well, a sexy party favor would let that all down. She'd show that off along with every bit of her skin."

"Oh my God."

"That's being touched everywhere."

"Oh my. Um . . ."

Laura waited a few seconds, then said, "Ha. You're already thinking about it."

"I, uh . . ."

Laura only laughed again, so Lenore said quickly, "Maybe I am! Got to go! Bye!"

Grinning, she tapped to end the call and stowed the phone just as the back door squealed open.

Chapter 6 – She's Always Blindfolded

"You should be nicer, Emilio."

He scowled while looking up from his seat at a picnic table in the park, a hot dog wrapped in a napkin poised for another bite.

"Lindsey, you don't know shit. You mean with that new guy, right?"

"Professor Amos, yeah. He's nice. Give him a chance."

"I don't give anyone a chance."

He glanced down with a smirk at her bare legs, bounded by shorts up top and sneakers at the bottom.

"Hey, I'd give you a chance, though."

Looking into her eyes, which moved with her shaking head and lack of a smile, he added, "Private tutoring is what you need. How about it?"

"That line works for you?"

He grinned and said, "There has to be a first time."

"Huh. Not today. Really, he's a nice guy, and you should—"

"Make an important call, yeah," he said while taking out his phone. "Beat it. Unless you need some special schooling. Don't ask for what—you already know."

With a scoff and exaggerated rolling of her eyes, she turned and strode away, and he postponed dialing to leer at the backs of her legs until she was well along the asphalt path.

"Hey," said Brock through the phone. "What's up, Emilio?"

"Usual. Dodging a class. Hanging in the park. Almost scored a fine little thing named Lindsey."

"Good for you. Almost isn't anything to celebrate, though."

"Yeah, for sure. Hey, when's the next party night at your house?"

"Coming right up. Got one scheduled for Saturday. Shit, biggest one ever."

"Numbers, you mean?"

"Uh-huh. Big turnout. Like, unbelievable."

"That's hilarious—you don't really sit around talking."

"No, man, we call it the Frat Chat, but that's a lie. No one is there to talk. Shit, if word got out about what we're really doing."

"I'm surprised you ever told me."

"Beer. Makes for all kinds of surprises."

"So, this Saturday, huh? Who's the, uh, guest of honor this time?"

"Same one."

"It's been a while for me. I don't even remember her. What's her name?"

"Shit, like I'd tell you. I don't tell anyone. Man, I'm the only one that sets it up, and I barely spend any time with her. That's how our deal works."

"Do I know her? She in classes?"

"What? You really don't remember. God, no. Maybe a hundred years ago. That's exaggerating. She's older but has a killer body."

"How much older?"

"Like, twice our age. She loves the young studs," he said, laughing.

"Uh, that sounds kind of—"

"No, you don't get it. This woman is built and more importantly, she'll do anything. I mean, anything."

"My kind of woman."

"So, what's your interest? You going to finally drop by again?"

"I'm thinking about it. Saturday, huh?"

"Yeah. Why now? You've had a standing invite since I met you."

"It's like this: I have someone I'd like to bring. Does that sound alright?"

"Could be. Let's hear the story."

"Leverage. I can't keep flunking classes like you jocks."

"Hey, now. I'm pre-med too."

"Oh, I don't mean you, then. It's just that I have zero value to the school. Really, no one gives a shit."

"Yeah, I get that. How does bringing a buddy help you with flunking classes and getting your ass tossed out?"

"Because he's a professor."

"Oh, no way. Seriously?"

"Oh, yeah. If I get him there, even just showing up, I got leverage. And if he joins in the fun, I got his ass good."

"Top of the class for you. Shit, yeah. Alright, it's probably a stupid plan but hell, let's do it anyway. Bring your boy, and maybe he'll party like everyone else."

"Cool. Thanks. Hey, what about that babe I just made an offer?"

"What about her?"

"Maybe I should bring her too? Maybe that's more her thing."

"Oh, yeah, why else would a babe shoot you down, huh?"

"Wasn't even thinking that. But yeah, maybe that's it."

"Hey, I don't know. We've never tried that before. It's possible our star attraction might like that too. Who knows? She seems up for just about anything. That would be a hell of a surprise for her."

"How so?"

"Because she stays blindfolded. Remember that?"

"Oh, that's right. That kind of spiced shit way up."

"Yeah, exactly. So, she'd already be started on your cute little girlfriend from the park before she knows exactly what she's doing."

"She'd figure that out pretty damn quick, Brock."

"Yeah. The fun will be seeing if she stops. I'd bet she doesn't miss a beat."

"So, you think she'd like that, huh?"

"I have no reason to think that but shit, I've wondered. Just my perverted nature. Hell, maybe I'll schedule an all-girl Frat Chat for— no, wait, it would be some other kind of chat. Well, you get the idea."

"Oh, wow, yeah. You could sell tickets just to be in the audience for that. Huh, she's always blindfolded. You make her do that?"

"Man, it was her idea. She's a total sex freak. She says it's more exciting that way. Leave your would-be conquest out in the cold somewhere this Saturday, though. Maybe I'll sneak a babe into the mix next time. We'll see."

"You really do have some kind of perverted nature going on."

"Thank you."

Chapter 7 – A Crazy Idea

Lenore blinked a few times and looked around the room, which had the benefit of only the weak night light plugged into the far wall. Sitting against a stack of pillows, clutching the blankets high up to her chin, she scoffed silently at hearing Amos treading around the house before joining her.

Before his footsteps hinted that he was on his way there, she tipped the blankets out and looked down at her chest. The thin line of lace along the top wasn't even close to allowing any cleavage to show, and she drew in a deep breath, expanding her lungs.

She held it for a few seconds, then scoffed and let the air seep back out, then she resumed the full blockade of blankets up high.

But she stayed seated, her eyes on the door.

Through which she heard approaching footsteps, then a light turn of the knob, and Amos paused there, eyes not ready for such low levels of light.

"Oh," she said, "watch you don't trip. Hit that switch if you need it."

The clock from the living room wall reached out and kept Amos's pause from being too silent. It couldn't shorten the duration of it, though.

"Uh, really?"

"I, uh, might have left a shoe out there somewhere. You could trip."

His silhouette remained partway in the hall, partway in the bedroom, and with a hand still on the doorknob.

"A shoe?"

"Mm-hmm. Oh, and with the lights on, you might have a view since this blanket is somehow too warm for me tonight."

More ticking from the clock.

She saw his free hand reach for the switch, but he froze into a cardboard cutout of himself.

"Yeah, too warm," she said. "You want some light, right? In case I, um, you know. Didn't feel so shy or modest."

"But you, uh, really don't ever, I mean . . ."

"First time for everything?"

"Um, you, uh, you—"

"Bad idea. Never mind. Just watch for loose shoes."

"I didn't mean that—"

"It's okay, Amos. Come on. The lights off are fine."

"Alright."

She leveled the pillows and laid herself back down, kept the blanket pulled up high, and listened as he closed the door and trudged slowly toward the bed. With the sounds and jostling of him pulling back his side of the covers and sitting, she shifted over onto her side, facing away.

Still seated, he said, "It's just that—"

"Amos, it's okay. You know how modest I am. It's a, um, relief to not try pushing myself like that."

"Maybe next time, if you really want to, uh, if you—"

"You want to hear what I was going to try?"

"Uh, sure. I am curious. You sure you want to even talk about it?"

"Well, I guess I could try. I was nervous, but I was going to—oh, I was sitting up when you opened the door."

"You were?"

"Uh-huh. And my plan, if I could get myself to do it, was to let the blanket down after you put on the light."

"The blanket."

"Yeah. So, you'd see my nightgown pretty clear."

"That's, uh, that would have been—"

"I probably couldn't have done it, but I was thinking of slipping the straps down too."

"You were going to do that? With the lights on?"

"Mm-hmm. Well, I don't know if I really would have. But you would have had a, well, a pretty good view. Of them."

"Them. Wow. Um, but you're not really—"

"Not an exhibitionist, no. Uh-uh."

"I kind of like that you're—"

"That I'm not. I know. You weren't just saying all that stuff when we were just getting to know each other."

"Well, no, I wasn't just, uh, making up stuff."

"Hey, it was just a crazy idea. Come on. It's late."

He leaned himself down on the sheets, kept his back to hers, and pulled the covers up over himself.

"Goodnight, Amos."

"Goodnight, Lenore. Sweet dreams."

"Okay. I think I'll have a few. You too."

Chapter 8 – Scared About Going to Hell

Amos had just taken a breath and was about to address the talkative, restless class when Lindsey spoke first.

"Hello, Professor Amos."

He turned his head enough to face her and said, "Hello, Lindsey. Good to see you here for class."

"I'm here too," Emilio said loudly from the high back row.

Amos grinned up at him and said, "And it's good to see you here, too, Emilio. How's that book coming along?"

"What book? I made that up."

Amos looked around at the laughing faces, then shook his head and grinned down at his notes.

"Well, one might say that you should consider writing it. If you—"

"Heck, professor, you could say it."

"I think I just did."

"No, not really. You kind of pushed that idea off on someone else."

Amos smiled and waited for the laughter and snickering to subside, then said, "Chapter 3?"

"Huh?"

"You seem to be generating a backlog of ideas for that book that I, not some unnamed individual, suggest that you write. We were up to Chapter 2 yesterday."

"Oh, I get it. Yeah. Well, since it's your suggestion, sure, I'll write the book."

Amos gave him a thumbs-up sign, then looked left to right at the rest of the students.

"So, I thought we'd begin taking a serious look at psychology by—"

"By living it?"

He grinned first, then looked up at Emilio, who also showed a generous grin.

"Ah," said Amos. "Roller coasters. Hot and cold. Things like that."

"Hey," said Emilio, acting like the thought just occurred to him, "maybe mix that all up. Extra points for that."

"Let me see," said Amos, looking up while scratching at his short whiskers. "I shiver in the seat while it's sitting still, then roast while I'm screaming down the hill?"

Most heads in the room turned toward the back to watch Emilio give his response.

But all he did was point at Amos and shake his head for a few seconds.

"Well, that's telling."

"What is?"

"You're scared about going to Hell."

The class squirmed into a mix of scoffing, giggling, and light swearing.

"I'm what? How did you come up with that?"

"Chapter 4? You're alright if I mix you up in Chapter 4?"

"Sure. Enlighten us, Emilio."

"Gladly. Some instinct, maybe a fear, got you to link unbearable heat with traveling downward, which is a common way to describe the path to Hell."

"He's a philosopher!" said Lindsey. "Kind of a butt-head, though."

"Hey," Emilio said, pointing toward her in the front row. "You might be headed there yourself. Sooner than you think."

"I think you're reaching just a bit," said Amos.

"Oh, am I? Consider your choice of words, which you can be sure will appear in Chapter 4. You could have been only warm as you traveled quickly down the hill. Oh, no. That wouldn't describe your mad descent. No, you were roasting. And screaming? Yeah, you were screaming. Screaming and roasting. Sorry, professor. Sounds like you're going to Hell."

Only a few were laughing, and nearly all were watching Amos, who looked around the room calmly before smiling up at Emilio.

"Chapter 5 shouldn't take you much time, philosopher Emilio."

"No? Why not?"

"Just one letter."

"Uh . . ."

"Yes. The letter 'F.'"

Emilio waved both arms up and down as he looked around the room at the cheering and laughing, then he focused again on Amos.

"Well played, professor. Well played indeed. Chapter 6 should then be the real fun."

"How so?"

"Once one accepts that they've failed, they got nothing to lose. Shit, they just go nuts after that."

"Uh-oh," said Lindsey. "You said shit."

"I heard him," said someone across the room. "He did say shit."

Amos was grinning and shaking his head, and they continued.

"He shouldn't be using that kind of language," another said while laughing.

Lindsey raised her hand, and Amos scoffed and gestured toward her.

"What was that word you shouldn't have used yesterday, Professor Amos?"

He blew out a deep breath as the entire class waited quietly.

"Shit. That was the word."

From the back row, Emilio laughed and called out, "Going to Hell!"

Chapter 9 – They Call It the Frat Chat

"Thanks for the coffee."

Amos leaned his straight back against the tabletop, much like Emilio was doing, and took a sip while looking around the park.

"You earned it," Emilio said. "I kind of got on a roll today."

"That's not an apology."

"Nope. Avoid that like the plague."

"Huh," said Amos. "You could probably plan on rewriting Chapter 5, you know."

"Thanks. Chapter 6 is where all the real action is, though."

"Oh, right. Where I go to Hell."

"Yep. Well, no, I only suggested that you might think that. You seem like a decent guy. You still have a chance."

"You're too generous. Not just with the coffee."

"Anytime. Hey, that fun back in class didn't get to you, did it? You seem a little down."

"Maybe it's the chaos of moving. Yeah, I am kind of dragging a little."

"The word 'maybe' almost always precedes the exact truth."

"Alright. It's just that relationships sometimes take some extra effort."

"I hear you. You're giving me another chapter, aren't you?"

"Yes, Emilio. That's what it's all about. I can't wait to read that book."

"In the meantime, ride that coaster."

"Yes. I'll ride that coaster."

"Hey, that guy I was talking with yesterday right here, Brock, is the head guy at a frat house, a big one. He—"

"Isn't a psych major?"

"Not even close. Unless you call football psychiatric. I think he does pre-med just for kicks too. Anyway, he puts on this, uh, get-together thing at their house, and they call it the Frat Chat. Just a hang out, good talk, a few drinks. Stuff like that. Maybe you should drop by."

"Oh, thanks, but I don't know. I mean, I—"

"You want to stay buckled up in your safe little coaster car. Ooh, no scary hills—afraid it might be just a hot ride to Hell."

Amos could barely stop his smile long enough to take a long sip of hot coffee. With that finished, he scoffed, still looking out at the scene.

"Nothing is ever that safe."

"Or that overheated and making you scream. Yep. For sure, professor. Hey, just so you know, it's not just all guys. There are girls there, too, and no one can say that things somewhere, in some room somewhere, will stay all nice and clean."

"Huh. So, the girls might not be there to chat?"

"God, the guys hope not," Emilio said, laughing. "But that scene is easy to avoid. Just come by. Hang out a while and have a cold beer. Get your mind off of your one-way trip to . . ."

"Marital bliss?"

"Your words," said Emilio. "Not mine. Very revealing."

"Great—I'm writing your next chapter already. Huh. When and where is the Frat Chat?"

* * *

Dressed in a tasteful, muted color pantsuit and with her hair up, Lenore sat in her small office, a printed report in her left hand while her right kept data scrolling on her laptop's screen.

She looked up when an employee of her small custom software company appeared at her open door and said, "Coming, Lenore? Working through lunch will just wear you down."

"Oh, Shirley, I don't know. What's on the menu for you all today?"

"We were thinking that taco place over by—"

Her silenced phone buzzed softly and vibrated around beside her keyboard.

"Never mind," said Shirley. "Could be a client. Better take that."

Lenore picked up the phone while saying, "Bring me back some kind of sampler, alright? Some variety sounds good."

Shirley pointed and nodded, then backed away while closing the door.

"Oh boy," Lenore said, smiling at the caller ID while tapping it. "Laura. What's going on?"

"You tell me, Lenore. Made up your mind yet?"

"What? No, you can't be serious. That's fun to hear you talk about it, but I don't think—"

"So, you're saying things are improving at home? Like, in bed?"

Lenore scoffed and said, "You sure get right to it, don't you? No. Since you asked, I'll tell you that if anything, it's getting worse."

"Tell me. What happened?"

"Well, I was thinking about what you said, the whole idea of—"

"You taking my place. Uh-huh. That's a good start—it's on your mind."

"It's not on my mind. I just kind of, I don't know, remembered our conversation."

"Sure. Uh-huh."

"And then, I thought I'd, um, try with Amos again, just to see what would happen."

"Try again how? Come on, don't make me fight for details."

"Okay. It was bedtime. Like always, I got ready first and got in bed. I was—"

"Details, Lenore. What were you wearing?"

"I guess that's kind of important. Alright, just one of my nightgowns that I wear to bed."

"Like some tiny little thing that barely covers anything? Something to drive him crazy?"

"Uh, no," she said, scoffing. "Uh-uh. It's, uh, modest. It, uh, covers everything."

"That's horrible. What a waste."

"And I was under the covers."

"I'd call that more of a crime. That's how your so-called bedtime starts? You sneak into bed, hide under the blankets, and he just wanders around the house and drops in to see you?"

"You make it sound so pathetic. It's not like—"

"Sorry, it's pathetic," Laura said, laughing.

Lenore laughed, too, and said, "Alright. Yeah, it is. So, anyway, the lights were off and when he opened the door, I made up some reason for him to have to turn on the lamps by the bed."

"What reason? You didn't just tell him you wanted to show off your naked body?"

"Laura! No, I told him that I might have left a shoe on the floor, and I didn't want him to trip on it."

"Reasonable. Alright. Let me guess: he didn't turn the lights on."

"No, he didn't. He—"

"Back up. What were you going to do if he did flip the switch?"

"I was just going to show him my breasts."

"The lucky bastard. I can tell they haven't changed since college."

"Oh, they kind of have," she said, then giggled and added, "they're bigger. I'll take this chance to say they're actually, um, perfect."

"Well, that would be one hell of a sight. So, if he had hit the lights, he would have had a good look, then maybe he would have jumped right—"

"Oh, no, Laura. He probably still wouldn't have jumped on me. I had to try, though."

"Sorry, Lenore, but he's a dumb bastard. Maybe he would have stared, at least."

"Well, that would have been fine too. I was all psyched up for it."

"Tell me about that."

"You were a psych major before you dropped out, right?"

"Yep. That hot professor paid me to leave after the stories about us got out."

"Oh, I remember him."

"The other one too."

"Oh. Yeah, there was—"

"There was that counselor too. I guess I didn't have a good focus on the books, huh?"

"No, you didn't. Alright, yeah, I was psyched up. I was sitting up, the blanket was out of the way, and I was going to be a tease, slip the straps down, then just show them."

"Because you wanted to show them off. You wanted eyes on them, right?"

"Well, yeah. I mean—"

"You wanted to strip that nightie out of the way and just get those breasts, which are even bigger these days, out for some appreciative eyes?"

"Yeah. Is that so much to ask?"

"Not at all. Sorry, but he's a fool. You know who isn't a fool?"

"Who?"

"Every guy that you'll show them to at the frat house."

"Laura! I never said I'd do that."

"True. But can you imagine it? Just imagine the look you'll see in their eyes when you offer those to—"

"Showing. We were only talking about showing."

Laura scoffed and said, "You think that would be enough for those young studs? Oh, please, Lenore. No, just you being there is already offering. And not just your breasts."

"What exactly happens when you, uh, offer yourself?"

"A lot. That's all I'm saying. You'll find out for yourself."

"I never said that—"

"A lot while you're wearing your cheerleader uniform."

"What?"

"Uh-huh. You still have it, right?"

"Well, yeah, but I—"

"All of it? That sexy t-shirt top too?"

"No, not that. I replaced it with something similar. But it's, um . . .."

"What?"

Lenore giggled and said, "It's tighter. I told you, they're bigger now."

"Okay, good, plan on that. No bra, though. Then, when—"

"Laura! I never said I was going to take your place Saturday."

"You're thinking about it. Don't try lying to me, Lenore. I know you too well."

Lenore sighed and said, "You do know me well. Okay, sure, the thought crossed my mind."

"What thought? Give me some details."

"You're too much. Alright, just the excitement of, um, something new."

"Dressed like a cheerleader?"

"You did say that. And if I was going to take your place, I'd have to."

"Yep. Hey, you think college guys would like your breasts?"

"Laura, you're impossible."

"Answer."

"Fine. Yeah, they'd like them."

"Try again."

Lenore cleared her throat, then said, "They'd, um, love them."

"Yes, they would. Oh, Lenore, they sure appreciate mine. It feels damn good to be sexy and appreciated like that. So? Saturday?"

The seconds crawled past as Lenore closed her eyes and leaned back in her swivel chair. After a modest scoff, a smile appeared.

"I'll meet you for a glass of wine Saturday. How's that?"

"It's a good start. I'll get you prepped, make sure you could pass as me, then—"

"Only the drink, Laura. That's all I'm promising."

"Good girl. You're going to have to kick the guy out soon anyway. You deserve a break."

"That might all be true. I'm not done trying, though. I'll see how things go. But I don't know about what you're—"

"Hey, no pressure. Just a drink. But, uh, maybe, until then, you should . . ."

"I should what?"

"Let your imagination go."

"I can do that. And I can have a glass of wine with you."

"Yep, I heard you. You said just a glass of wine."

Chapter 10 – Made to Attract Attention

She tipped her head from side to side, then shook it a few times, getting her long, thick blond hair to sway around behind her. Then, Lenore picked up her efforts, snapping it around, and got strands of it to bounce over to the front and lay on her chest.

With both hands, she reached up and raked her fingers in, then puffed it up and let it drop onto her back, then she brushed at each side and tucked stray strands behind her ears. She'd just begun a smile and a closely watched unbuttoning of her blouse when someone rapped on the front door.

"Oh, dammit,"

She redid the button, grabbed a plain brown scrunchie from the dresser, then hurried out of the room and toward the door while gathering it all up with one hand.

Still gripping a thick bunch of hair near her scalp, she flipped the dead bolt with a clunk. Seeing the doorknob turn immediately, she stepped back just as Amos swung in the door.

"Lenore. Hi," he said, looking up at the hair gathered up in her hand.

"Hi, Amos. Just, uh, redoing the hair. It loosens up sometimes."

"No one would doubt that. It's a lot of hair to keep under control like that."

He glanced back at the door, then said, "Didn't expect the dead bolt. Are there burglars running loose out there?"

She laughed and said, "No, of course not. I must have hit that by accident."

After a quick turn, she began walking toward the kitchen and finished up her hair with both hands, confining almost all of it into a neat bundle. He followed closely behind after dumping his keys on the table near the door.

"The hair looks good. Up like that, I mean. It matches your professional persona."

"Oh, that. Yeah, it sure does."

"When's the last time I saw it down?"

She turned to sit at the kitchen table, and he paused in the doorway to glance around the kitchen.

"Why, just the other day, I think. You see it down all the time. Don't tell me you don't remember."

"Oh, uh, yes. Of course, I remember. It's quite a sight. Glamorous, even, one might say. But up is good too. I like it up."

"Of course."

She tipped her head toward a large pot on the stove, where a lid was getting rattled lightly by thin wisps of steam.

"I hope soup is alright. There's garlic toast going into the oven soon too."

"You're remarkable. Yes, that all sounds good," he said and took his usual seat opposite her. "Maybe we should break tradition and have a glass of wine with dinner too?"

"We could. Sure. What's the occasion?"

"Nothing big. Just, you know my general perception of students these days: kind of lazy, uncaring, and not really deep thinkers."

"Yeah. You have mentioned that. You just had enough of them and decided to have wine with dinner?"

"What? No, that's not it. There's just this one fellow in the intro psych class that kind of breaks that stereotype. He's definitely a deep thinker, even in class. We've had coffee in the park, and he's got some interesting perspectives."

"Maybe it's from your excellent teaching? He might have been an actual dope until you put him on a path to excellence."

"Hey, that was nice. Path to excellence. You think I could do that?"

"Sure. You're a truly dedicated professional and a good role model too."

"I do try. God, I really do try."

"I know."

"So, anyway, that just made me think of having a glass today, just for the heck of it."

"Sounds good to me. Oh, and speaking of wine. I don't think I ever mentioned my friend Laura, have I?"

"No, I don't think so. I'm sure I'd remember, especially because your names sound almost the same."

She stared for a second, then grinned and said, "You're right. I never even thought of that. We kind of look alike too."

"Well, one would have to say that she's quite attractive, then."

"Yeah. Quite attractive. Yep. She and I agreed to get together Saturday evening for a glass of wine. Yeah, another glass for me—it doesn't have to be just with dinner."

"No, one should say not. It's good to keep up with old friends."

"I wouldn't say she's an old friend. We've kind of had a regular get-together up until you and I started spending actual time together."

"Oh, I ruined that?"

"No, Amos. No, it's just been a different focus for me. That's all. We just talked and decided we'd get out for another drink, just catch up on stuff."

"Saturday? Heck, I'll probably be busy with reading and lesson plans and things anyway. I hope you have a good time."

"We should. We've been friends since college."

"Oh, classes together. That's kind of—"

"Well, actually not classes so much. We were both cheerleaders and got to be close friends."

"Those were the days, huh?"

"Oh yeah. I mean, kind of. Studies were always important to me too. Did I ever tell you that I still have my old cheerleading outfit?"

"No, and I'm sure I'd remember that bit of info. Where is it? Packed away in the attic?"

"Uh, no. I just never seem to get around to storing it away."
"Well, I must admit to having some curiosity. Can I see it?"
"Hey, it's kind of made to be seen. So, sure. Uh-huh."
"Made to be seen. Hmm. Yes, I guess it is. Made to attract attention too."
"That's what cheering's all about. Yeah. How about after dinner?"
"Okay," he said. "Yes, thanks.
"Soup and wine. Yum."
"Garlic toast too," he said, pointing toward the oven.
"Even better."

Chapter 11 – I'll Always Wear the Ring

Lenore stooped down and yanked open the lowest dresser drawer with Amos looming nearby and watching intently.

"It's just . . . right . . . here."

She'd pushed aside the top layer to reveal a neatly folded plain white shirt, and there was something multicolored below it. She lifted it all out, then stood with both garments in her arms.

"That, uh, really hasn't made it to the attic."

"I'll get around to it. One of these days. Anyway," she said while laying it on the dresser, "there it is. Well, today's version anyway."

"What do you mean?"

"Just that the original shirt got torn long ago, and I had to replace it with this one."

She unfolded it and held it up against herself.

"There's no college logo, but it's about the same as the old one. What do you think?"

He reached a hand out, then stopped himself short of it.

"Uh, may I?"

She laughed and said, "May you touch the shirt? Amos, come on."

"One shouldn't assume."

"Oh, of course."

He pinched the material and wiggled it around.

"That's, uh . . . that sure is thin."

"Yeah, and so was the original. I think we knew we'd almost always be in indoor stadiums, so it didn't matter. What do you think?"

"It's nice. That's the skirt?"

He pointed at a pleated, striped skirt with alternating university colors.

"Yep. That thing is for sure the original."

"It's nice too. It doesn't look old at all. I thought all of it would be rolled up in an old bag somewhere."

"Oh, uh, I try to take care of it. You know, wash it once in a while. I read that it keeps clothes lasting longer if you do."

"Hey, you feel like trying it on? Does it still fit?"

"You're silly, Amos. Of course, it still fits. I haven't gained weight. Uh, how about just the shirt?"

"That would be splendid. Okay, the shirt.

"Fair enough," she said. "Okay."

She waited, shirt in hand and watching him as he watched her back.

"Amos. Run along."

"I probably should, huh?"

She scoffed and said, "Unless you're asking me to kind of do a striptease for you."

She hurried to add, "Are you, Amos?"

He lost his smile and said, "Oh, uh, no. No striptease requested. I'll, um, be right back."

"Okay."

She monitored his steps toward the door and whispered, after he'd closed it quietly, "I could, though. I'd strip."

After a few seconds of watching the knob not turning, then hearing his footsteps signaling his walk back to the kitchen, she sighed and faced the mirror. With the garments dropped onto the dresser, she quickly unbuttoned her shirt, removed it, and tossed it over her shoulder onto the bed.

A second passed as she tipped her head each way, studying the sight of herself wearing only a bra, along with the baggy denim pants. She gave the door a quick glance, scoffed quietly, then unclasped it between her breasts. It quickly got added to the shirt on the bed.

And she paused again, eyes fixed on her bared breasts. The serious pause came to an end when she giggled softly, just once, and shook them from side to side.

"Oh my God. Laura, you're terrible for even suggesting such a thing."

She snatched up the shirt, carefully pulled it over her bunched up mass of hair, then tugged down on the bottom hem, stretching it tight against all that was under it.

"Hmm. Shame on you, Laura, for making me even think about it."

But she let go of the hem and cupped both breasts with her hands, then squeezed them while squinting at her reflection.

"You're right, though. They'd absolutely love them."

* * *

While walking toward the closed bedroom door, Amos heard Lenore inside the room call out, "Just about ready."

He waited there, hand on the knob, and said, "Me too."

"Got your second glass of wine, huh?"

His laugh wasn't loud enough for her to hear, and he said, "I cheated myself on that glass with dinner."

Grinning, he listened to her saying, "Probably not good to ever cheat yourself out of things, huh?"

"No, never. Tell me when."

"Okay. You can come in."

He swung in the door and saw Lenore standing near the dresser, wearing her usual sneakers and baggy jeans, and her hair was still all tied and constrained in an orderly bundle.

But she was wearing a shirt that was too tight and thin to hide any detail at all. And those two important details were hinting that it had somehow become quite cold in the room.

His look at her eyes didn't survive long, and he lowered his gaze to her breasts. Even as his mouth opened but said nothing, his eyes sank down quickly to study her sneakers instead.

"That's, uh, a nice uniform. Um, shirt."

"Amos. You're not even looking at it."

He didn't offer a trace of a smile as he looked up into her eyes.

"Sure I am."

He gave some vague area of her shirt a quick glance.

"It's, um . . ."

He let his eyes focus on her breasts and linger there, and a slow sigh hissed out.

"That's quite a sight. It's so, um, thin. You'd never, you know, actually—"

"Go out in public like this?" she said, laughing. "No, of course not, Amos. I promise you that I'll never, ever lead any cheers like this."

"That's probably good."

"I just, uh, thought I'd start getting ready to dress for bed, that's all. You like it?"

"Yes. Yes, I do."

"It fits better without the bra."

"Uh, yes. No one would debate that. Uh-huh."

She grinned and covered her breasts with both hands, saying, "I almost feel naked standing here like this."

"Well, not anymore. Your hands are contributing to some modesty. Oh, and the engagement ring looks good. I like that you wear that all the time."

"Well, of course. I love it. I'm not taking it off."

"Promise?"

"Of course. Promise."

She waited with her eyebrows raised as he seemed to be studying the ring on her finger, then he looked up at her eyes.

"Well, Amos, that's it. The boring old uniform. No big deal, right?"

"Well, there's a skirt too. But you don't, uh, need to, um—"

"No, I suppose not. Maybe if there's any real cheerleading going on. How's that?"

He laughed and said, "Okay. You, uh, want some privacy to, uh, get—"

"Ready for bed. Sure, thanks."

He finished what was left of his wine, then quickly left and closed the door. Lenore shook her head, then faced herself in the mirror again.

Her hands were still covering her breasts, and she focused on the sight of her ring. She rubbed both hands around, squishing her breasts, moving them from side to side as the diamond on her ring glistened.

"Oh, the ring—that's . . . intriguing. But I'm not doing it. No way, Laura."

She squeezed a few more times, then held them still and looked into her reflected eyes.

"But if I did, which I never would, I promised that I'll always wear the ring."

She looked down again at how her hands could barely cover them. "I promised."

*　*　*

In a room lit by only a dim night light on the far wall, low near the floor, Lenore waited beneath the thick blankets. When footsteps approached and the door opened, she didn't suggest anything about lighting up the room.

With the door closed again, and while he was tiptoeing through the dark, she said, "No cheerleading for me."

"Good," he said, not laughing. "You look, uh, too good."

"Well, I guess that's a compliment. But you're right—it's probably not the best idea to look too good."

He folded back the blankets and sat on his side, back straight, then said, "I just . . . it's just that advertising too much about—"

"Amos, I know. There's no good that comes from that. You know I'm basically a modest girl anyway, right?"

"Well, yes. It's one of the many things I adore about you."

"And I don't feel any need to traipse around in a tight shirt with no bra."

"That wouldn't be modest at all. No."

"I mean, really, under what kind of circumstances would I ever want to do that?"

"There couldn't ever be a good enough reason for that. It does look good, though."

She giggled and said, "What about it? You just have to tell me."

Still seated, facing the wall with only enough light to cast him as a silhouette, he laughed once, then said, "Your, um, your breasts, of course."

"Oh? Hmm. What about them?"

"Lenore, they're unbelievable. I just don't ever want to—"

"To let the whole world know?"

"Yes. Not even just a small part of the world."

"And they sure would know if I dressed like that for some reason?"

"Dressed like—"

"Like a shameless harlot, with a really tight, stretched-on shirt and no bra."

He sighed, and she could see the outline of his nodding head.

"Yes. Oh, yes, they would know. And there would be talk too."

"You can talk about it, though, right? What about that shirt did you like?"

"Lenore . . ."

"Oh, come on. What exactly did you like that no one else should know or talk about?"

He scoffed loudly enough for her to hear, then said, "Your breasts are quite, uh, large."

"Oh?"

"Yes. And with your waist being so slender, the contrast is, uh, it's almost too much."

"Aw, too much for you, you mean?"

He turned enough to give her a profile view and said, "Too much for the rest of the world. If I can keep you a secret, then, I don't know, maybe—"

"Amos, we're engaged. I promised I'd never take off that wonderful engagement ring you put on my finger, didn't I?"

"Yes, you did. No matter what?"

"No matter what. A promise is a promise. It's not coming off."

"Good. Me too."

She saw the shadow of a left hand shaking with the lit wall backing it up.

"So," she said, "the world knows I—I'm marked as belonging to another. It's right there on my finger, obvious as can be. Even if someone somehow happened to notice my . . . what?"

He laughed and said, "Breasts?"

She giggled and said, "My very large, round . . ."

"Breasts. Your breasts."

"Which, because my waist is tiny, look even . . ."

"Bigger," he said, laughing. "They sure look big."

She laughed, too, and said, "Yeah, even if someone else noticed my breasts, they'd also see that I'm taken. Because I'll be wearing that perfect engagement ring. Which means my . . ."

She gave him a few seconds, he didn't answer quickly enough, and she continued, saying, ". . . both of my . . ."

Almost giggling, he said, "Breasts."

"Yeah. Which means my breasts are strictly reserved for someone else."

"Yes. I like that."

"You know what else?"

"What?"

"When I had on that thin cheerleader shirt, that was only for you. What did you get a good look at?"

He laughed softly and said, "Your breasts."

"That shirt is so tight and thin that what is obvious?"

His sigh filled the room.

"Them. Your big breasts."

"Are they big enough?"

"Oh, God, yes. You have such nice, big breasts."

"Hmm, I don't think you're serious. They're not all that nice and big, so you probably wouldn't care if I went out in public like that. Tight shirt, no bra, just—"

"Yes, I would care! Lenore, promise me you'll never—"

"Maybe I'll just wander around somewhere, with just a really thin, tight shirt that has no chance of hiding my—"

"Don't even think about it!"

"Amos, I'm teasing! You can be sure I have no plans to wander around like that."

"Good. You're scaring me."

"I shouldn't tease you, I know. And Amos, guess what?"

He froze and said, "Uh, what?"

She tipped the covers back farther and said, "I'm not out where anyone else can see. See my big . . ."

He giggled once and said, "Your big breasts."

"Uh-huh. They're right here."

He turned to look, and she slipped the straps down over her shoulders, then quickly, before he could get a good look, put her hands over her exposed breasts. The ring on her finger sparkled even in the meager light.

"See the ring?"

"Uh-huh. Oh, yes, I do."

"See how the ring is always there along with those nice, big breasts?"

"Mm-hmm. Yes, it's there. Always?"

"Mm-hmm. And I'd bet you think they look even bigger and nicer because that ring is there, too, right?"

"It does help. Yes."

"Like it's guarding them? Saying don't even look at them?"

"Yes. The ring is good. One could be sure that it's indeed saying that."

"Not to you, though. Better hurry and get a closer look."

He started leaning toward her, and she added, giggling, "Before someone else does."

He snapped himself back up and said, "What? What do you—"

"No, no, no! Oh, sorry, bad joke!"

In a pouting voice, he said, again just a silhouette, "Yes, a humorless joke. One completely lacking in humor. God, I think maybe I need another sip of wine. It's, uh, the wine is good. I'll be right back."

"Amos, it was a stupid joke. I'm sorry."

He was up, in the dark with a hand on the doorknob.

"It's quite okay, Lenore. I think I'm experiencing just the stress of starting a new position. I'll just, uh, get another taste of that wine."

With her hands still on her breasts, she watched the dark shape swing the door in and then step out into the hallway. He took a long time to be sure his closing of the door was as quiet as it could be.

"Dammit," she whispered.

Still holding both breasts, she looked down and rotated her left hand, playing with the thin traces of light seeking the shiny stone on her finger.

"That kind of is a sight. It's . . . something. With that ring."

Chapter 12 – Parade Me Through Town

Amos stumbled but maintained admirable posture as he walked into the kitchen in his pajamas, which weren't nearly as cumbersome and insulating as Lenore's. He yawned while scratching at his scalp, then stopped to view her standing near the stove, stirring around in a pot.

She saw him and said, "Oatmeal," then turned back to her work.

"I heard you waking up," she added.

"Good morning. Thanks for cooking."

He resumed his shaky walk toward the table and sat, then smiled up at her as she approached with a cup of hot coffee.

"Sorry about last night," she said. "Sometimes, I can say some dumb things."

He rubbed around his face with the hand that wasn't clutching the mug.

"One might say that jokes, by their nature, have to border on the limits of reasonable discourse to have any worth."

Facing the stove again, she nodded and said, "Yeah, like that. I tried staying awake, but I was so tired. I didn't hear you come back to bed."

"Oh, that's my fault."

He took a big swig.

"I did pour some wine, then I got to reading, and I thought it'd be for just a second or two. Well, you know how that goes."

"Yep. Sometimes one just leads to the next. You hungry?"

"Yes. Very much so."

She scooped some into a bowl and delivered it, setting it on his placemat."

"Thanks. It looks and smells quite good."

"Liar," she said, laughing once.

She brought her own to the table and sat across from him.

"Do you have any special plans for your day off?" she said.

He swallowed a fairly good amount, winced from the heat of it, then scoffed.

"Ooh. That's hot. Very good, though. Um, how about if you phone in and take a day too? We could just hang out, get some coffee and then some lunch, and just have a laid-back day."

"You know, I could. We were working up to that possible contract on Monday. And since that went bust, we're doing nothing but regrouping. The staff can handle that without me for a day."

"Terrific. The weather's expected to be good too."

"It's not a bad part of the country to live in. I can't complain that I grew up here."

"You went to college here too."

"Yeah, how convenient. Starting that business hasn't been the easiest, but it's been worth it. I'm glad it's done well enough that I could buy this house."

"And I'm glad I found you out in that Internet wasteland. What are the odds?"

"Pretty low if you were—oh, no, never mind."

"No, go on. What?"

She scoffed and stirred her steaming oatmeal for a few seconds, then looked up.

"Just a stupid joke. I have to stop."

"Lenore, I overreacted. Your joke wasn't all that bad. Your joke right now, with traces of oatmeal packed in there,"—he grinned and pointed at her mouth—"is probably just fine too. Come on. Give me another chance."

"Alright. I was going to say that the odds of finding me were low if your search was for a cheerleader."

"Oh, a cheerleader," he said, grinning down at his bowl. "No, I didn't search for that. It's not an unreasonable strategy, though. Maybe I should have."

"No," she said, more seriously. "Because then, I'd have been putting myself out there as a cheerleader type. You would have passed on that real quick."

"I would have?"

"Uh-huh. No, Amos, you like the modesty vibes my profile gave. Admit it."

"You got me there. Yes. It's, uh, important to me."

"I know. And it just so happens I was a cheerleader too. Imagine that."

"I am."

"Hmm. That tight shirt, right?"

He shook his head, grinning.

"Uh, not exactly the shirt. Oh, see? Now, you have me open to outright discussions of such things."

"Hmm. Tell you what: let's delve into more details about that later, alright?"

"One might say that the devil is in those details. Those obvious details."

She stared for a few seconds, then looked down at her slowly stirring spoon that prompted trails of steam to rise from one side, then the other.

"Oh. Like the devil's work."

"It's just a phrase. It doesn't mean anything or have any direct bearing on any of this."

"No, of course not. How's your oatmeal?"

"Scrumptious. The coffee's good too."

"Oatmeal details. Coffee details."

"Those matter. You seriously do look beautiful in a robe and with your hair up. You're just a classic beauty. No style of dress could ever hide that."

"So," she said, grinning again, "you're planning to parade me through town like this?"

"If it's a choice between that,"—he jabbed a finger at her a few times—"or parading my fiancé as a sexy cheerleader, take a guess."

"Well, the robe, of course."

"Of course."

Holding his gaze, not smiling, she said, "Only because it's chilly today, though. Otherwise, I'd have to . . ."

He scoffed and said, "That sense of humor of yours. You're incredible."

Chapter 13 – They'd See Everything

As they walked in the cool sunshine, crossing a mostly empty park in the unusually quiet college town, Amos reached for Lenore's hand and found it.

He shifted it around, smiling at the feel of her thick denim jeans, then he turned just his eyes and smiled more at the sight of her baggy flannel shirt under a zipped-up hoodie and hair twisted and tied and doing no hanging down at all.

"It's a beautiful day to take off," he said. "It seems that Wednesdays are days off for a lot of majors. It's kind of nice and calm out here."

"I've seen how it usually is—more like a circus. You said you met with that student here? The deep thinker?"

"Yes, Emilio. He might not truly be all that deep. Maybe he's just good at faking it. I'll need to gather more data to be sure."

"He's older, though?"

"Yes. Another student in the same class, a young lady named Lindsey, said he's prone to failing classes. But he's still giving it a try, so I wish him well."

"The old college try, as they say. So much enthusiasm, huh?"

"Uh, sure. Good for him, I suppose."

"This seat," she said, pointing at the bench directly abutting the asphalt walkway. "In the sunshine is nice."

"Excellent choice."

They sat, her leaning and him not, each took a sip, then he said, "It really is a beautiful town. These old buildings, Lenore, are quite impressive."

"Yeah. Quaint. There's a frat house area, too, which is kind of historic. I mean, I've heard that. I tend to avoid all of this if I can."

"Oh, yes. I believe they call it Frat Row or something similar."

"Uh-huh. Frat This, Frat That, and on and on. But that's university life, I suppose. I think it's extraordinary that you were able to get a position out here. It's like it was meant to be."

He set the cup on his knee and waved his free hand out across the expansive lawns and toward the majestic buildings beyond.

"Sure, this is all nice. But making the move here is only about you. That's the big prize."

"Oh, I'm a prize?"

Quickly, he said, "Well, no, not like that. I only mean that you're appreciated and valued."

"Well, thank you, Amos. Ditto. It's kind of funny, in a way, that when you were leading up to proposing, I saw it coming. But you know what? Even though I didn't expect that so soon, there were never any alarms going off. It was just nice. And you offered me such a nice ring."

She held out her left hand where they could both see it.

"I sure like the sight of that," he said.

"It's so nice—it doesn't really go well with these baggy clothes, hair in a knot, slurping coffee on a bench while—"

His laughter got to a level where she had to laugh herself.

"Lenore, that's all very good and appropriate for a day off in the park. I'd say, the ring goes with that outfit quite well. Any outfit, really. It's universal."

"Oh, like cosmic? Like, meant to be? Hmm. I think you're right. And yeah, the ring had better go with everything."

He turned and waited for her to meet his gaze.

"Uh, what do you mean?"

"Well, Amos, because I promised that I'd always wear it. And I can't take back that promise, can I?"

"No. Uh-uh. No way, Lenore."

"It's a promise. Oh, until we actually get the real ring. Someday."

"Oh, yes. Someday soon. You wearing that ring will really be—"

"Looking good enough to parade around?"

"What?" he said, laughing. "No! It'll just be a perfect ending."

"Ending to what?"

"To my long wait to meet you and keep you for myself."

She sipped her coffee while gazing out across the park.

"Keep like a prize."

"No, it's not like that at all. It's more like appreciating a fine work of art."

Laughing, she said, "Huh. A prized work of art at the parade. As long as no one's there to watch."

"Stop," he said, snorting out a laugh. "Just stop."

She giggled, took a sip, then slowly turned enough to look to her left.

Where she knew without any doubt waited Frat Row, a raucous, shadier part of town that lurked just a block from the roads laid out in a square and keeping the park much more safe and civilized.

* * *

Pointing while they walked, Lenore said, "I've become too used to those amazing buildings on campus. They really are something."

"They're new to me. I guess a couple of months isn't long enough to get numb to them."

With a gentle tug on his hand, she steered the two of them toward the walkway branching to the left.

"Those up ahead," she said, "I'm not sure I ever really noticed those."

"Magnificent. Incredible stone work. I'm not sure what classes even go on in there."

"There's probably a map or a directory somewhere, right? Maybe we should make more of an effort to know our way around here."

"We could. One should have a sense of their surroundings."

Sipping coffee, hand in hand, she kept them moving toward a quiet street that led away between two of the older, taller structures.

"Let's see the sides of these things too," she said. "The architecture, Amos. It's incredible."

She noticed him tipping back his head, studying the array of windows and the fire escapes installed in more recent times, then turned just her eyes to look ahead to the next block.

At the sight of many students milling around in the distance, she wedged her coffee under her arm, freeing up that hand to slip sunglasses out of a pocket. She snapped them open, then stopped with them close to being installed.

"Now, you're putting those on?" he said, laughing. "It was way sunnier in the park."

"Oh, uh, yeah. I just didn't think of it till now."

She finished poking the tips into her tight mound of hair, then pushed the large, dark lenses up along her nose.

"Better late than never. Ooh, it's chillier here too."

With her hand still free, she flipped up the hood of her sweatshirt, then alternated tugs at each side, pulling it all forward before she again held her coffee.

"Now, you're ready. For sunshine, cold, anything."

"Huh, ready for anything. Yep."

He squeezed her hand and looked up as they began to pass between the looming walls.

"They're tall, that's for sure," he said. "Imagine the upkeep. Whenever I look at the outsides of buildings like these, it makes me wonder about all the things going on inside there."

"Hmm, yeah," she said, still looking ahead. "If walls could talk, huh?"

"Yes, exactly."

"Maybe it's better if they sometimes keep their secrets, though, right?"

He laughed and nodded, still looking high above the sidewalk level.

"Their secrets are probably mostly boring anyway. College towns are pretty tame compared to the wilder places in the world."

"Oh, yeah, that's true," she said. "There's probably nothing noteworthy going on in these buildings. Certainly not uncivilized stuff."

"Yes. Well said."

As they began to walk beyond the back reaches of the taller university buildings, Amos looked ahead, too, and stopped her with a gentle pull of her hand.

"I don't believe there's anything worthwhile up ahead," he said. "I'm ready to go back."

She stayed silent, looking at a series of old residential buildings that appeared to have been single-family at one time but had become hubs of activity, with small parking areas, fire escapes from the upper floors, and yards full of litter and forgotten sports equipment.

"Wait," she said. "These are the, uh, dorms?"

"Well, no, the dorms are somewhere in the bigger buildings on campus. We can go look for them if—"

"So, what are these, then? Oh, for the sororities and stuff?"

"Well, Lenore, mostly for fraternities. At least on this street. I think this is what they call Frat Row."

"Oh. Frat Row."

She spent a few seconds looking one way, then the other, and he said, "Come on. My coffee needs a refill."

He pulled, but she didn't budge.

"I'm, uh, just checking out the architecture of these giant old houses. That's what these were at one time, right? Just people's houses?"

"I would think so. Hey, it's your hometown."

"Yeah, but I've never paid attention much. Really, Amos, these houses are kind of extraordinary. Kind of makes me wonder."

"Wonder what? About how quick we can get another cup of—"

"Yeah, just a sec," she said and held them both there. "Coffee sounds good."

She giggled and said, "Oh, Amos, the secrets some of these buildings could tell, huh?"

"Uh, sure. Like all-night studying, eating too much pizza, drinking too much beer, playing music too—"

"Uh-huh. Yeah, stuff like that. Oh, maybe a few parties too."

He stopped pulling on her hand and studied the line of aged and weathered buildings with her. Nearly everyone they could see—sitting on porch steps, standing near bicycle racks, calling out of windows— was a male student, and only a few young women were walking around.

"Oh, well, yes. We can't forget the occasional party," he said.

She pointed up at the second- and third-story windows of the closest frat house and said, "Anyone in those rooms would have a good view up there. They could probably plan on, um, seeing everything."

"Uh, yes. Everything of what?"

"Oh, just wondering if there are ever any street parties out here, anything like that."

"I wouldn't be surprised. Yes, Lenore, anyone in a room up there could reasonably expect to see it all."

She turned and turned him around with her to face back toward the park centered within a sprawling square of stately school buildings.

"Yeah, even of the—oh, I forget sometimes that this is your first year here. I'm just thinking of the fall parade that travels all around the park."

"Oh, yes, I didn't know about that. That sounds like a very noteworthy event."

She looked back over her shoulder and said, "And even from a room up there, one of those old frat houses, the view would be . . . pretty good. They'd see everything they'd want to see."

"Uh, yes. And they'd likely fully expect to see everything too. You're making me kind of eager to see this parade. When is it?"

"Soon. I think. I'm not . . . sure."

* * *

Lenore turned away from the frat residences and joined Amos in looking back toward the park.

"You're probably starving for something by now."

"What?" she said. "What do you mean?"

He still held her hand and looked from one dark lens to the other, then scoffed.

"You barely touched your breakfast. You're probably starving for lunch. Want to get something in town while we're out?"

"Oh. Lunch. Yeah, I, uh, wasn't even thinking of that. But you're right—I'm about ready for something."

She gave a quick look back while holding her sunglasses in place, then faced the park again.

"Sure. Let's get something."

"Can we agree to strike from our menu another round of oatmeal?"

She laughed, then scoffed and said, "Yeah. No more plain old everyday oatmeal. Maybe something spicier."

"Now, you're talking."

Walking through the canyon between the tall college buildings, back toward the park, Amos glanced at his watch, then lowered it and looked ahead again.

"There's a college bar kind of place that's probably open. Let's check it out."

"Oh, a college place? I don't know. I mean, it's probably packed, and it'll be loud, and there could—"

"No way, Lenore. They're young and if they're not in class, they're probably still snoozing."

"Oh. Yeah, college kids. Uh-huh. Up all night."

"That, I believe, is a fair description of them."

"Yeah. Hey, can we take it to go and maybe sit in the park again?"

"Yes, of course. You have the most delightful ideas."

"Sometimes, I do. Yep."

* * *

Standing outside the storefront restaurant, up against the brick wall and watching the foot traffic passing, Lenore said, "Hey, Amos, you want to just run in? I, uh, should probably check with the office."

"Oh, sure. I'm in the mood for tacos."

"Me, too, then. Get a bunch of them."

"Mm-hmm. Alright. More, as is often stated, is many times better."

"Yeah, for sure. I'm thinking the same thing. Something to drink too."

"Yes, something to drink too. See you in a moment."

With her back to the wall, Lenore tapped her phone a few times then held it to her ear.

"Laura. I just had to call you."

"Hi, Lenore. Why? What's up?"

"Just to vent again. About last night."

"Go on. Tell me. Vent all you want."

"Okay. I think it's because I'm frustrated, but I tried teasing him last night. But really, it was more about just wanting to kind of show off."

"Show off what? Come on. Tell me."

"My breasts. I just wanted to bare them and have him appreciate them, then get him to go crazy."

"Ooh, good plan. He didn't go crazy?"

"Huh. He mostly just talked about wanting me to stay modest. It mostly seems like he thinks I'm too pure to even touch. Or like he wants me to be that pure. He likes them, I'm sure, but he—"

"He didn't just go crazy."

"No, and it didn't go well. I mean, it started off okay, then . . ."

"Then, what?"

"Laura, I was teasing him and I slipped up. I started thinking about doing, um, what you said. And I said something kind of stupid."

"What were you thinking?"

"About having the sight of me really appreciated. Not being so modest about them. Like—"

"Like at the frat house. Yeah, you'd get more appreciation than you can imagine. What were you thinking exactly?"

"You sure you want to hear this?"

"Of course!"

"Alright. I'd dropped my nightie, and I was holding them, one hand on each. And I'd just said something about my engagement ring being right there on my finger."

"Oh, I can picture that. Go on."

"I'm not doing this, but I thought of how wild that would be, uh, for some frat guys. Holding my breasts while they're checking me out, I'm knowing what's about to happen, and I'm still wearing that ring. It's kind of obscene."

"Yes, wearing that ring is so obscene that you just have to do it."

"I can't do that, Laura. So, I was thinking about it, though, then I just blurted out something dumb."

"You told him our plan? Lenore, you—"

"No, I didn't. But it was still just kind of a dumb joke. I just have to stop thinking about it or—"

"Or just do it. Yeah, you should—"

"Laura, that's not what I'm saying. The thing is, it all kind of fizzled out after that. He's nice enough to walk around town with, talk with, stuff like that. But he's got this notion that he owns me."

"Like a slave or something?"

"No, that could maybe be exciting somehow. No, it's even worse: like I'm a prize or a work of art."

"Shit, that's not flattering at all. Well, it'll just get worse if you get married."

Lenore sighed and said, "I don't know if I can do it."

"The frat night thing?"

"I was talking about the marriage. That. I don't know if I can—"

Laura laughed and said, "So, twin cheerleader girl, you're still thinking about—"

"Laura, stop. Oh, he's coming back out. Got to go."

"You're going to look just like me. No one will ever know except you and I. You won't believe how exciting it is to—"

"I got to go! Bye!"

The glass door swung out, ringing the bells, and Amos saw her stowing away her phone.

"How are things?"

"Good. Glad I checked. Just some, uh, decisions pending."

"Oh, that sounds serious."

"I guess. I'll figure it out. I already kind of made up my mind on some things."

"Good. Trust your instincts. One might say that hard decisions should be approached without any hesitation. One should just go with what seems right."

"Yep. That's probably the best approach for hard decisions."

She stared for a few seconds, then said, "Uh, tacos are way easier to decide."

"Agreed."

He handed her a bag and a drink, then gestured with his own drink toward a bench farther down along the sidewalk.

"I can't wait, Lenore. I'm starving. How about you?"

"The more I think about it, yeah. Kind of starving."

* * *

Still chewing, Amos stuffed the last of their trash into a can near the bench, and they began a quiet walk home.

"That was good. Some things, like tacos, are simply too scrumptious to not consume."

"Yeah," she said, then sipped her drink. "Uh-huh. Some things."

She noticed his eyes darting around toward the park.

"Looking for someone?"

"Oh, uh, just curious if that student I told you about is lurking around somewhere."

"That interesting, deep-thinking one?"

"Well, he seems that way but that girl in class, Lindsey, said he's some kind of fitness model too. Who knows? Young guys usually have much shallower things on their minds."

"Yeah. I can imagine."

"You can? What is it that you—"

"Miss Lenore!"

They both turned at the sound of someone coming up behind them as they traveled away from the restaurant. A grinning young man was taking quick steps toward them and waving.

"Oh, Jeremy, hello," she said. "You recognized me?"

"Kind of. Yeah. Oh, you mean because of the glasses and the hoodie?"

"Yeah, I'm hiding from the sun. Jeremy, this is my fiancé, Amos. He's a professor here at the college. Amos, this is my lead programmer's son."

"Hello, Jeremy, nice to meet you."

"You too, professor. Wow, a professor—that's cool!"

"Jeremy is the young fellow that's been doing the yard work up until you took over."

"Oh, nice work, Jeremy. You even kept the mower and tools and stuff all clean and organized. That's very admirable and responsible."

"Thanks. I try," he said, grinning at Amos.

Looking again at Lenore, he said, "If you ever need any kind of extra help around, just tell my mom. I'm always happy to earn some extra money."

"We'll surely let you know," said Amos. "I'm pretty sure I have things under control, though. Are you a student here?"

"Oh, me? No, I just graduated high school. And I don't know what I want to do anyway."

"Well, one might say it's a good time for you to give it some thought."

"You're right. I will. So, good meeting you. Bye, Miss Lenore."

"Bye, Jeremy."

They watched him run back toward his group of friends, who were all watching them.

"Energetic young fellow," said Amos.

"He certainly is. Or was, I mean. With the yard. I think he's disappointed to be missing out on that part-time work since you took over."

"It seems so. Yes. You really are disguised pretty well. I'm surprised that he—"

"I'm disguised? No, I'm not, not really. It's just the sunshine and chilly air."

"Well, whatever it is, you're still looking just as lovely as ever."

"Aw, thanks, Amos. It's like there are extra layers of modesty, huh?"

He continued to walk with her, offering no response.

"Amos?"

"You're mocking me. And I deserve it. It's just that—"

"I'm not mocking you. It was kind of more just like a joke about it. I guess it wasn't too funny, huh?"

He managed a pained grin and said, "You and your jokes."

She elbowed him and said, "Amos. I apologized for that joke several times already. It was a stupid joke, and I never should have—"

"It's fine. Really. I should be apologizing. It's just, um, I really do feel better when—"

"When I'm covered up. I mean staying modest. I know."

"Modest is good. I'm glad we agree on that. I mean, sort of anyway."

"We do, Amos. Truly."

"I mean, just imagine if you were wearing that, um, your—"

She scoffed and said, "Tight shirt?"

"Yes, and—"

"No bra. Okay. I'm imagining I'm wearing that skin-tight shirt with no bra. Are you imagining it too?"

"Lenore. Um, yes. Of course. Do you think that Jeremy would have ever even made eye contact with you?"

She sighed, hesitated, then said, "No, I suppose not. And he never would have seen you at all."

"No. So, that's all I'm saying: unless you want every guy just ogling every intimate little part of you, then staying kind of modest is the smartest plan. Otherwise . . ."

"Otherwise, what, Amos?"

"Well, can you imagine if all they could think about was your body? Would they go so far as to even imagining you naked? I mean, think of that . . ."

"No, I wouldn't want that. I'd feel just like some kind of . . . object."

"That is exactly my point. They'd be totally ignoring that you're an accomplished business owner and future professor's wife."

"Yeah, that's . . . they wouldn't even care about any of that. Those things."

They took a few steps in silence.

"Well, it's a good day for a walk through town, wouldn't you say?"

"Yep. The sunshine and crisp air is so, uh, stimulating."

"Yes. Yes, it is."

Chapter 14 – I'm Just Something Soft

Lenore had just closed the bedroom door, and Amos spoke from the other side.

"I'll be just a minute or two, Lenore. There's something I forgot to check for tomorrow. A passage I'm curious about that will bug me all night."

"Oh, we couldn't have that. Have a sip or two for me too."

"What? No, I—"

"Amos, I'm just being silly. But I wouldn't blame you. Wine is a good thing."

"Yes. One would surely agree with that. Uh, I might have just a sip. I'll be in in a few minutes."

"No rush. See you."

With an ear to the door, she listened to his footsteps retreating toward the kitchen, held her breath until she heard a chair drag away from the table then scrape several times, and then she let the air out.

After a quick glance at the alarm clock, she turned the door's mostly ornamental locking mechanism, then hit the wall switch, lighting the dim lamps on both nightstands. It took only a few short steps to get her to the dresser, where she faced the mirror and looked into her own eyes.

While untying the loose knot of her thick robe's belt, she said softly while shaking her head, "I can't be just a chaste, respectable business owner."

She flapped it open, revealing a less-than-daring baby blue nightgown, one with only stingy lines of lace along its edges. But she held the robe to each side and studied how that rather plain garment, which began high on her chest, up near her throat, covered every hint of every detail beneath it. But it failed in hiding the size and shape of her breasts, which she saw were indeed quite large and round.

"Maybe someday."

With her eyes still on them, she slipped off the robe and tossed it back onto the bed. Her hands immediately went to her breasts, and she held them through the thin cloth without attempting any squeezing.

But she did turn herself enough that her engagement ring caught the lamplight and sparkled it back out, like a beacon signaling that there was something worth noticing there.

"Hmm. That does draw the eye. That ring . . . there."

Her sigh was almost a groan as she took slow steps backwards, turned enough to climb up onto the bed, then rose to her knees and faced the mirror.

She reached for her hair, all woven together and clamped into a tight, thoroughly organized mass but then, she only turned her eyes up, scoffed at it, and left it like it was. Her hands found the silky garment's thin straps on her shoulders, and she pinched them and paused, again looking into her eyes.

"I can't be just a . . ."

She smirked, shook her head.

"Not just a professor's . . . demure and proper . . . future wife."

She scoffed and added, "Just some work of art too prized to ever be . . . touched."

She slipped both straps down far enough that the fabric on her chest had begun to fall as well.

"Touched? Hmm, no. Maybe I'm not too proper to be . . . used?"

She hesitated for a moment, then kept going but much more slowly, teasing the lace border lower.

As more of the smooth skin was exposed, every slight advance showing just how generous were the curves, she was saying, "No. I'm not a future wife or a business owner. I'm an . . . object. Hmm, maybe more like . . . *just* an object. One with a tiny waist and big . . . hmm . . ."

She let the thin cloth fall past her breasts, revealing them completely, then released the straps. With the backs of her hands toward the mirror, she used just her fingertips to trace patterns around on her breasts—high up, all around the insides and outsides, and the soft skin underneath.

She closed her eyes, tipped her head back, and said, very quietly, "I hope you like them. Is looking at me a good start? Are these acceptable enough for you to . . . use? All . . . all of you?"

She gave them both a gentle squeeze and held still, then rubbed her palms down to support them from the bottom, lifting them up and out toward the mirror and her imaginary audience.

"Tell me you like them. Tell me I'm nothing more than an object to you. Maybe that's . . . all I really am."

Scoffing and shaking her head but grinning, too, she looked down again to where her fingers were still touching softly all around. She let her right hand drop to the bottom hem of her gown.

"Maybe that's all I want to be."

She lifted it up, just high enough to show the bare, smooth skin of both thighs.

"Just an object."

She raised it higher.

"I was instructed that I'm not allowed to say no."

Still holding up the hem, and still gently rubbing a breast with the hand wearing the ring, she added, "Uh-uh, that's not right. No, I was ordered, and I have to obey. I can't say no to anything at all. So, I guess I really am just an . . ."

She pulled the cloth up higher, up near her waist and showing so much more. And she leaned her hips forward and kept her shoulders as far back as she could.

"Oh, I'm . . . just an object. Something soft for . . ."

She let her ringed hand move from one breast to the other, then back.

"I'm just something soft, a soft object for . . . sex."

She moaned and alternated long, determined squeezes for each of her breasts.

"I'm a very soft object *just* for sex. Any . . . *any* kind of sex. Objects like me don't dare say no to anything at all."

She watched her tongue slip slowly across her upper lip.

"And such a soft object, one that is *only* for sex, has no choice but to . . . undress. She has to show how soft she is everywhere. How her only true purpose is to be used for sex."

Scanning all that she was offering to the mirror, she couldn't stop the soft, barely noticeable moan.

"Oh, no, she has to undress so she can be used, like the object she is, for . . . whatever you want . . . no matter how many of you—"

She scoffed and let the garment fall, covering her thighs entirely.

"Oh, Laura, no way. Thanks for the fantasy, but I just couldn't. Damn you for making me even think about it."

Even while damning her look-alike friend, her eyes were drawn to the hands covering her breasts and the bright diamond that she'd agreed would tell anyone close enough to touch her that those breasts, those very nice, big breasts that contrasted so strikingly with her slender waistline, were already someone's property and not to be used or even seen as objects because—

There were footsteps in the hall. Coming toward the bedroom.

Lenore shot a quick glance at the clock and whispered, "Dammit!"

She pulled the straps up even while hurrying off of the bed, then she wrapped the robe around herself while rushing toward the door.

The footsteps were close. Just about there.

Wincing, she turned the lock as quietly as she could, then stepped back.

Just when the door swung in.

"Oh, Amos, I was just going to switch off the light."

"Perfect timing. I'll get it."

He got it.

Walking back toward the bed, dressed modestly and again in the darkness, she said, "Did you get your stuff done?"

"Yes. I even took a sip of wine, just because you suggested it."

"I kind of did. Yeah."

She pulled back the covers and slipped herself in, then pulled it all up high as he walked to his side of the bed.

"It's good for you," she added. "Especially if you think I'm going to make any more bad jokes. I promise, I won't."

"Okay. Thanks. You, uh, looked really good just now. At the door."

"What, these plain old bedclothes?"

He laughed and said, "Yes. Really, it's you. It's you that always looks good, no matter if—"

"If I'm making dumb jokes and teasing you about things."

Undressed except for his boxers, he rolled the covers back enough to sit.

"Not about the ring, though," he said. "That wasn't teasing. That wasn't a joke, right?"

"What? No, of course not. It's a real promise. I'll always wear it. I think it's a, um, very fashionable kind of statement."

"You think so?"

"Yeah. I think I look even better wearing it. There's something extra special about a ring on a finger."

He turned, just a silhouette, and said, "I'm so happy to hear that. Yes, it's very special."

She was holding it up, playing with the light, and he took her hand, then kissed it.

And when he didn't let it go, she gently pulled it back.

"Oh," she said, "I think all that walking today kind of tired me out. I think I'm almost already asleep."

"Busy day. Yes."

"Sorry."

"For what? No, you need your sleep."

He rolled himself in and tucked up the blanket while she was rolling onto her side, facing away.

"Sweet dreams, Lenore."

"Mm-hmm. That's my hope. Goodnight."

82

Chapter 15 – No Denying the Divine

Standing at his lectern, an array of notes at his disposal, Amos wore a tweed jacket of grays and darker grays and looked around at the rows of students who seemed to be in no hurry to give him any of their attention.

He scoffed, then looked toward Lindsey, who shrugged with her eyebrows locked up high then smiled at him.

After smirking and shaking his head, he devoted a few seconds to organizing his notes and other items, then he nodded while looking out over his students again.

"Class, we really should get going. Class."

Most of them let out their last whispers and laughs and more contentious comments, then remained quiet and looked his way.

He sighed and said, "Thank you. Close enough to get started."

"Starting is the easy part!" said Emilio, causing most heads to turn toward him, and a mix of murmuring and chuckling swept around the room.

Amos gave Lindsey another look, and she held one finger to her temple, twisting it like a drill bit, and scrunched up her face, mouthing the word, "Crazy!"

Coughing and grinning her way for a second, Amos rapped a pen on the hard wood surface and focused on Emilio.

"We're in some kind of new routine here, Emilio."

"Yep. You like routines."

"Healthy routines are good. One should never even try to deny that. The problem is that we—"

"That we get stuck like thin bicycle tires in deep muck? That's what you were going to say?"

"No. That's a valid point, to be sure, but no, I was aiming for a different retort."

"Please, proceed."

"In your mind, we've swapped roles, Emilio? You're granting me license to address your class?"

"Hurry before I change my mind."

Everyone laughed, including Amos. It took a minute for enough quiet that the actual professor could continue.

"Well, class, it seems that our resident, self-appointed substitute professor is compelling us to launch into an impromptu discussion of—"

"Divinity!"

Amos squinted at Emilio's big grin and finger pointing toward the ceiling. His first look anywhere else gave him a view of Lindsey shaking her head slowly and rolling her eyes.

"Divinity?" Amos said. "Is that word or even concept allowed at this university?"

He looked around, grinning while basking in the sights and sounds of his having scored some comedic victory.

Emilio shook his head, pausing just long enough to have the majority of eyes on him, then said, "Doesn't matter. There's no escaping it."

"Enlighten us, Professor Emilio. I believe we left off at some cryptic comments about roller coasters and temperatures."

"That we did. And divinity—"

He paused, giving a dramatic point toward Amos with one shaking finger.

"—is hardly ever even imagined when you're slacking in a clean coaster car, all buckled up but not going anywhere."

"Alright. And what of the temperatures?"

"Same thing. Just sitting there, all cold and shivering, wishing you had some heat. You should already see divinity calling to you. Yeah, you should hear it calling you by name."

"Anything else, stand-in professor?"

"Yeah. There's no denying the divine once it calls you. Your ass is locked in."

"We probably can't bandy that word about either," said Amos.

"It's a word that shouldn't be bandied about. True."

When he heard, "Told you," he looked over at Lindsey, who was only shaking her head.

"Perhaps we'll have to wait for whatever chapter of your book will outline those thoughts in more detail. What do you say, Emilio?"

"Alright. I haven't really thought through all that too well. Just kind of thinking out loud."

"During class."

He looked around, meeting eyes of some that were giggling and others that were scoffing and agreeing with Lindsey.

"It's just, uh, where I happen to be. At the moment."

"Right. Working on a chapter about coasters and cold and divinity. Nice."

"Okay, that's accurate. Fair enough too. This might not be the best time."

"I should say not."

"Okay."

Amos shook his head and grinned up at Emilio, who had started to grin himself.

Then, Amos said, "Not."

Emilio stood, cupped his hands into a megaphone, and called out, "Class dismissed!"

Chapter 16 – No Third Floor for You, Professor

"Your student loans are being put to good use. Thanks again."

Amos took a long swig of his hot coffee right after Emilio handed it to him.

"Aw, you're welcome, professor. I'm just busting your balls in there sometimes."

"No, you're not. Come on."

"Alright. Yeah, I have things on my mind that aren't exactly sorted out yet."

"Have a seat," Amos said, pointing toward their usual picnic table. "Do expound on that."

"Spoken like a considerate educational professional."

"Huh. More like a psychiatric counselor."

"Oh, good one—not much difference."

"Funny."

"Busting your balls again. Look, I'm onto something, I just don't know what. You got to work with me here."

"I do?"

"Well, shit. I'm buying the coffee."

"The philosopher has a point. Okay, what do you think you're working on?"

"Going from the motionless to falling down a hill. Going from too cold to too warm."

"And back again."

"Yeah. It never ends. There's something . . . I don't know what else to call it. It's not magic. It's something built into the system. Might as well call it—"

"Divine?"

"Good thinking. Glad you suggested it."

"Huh."

"You're the learned one. You even have fancy papers swearing to it."

"Maybe I'm out here just for the coffee."

"Fair enough. Hey, about that Frat Chat this Saturday. I'm glad you're coming. And this has nothing to do with anything divine, but there's some, oh, let's call it entertainment scheduled."

"A live band? What?"

"Uh-uh. The female kind of entertainment."

"Oh, I don't know if—"

"Look, I know you're not the type to get involved with such things, so just plan to hang out, like you said you would."

"I did say that."

"Yeah, and a promise is a promise."

"Well, one would surely state that that's a worthwhile value to uphold. Once spoken, it should never be disregarded. Sure."

"So, we'll just finish off a couple of beers, shoot the shit, just hang out."

"This female entertainer is probably, one might say, of the quite attractive variety?"

"Well, shit, yeah. Of course."

"And it's probably a safe wager that she makes no attempt to, uh, disguise it?"

"Not going to happen. Uh-uh."

Amos rolled his shoulders a few times, then sat up straighter. Then, he scoffed and tended to his drink while looking out over the park and incessant activities.

"What was that for?"

Amos turned to hold Emilio's gaze, then resumed his study of the grounds.

"Nothing. Well, nothing important. That special guest is probably more suited to such exploits than, shall we say, to more mundane expectations."

"I'm not following."

"Oh, I'm just thinking back to some of the countless psychology case histories I've studied. Many outlined the potential difficulties one might face when attempting any meaningful, oh, let's say relationships with such a woman."

"I'd say, bring on those difficulties," Emilio said, laughing. "Sign my ass up."

"We're back to the roller coasters, Emilio."

"We are?"

"When one digs deeply into the literature, one often finds detailed discussions of—"

"Shit, I'm going to need more coffee. You too. Be right back."

Amos finished what he had left while watching Emilio hike back toward the nearby coffee shop window.

* * *

Lenore picked her silent phone up off of her office desk and scoffed at the time.

"Well, Laura? What's taking you so long?"

She rolled her chair back, then rose and stretched, then walked over to the door. After looking around at several employees motionless at their screens, she closed the door quietly and returned to her seat.

Just then, her phone began its muted buzzing and light rattling.

"Laura, I was just wondering if you'd call. How are you?"

"Doing alright, Lenore. Just checking in. Seeing if we're still on for that glass of wine Saturday."

"Yes, of course. But Laura, I still don't know about anything more than that."

"Sure. That bum you're about to throw out, he—"

"Laura, come on. He's not a bum. And we had kind of a nice day yesterday. His Wednesdays are off, and I called in myself. We spent time in town."

"Spent time how?"

"Well, coffee. Lunch—I called you while he ran in for tacos. We, uh, did some walking around too. I led him over to where I could look at all of the frat houses."

"Ooh, Frat Row. Uh-huh. Did you wonder which one of those houses you'd soon be—"

"Laura, I never said I would. But, uh, I did wonder."

"You probably looked up at a bedroom window on the third floor of one of those gigantic old houses, and you imagined yourself up there, alone except for a bunch of horny young guys."

"You're too much sometimes. No, I didn't, not while I was standing there with Amos. That would have been—"

"Wait a second. You're clever, but I know you too well. So, what you're saying is that you *did* think about exactly that just not right then?"

"Laura."

"You can't keep secrets from me. Spill it, girl."

"Oh, sure. It was later, at bedtime, when—"

"When you were hiding yourself in some boring nightgown."

"Yes, actually."

"And burlap sacks, and an old tarp, and surplus quilts that were—"

"Laura, you're too much! I was trying to say that Amos didn't want to come to bed right away."

"Because of that boring nightgown?"

"What? No, not that. It was just, uh, awkward the night before."

"You told me some of it. What else?"

"Oh, Laura, it was probably mostly my fault. I was kind of, um, testing him. Teasing him. Seeing how things would go. I wanted to see if I could loosen him up—get him to act crazier."

"How? What were you doing?"

"I was talking about my breasts, and I got him talking about them too. I was talking about my engagement ring, too, about how it sent out the message that my breasts were his. Hell, I was telling him they were his, right?"

"That should have got him going. So, what happened?"

"Oh, God. I had the ring close to my breasts, and I was teasing him, telling him to get a closer look."

"He sure as shit should have. Hell of an invitation, huh?"

"Yeah. But then, I must have had some thoughts about, um, what we—"

"Oh, I know. You were thinking about how you're going to share those fantastic breasts of yours with all the—"

"Hey, I wasn't thinking exactly that. Just, you know . . . something exciting. Then, I made a joke about him getting a closer look before someone else does."

"You said that?"

"It's your fault, telling me about all that. Inviting me to take your place."

"I'll take the blame. Yep. So, that's what ruined things?"

"Yeah. He took off for the kitchen. So, last night, I guess he still felt weird, so he stayed in the kitchen for a while. And I, um . . ."

"You what?"

"This is your fault too. I let myself imagine what might happen there. I kind of, um, acted it out. In front of the mirror."

"Oh, good for you! And of course, it all just felt boring as hell, right?"

Lenore laughed and said, "No, just the opposite."

"I know. I'm just messing with you. What did you imagine?"

"I kind of did a striptease for the mirror, imagining that it was for, you know, whoever."

"Not just one whoever either."

"Uh, no. That was, um, kind of—"

"Hot. Hot and exciting, right?"

"Well, yeah. I kind of, um, didn't want to stop, but I heard Amos coming down the hallway."

"That bum ruined it. Well, I can guarantee you one thing."

"What's that?"

"He won't ruin it for you Saturday night."

"Laura."

"At the Frat Chat."

"I never said—"

"When you're doing it for real. Not just for a mirror."

"But I—"

"But you deserve it. Lenore, it's just about over with him. You know it. I know it. Shit, he probably knows it."

"It's not looking good."

"Besides, I can't make it. Something came up, and I have to be out of town that night."

"Laura, no. I just . . . couldn't."

"You could. Say you will."

Many quiet seconds passed before Laura spoke again.

"It's simple, Lenore. Just say yes. Right now. Say it."

After another few quiet seconds, Lenore said, "Yes."

"Good girl."

Lenore laughed and said, "Uh-uh, kind of the opposite."

"Yes, that's right. Ooh, bad girl. Such a bad girl, Lenore."

"You've been kind of a bad girl since college."

"Yep. Won't deny it."

"Want to know a secret? I've always been kind of jealous of that."

"That's no secret. It's been obvious as hell. So, for one night, you can—"

"Be a bad girl. Oh God, Laura, I can't believe you're talking me into this."

"Huh. Didn't take all that much. Let's go over more of the details. You'll need to—"

"Oh, wait. Someone's at my door. Can we talk later?"

"Shit, Lenore. Plan on it."

* * *

Emilio was grinning as he took the final steps toward the picnic table, where he handed a fresh coffee to Amos.

"Thanks. Again."

"Student loans."

"Yes," said Amos. "So, we were diverging off on a tangent about—"

"Roller coasters," Emilio said. "This might actually be pretty good."

"Well, give me a chance with this. One might even request more of a chance than what I'm given in a lecture hall."

"Fair enough. I might even crank out another chapter for whatever you're about to spout."

Laughing, Amos said, "We professors do tend to spout."

"And spout and spout and—"

"Alright, I get it. Okay, so, there are numerous case studies of a specific situation, all slightly different. But for simplicity, I'll just liken it all to owning a very shiny, fast roller coaster car."

"Which you want to sit in, as long as it's not moving."

"Uh, well, this isn't about me. We're talking about the literature here."

"Sure. Alright, what about this hypothetical coaster car?"

"Per the studies, many have found themselves regretting trying to acquire and keep such a car. They think it's what they want, so they focus on it—that's their goal—so they—"

"Let me guess: they get it, and they always want more? Something shinier? Faster?"

"Some might. But I'm talking about a different outcome. You're still grandstanding from the back row, even out in the park."

"Oh, yeah. Sorry. Go on."

"Thank you. So, many an individual finds that fast, shiny car, and they think they're set. All is good. But things very often go awry."

"I like rye toast."

"Quiet in the back row."

Emilio laughed, then used his free hand to gesture for Amos to continue.

"Uh, I do, too, by the way. Anyway, what often happens, using the same analogy—a roller coaster car—is that a line develops once the crowds see how fast and shiny the car is. Can't blame them, right?"

"No blame coming from the back row."

"No. So, all this competition develops, all because that coaster car is so extraordinary. Before long, the individual that wanted that car, then thought they had it, finds himself or herself way, way back in line. Most of them never get a chance to ride in that car again."

"That's profound."

"Well, one might say that it's just a natural fact of life."

Emilio took a deep sip, then scoffed loudly.

"So, professor, there's got to be a moral after all that. Lay it on me."

"There's not always a—"

"Here's one: go for the plain car. The slow one. Settle for that so the crowds don't swarm in and take the nice one that you really want."

"Uh, maybe. That could be a logical conclusion, sure."

"You got a better one?"

Amos cleared his throat, then said, "Well, without having given a moral too much thought, I'd say that maybe the keeper of the fast, shiny car could, I don't know, smudge it up. Maybe not let it coast so fast all the time."

"Oh, I get it. Keep it secret. Some kind of disguise."

"Off the top of my head, yes, that's one solution."

At Emilio's scoff, Amos turned enough to watch him grinning and looking out at the students and townspeople out for a day in the park.

"Huh," Emilio said, shaking his head. "Imagine if you took some time and gave it some actual thought."

"Yes, uh, but we, uh, we're back to that Frat Chat thing."

"The shiny car that's the star attraction."

"Yes, her. She, that entertainment, won't be roaming all over in the house?"

"No way. It's all like a secret thing up on the third floor."

"What exactly is she there for? Who is she? Is she—"

Emilio laughed and said, "Damn, you're sounding kind of interested after all."

"No, I'm really not. Curiosity isn't the same as interest."

"If you say so."

"Well, I do say so. And the distinction is supported often in the literature, where people often—"

"She's blond. That's all I know."

"Huh? I wasn't even asking. I don't even want to know."

"And you don't have to. That's the beauty of a Frat Chat. Well, from what I hear—this will be my first. The point is, stay in the lounge, have a few drinks, and just sit around with the guys and—"

"Chat?"

"Exactly. No third floor for you, professor."

"Uh, no. Of course not."

Chapter 17 – Some Lower Feelings

"Wine, Amos?"

He looked over his plate of spaghetti, across the table, and into the eyes of Lenore, who was chewing and waiting for a response.

"I should have asked before we got started."

"It's never a bad time," he said. "Uh, no, I'm good. Thanks, though."

She set her fork down after taking another bite and backed out her chair.

Speaking around the food, she said, "Don't mind if I do."

"Oh, sorry," he said. "I could have offered to get you some."

"Nonsense. Easy enough."

He paused his halfhearted dining to watch as she held up the bottle, using the afternoon light through the window as a backdrop.

"Huh," she said, then pried out the cork.

"I, uh, had more than I thought the other day," he said. "It's quite good."

"Yeah," she said while pouring. "It's one of those things where once you start, you don't always want to stop."

"One would have to agree with that. Reading is like that for me too."

"I've noticed."

She hadn't turned to say it, and she twisted the cork back in, then held the bottle up for another look.

"Oh, what the heck," she said, then uncorked, poured the rest into her glass, then pushed the empty bottle to the back of the counter.

"Like you said, Lenore."

"Yep. It's one of those things."

She turned and took the few steps back to her seat, then took another drink before setting down the glass and sitting.

"Beer is sometimes good too," he said. "Today, talking with Emilio, he invited me out with him and his friends to have a drink."

"Oh, well, that's nice. You think you'll have beer?"

"Probably. I so seldom have it, and it's a good chance."

"Where do you all plan on going?"

"Oh, uh, just somewhere in town. There are just so many places for the kids to hang out around town. I mean, even just around the park, there are—"

"Huh. I'm surprised he didn't say where."

"Well, Lenore, it's possible that he hasn't even thought about it yet. You know how kids are."

"Kids?"

"Well, they're young enough that they sometimes seem—"

"Like young adults. Yeah, you're right. Maybe not exactly kids, though."

"Probably not. No, they're mostly grown up and are certainly adults. So, he invited me today while we were having coffee, and I remembered that you were sneaking out for—"

"Sneaking, Amos? Who said I was—"

"Just a colloquial term to add some—"

"I told you about it. About, uh, having a drink with Laura, remember?"

"Oh, yes, you surely did. I remember you saying that clearly, about going out with Laura."

"So, there's really no sneaking going on."

"It was just an unfortunate attempt at more colorful language."

"Well, that's good about Saturday. I'm glad you're getting out and not just fiddling with research and lesson plans and stuff."

"Yes, one can't deny that it's good timing. And I'm free to go and not feel like you're being left alone with nothing interesting to do."

"Well, no, I sure won't be alone. And I expect that I won't be bored or anything."

"Good. I don't expect that I'll have—uh-oh, more colorful language—an enraptured time, but I hope you do."

"Enraptured? Uh, yeah. That's colorful. Where did that word come from?"

"Oh, I don't know. Emilio, that philosopher student that I talk with sometimes, has this theory or idea he's working on about contrasts. One of his examples is about roller coasters. Maybe I was thinking about that? You know, the absolute thrill of doing something like that?"

"Uh, yeah. That could be an enraptured experience, I guess."

"So, changing subjects, do you have any photos of Laura? I must admit, I'm curious since you said you two kind of look alike."

"Oh, sure, somewhere. I probably have a few photos I can dig up. After dinner?"

He grinned, nodded, and said, "Okay," then pointed at her wine glass.

"Be sure to finish. That might be the single most important thing one can't stop once they start."

"Huh. Maybe," she said. "Like if you've been thirsty for it for a long time."

"I like how you're so rational and make so much sense. Good for you."

"Thanks. That's me, all the time."

*   *   *

After finishing some minimal cleaning in the kitchen, Lenore walked past the entrance to the living room and paused to look in on Amos, already seated somewhat rigidly on the couch and scanning through some papers.

"Hey, I'll see if I can hunt down those photos. Give me a minute, alright? I've been wanting to redo my hair."

"That sounds good. I'll be right here."

"Okay. See you in a minute."

She made no effort to quiet her steps in the hallway, but she closed the bedroom door as quietly as she could.

And she locked it even more carefully.

The closet door opened quietly without any special effort from her, and she dropped down to wiggle out the bottom box in a stack of them. With that in her hands, she plopped backwards to sit, then popped off the lid.

Inside it were all kinds of odd things—mementos, beginnings of a coin collection, worn playing cards, and most importantly, an envelope not quite large enough to contain several photographs.

She slipped them out, then closed up the box and returned it to its place at the bottom of the stack. Already looking through them, she stood and walked to the dresser, the one with the voyeuristic mirror.

She laid them out and leaned over to examine the line of photos of her and Laura from their college days.

"Could be twins," she said softly as she took a few seconds to arrange them neatly. "Oh, there's no doubt about that."

Most were images of them from their shoulders up, their smiling faces filling the rectangle. One in particular, though, was taken with them back a step or two—not far enough to see anything below their waists, but certainly not what anyone would call a headshot.

She separated that one from the herd, which she shuffled together and left in a neat stack. That photo left out of the pack got leaned up against the mirror, and she took a step back.

From there, after confirming that the door was safely shut and listening but hearing no footsteps, she began looking from the photo of Laura to her face in the mirror.

Mostly the eyes, at first.

Then, the breasts.

"Hmm. Twins there too."

Looking at Laura's chest, she reached up to hold both of her breasts, then looked at her hands in the mirror.

"The ring," she said softly. "That's a difference."

She started to take it off, then came to a stop.

"No. I promised."

She sighed with her hands back in place but only for a second, then she glanced at the door before starting to quickly unbutton her loose shirt. Not bothering to get every last one near the bottom, she pulled it open enough to show part of her bra and her large breasts contained neatly there.

It was only a light scoff that accompanied her finishing off the buttons, then pulling the shirt wide open, and it stayed open.

"Yes, the ring," she said as she cupped both of her breasts again.

But a second later, she turned up her eyes and smirked.

Her hands rose up to the clips and bands that kept her hair all orderly and tame, and she quickly undid it all. Almost with a whooshing sound, it all cascaded onto her back.

"Huh," she said as she fluffed it up with both hands, then her eyes were drawn back to her breasts, which were also subjected to a level of order and tameness.

The door got another unenthusiastic glance, then she used both hands on the clasp between her breasts. It came open easily, and she hesitated with both hands holding it, ready to open.

"If I'm you, Laura," she said softly, "what's next?"

She grinned and pulled the bra open all the way.

"That's what. Just exactly like you would do."

She gave Laura's image another glance, scoffed at the smile that seemed aimed up at her, then focused again on the mirror.

And her hands, which had just tucked the open bra parts around to keep it all open, fluffed her hair forward, some on her shoulders and some on her chest. A few waves of it decorated her breasts in a teasing way.

"If I'm you, I have to really be you."

She placed both hands over them, not nearly covering them completely.

"Oh, I'd be you except for that ring. Wearing it, though, would be so . . . hmm. Maybe it's not really about some . . . promise."

She got her palms under her breasts, only slightly holding them up.

"And I'd have to . . . do whatever you would do."

She sighed as she began gentle squeezing, her eyes fixed on the shape of them changing as she squished them and seeing how much they filled her hands.

"These will have to be . . . for them. Hmm, *all* of them. You never even told me how many."

She looked up from her breasts, into her eyes, and said, "You can't say no, Lenore. Because, if you're there to be Laura, then you're . . . oh, what did I say the other day?"

Whatever trace of a smile she had vanished, and she said, while looking into her eyes and fondling her bare breasts, "If I'm there, then—no, *when* I'm there, I'm something soft, something soft that's there *only* to be . . . used . . . for sex."

She nodded and added, "Used."

She closed her eyes and tipped her head back, and she gave herself more ambitious squeezes and rubs all around.

Still aiming her closed eyes at the ceiling, she said, "I'll have to be an object. Just a soft object."

She tipped her head down and looked first at her breasts, which she noted again were quite large and were overflowing her hands, one of which was adorned with a sparkling diamond, then into her eyes.

"And I won't say no. Not to anything."

* * *

"Your hair looks good," Amos said while still sitting on the couch as Lenore walked into the room. "I always like it like that."

She turned her eyes up and scoffed.

"What, this? Easy enough. Glad you like it."

As she approached him, he glanced down at her hand.

"Oh, good, you found some photos. It must have taken some digging to get those, huh? It took a while."

"Well, sure. It took some, uh, looking through things to find them. There aren't too many."

While she was sitting beside him, he said, "One might say that even one is enough. It's really just to see how alike you two are."

"How alike we are? Um, maybe not totally. We kind of looked alike back then. That's all I said."

"Right. I remember."

"Here," she said, handing him only a few of the headshot variety. "Take a look. Me and Laura."

"Oh, look at that. I do see the resemblance. You had your hair up even back then. I guess that was always your preference, huh?"

"Uh, yeah. Kind of always."

He got to the last one, which showed Lenore smiling at the camera as Laura was turned toward her, lips puckered up and almost kissing her cheek.

"Well, she was quite the clown, huh? The things people do to be funny."

"Well, it wasn't just that. We really were good friends. She just—"

"Were, Lenore? That's kind of sad if—"

"Oh, no, I didn't mean that. We're still good friends. It's just different. Our lives are so different."

"Yes, well, time does change things. You can probably still share parts of your lives with each other, though."

"Oh, we do. I mean, when we can. Maybe it takes more of an effort to, like you said, share what our lives are like these days."

"Yes. And it's well worth the effort."

He handed the photos back to her, and she tucked them into a pocket of her shirt, then turned away quickly to button it up one higher. She was shaking her head about it when he spoke, then she turned back to him.

"So, you two went to college, graduated together, then—"

"Oh, no, I never said that. She, uh, dropped out kind of early. Like freshman year, actually."

"That's a shame. But college level courses aren't for everyone. There are many students that can't keep up and have to—"

"No, Amos, it wasn't grades. She, uh, kind of got into some trouble, and she figured the best thing to do was not be there anymore."

"What kind of trouble?"

"Like, well, getting caught messing around with staff."

"That's some bad judgment there, mostly for the staff member, who should know better. She could have just stayed focused on the work before her."

"Well, she wasn't really the type to follow rules."

"And where did that get her? I hope I don't sound like I'm being overly critical of your friend, Lenore, but—"

"No, it's fine. Go on."

"—but she seems to have let some lower feelings get—"

"Lower feelings?"

"Well, urges, maybe. You know what I mean. Really, why should it be so difficult to control oneself and think of the future?"

"I think she was always kind of thinking a lot of the moment too."

"Yes. And where did that get her?"

"Uh, dropped out."

"Yes, that's right. Now, look at you. You've stayed focused, got your education, and now are an esteemed and well-respected business leader of the community. Lenore, it's so commendable."

"Well, thanks, Amos."

"I don't mind saying that I greatly admire you. You're an inspiration in how you stay focused on what's productive and meaningful, and you do all that while looking quite enchanting too."

"Enchanting?"

"That might not the best word, I'll admit," he said with a light laugh. "How about like a vision of beauty? Yes, that's more what I mean."

"Well, thanks. That's very sweet."

He snickered and added, "But if you get in the habit of swilling that wine, that—"

"I've never swilled the wine!"

"I know. I'm only teasing. And I was going to conclude by saying that it would only serve to tarnish the image that you've crafted over the years. And that's a very good image."

"Well, you're certainly complimentary tonight. Maybe it's you that's been swilling the wine."

"Oh, I don't think so. I sure am looking forward to a cold beer on Saturday, though. I don't partake of that too often."

"No, you don't."

"You'll be doing some partaking Saturday too."

"Uh, partaking?"

"Wine? With Laura?"

"Oh, I, uh, forgot for a second. Yes, I'm looking forward to that too. And I do plan to do some partaking."

"That's fine because I know it would never be so much that anyone would think less of you."

"Well, no. Wouldn't ever want that, right?"

"No, neither of us would."

"Alright, well, it's late. Ready for bed?"

"Yes. I'll be in in a minute."

She got up and said, while walking out of the room and not looking back, "Okay, see you soon."

Chapter 18 – It's Just to You, Right Now

Lenore groaned as she leaned her back into the door to latch it. Already reaching up a hand toward her breasts, she turned and also reached for the small lock lever, but she paused and didn't flip it.

And she didn't follow through and grab either of her breasts.

She quickly changed into another of her nightgowns—different color, same lack of daring—and turned down the bed covers. A glance at one of the lit lamps evoked a light scoff, and the sight of the other led to a quick frown.

"Dammit."

After a quick glance at the light switch on the wall near the door, she frowned and climbed into bed, then pulled the covers up high.

Many quiet minutes passed as she stared up at the ceiling and still, no footfalls indicated anyone was coming down the hall to join her.

"Commendable," she said, shaking her head.

With her eyes on the door, she reached with both hands, snaking them along under the blankets, until she could place them on her breasts.

She kept her eyes on the door when she scoffed, then said, "Esteemed and well-respected?"

Fingertips found the straps up over her shoulders, and she held them.

"It's my image to tarnish, you know."

She wasted no time in pulling the straps down along her arms, and she made sure that the sturdy hem with only meager lace pressed down on her breasts as she dragged it down.

Stopping the unveiling, she said, "Mm, even just that."

She continued the tight drag far enough to free them. "And what if I'm mostly . . . something soft?"

She let go of the straps and squeezed both breasts.

"Something only for sex. Something to be . . . used."

Shuffling footsteps started out faint, then got louder as Amos approached the closed but unlocked door that led to a room with its lights on and something soft waiting under the blankets.

The door opened, and Amos looked first at the lights, never looked at Lenore, then looked at and reached for the switch.

"Leave it," she said, and he stopped.

"Leave the lights on?"

"Just for a minute."

She moved her hands enough to draw his attention to where she was holding her bare breasts under the covers.

"Guess what I want to show you."

"With, with the lights on, Lenore?"

She nodded and said, "Yep. Come closer."

He looked at the switch again, then closed the door and walked to her side of the bed.

"You don't have to, um, do—"

"No one said I had to."

"No, I never did. So, there's no reason to—"

"What if I wanted to? What if I just wanted to lie here with my—"

"Lenore. You don't have to—"

"Just for you to look at? Just leave them uncovered for—"

"But Lenore, there's no need to—"

"Would that tarnish my image to you, Amos?" she said, grinning like it was only for fun.

"Uh, no. Of course not. I know you're not, um, the kind of woman that would . . ."

"Hmm? That would want her bare breasts looked at?"

"Lenore. Just—"

"Who would want them admired?"

"I already admire you. I just told you so."

"Hmm. You weren't talking about my breasts, though, were you?"

"Why would I have to? Lenore, what is this?"

"Why, Amos, it's just me, lying in bed."

She giggled and sat up and with both arms out, she held the blankets up high and close like a curtain, still making the sight of her breasts under all of that obvious as two bumps in the thick cloth.

"Sitting up in bed. Wondering if you'd want to watch me show off my—"

"Show them off? Really?"

"Well, it's just to you right now."

"What?" he said, his voice rising. "Right now? What does that mean?"

"Nothing! Amos, it's just that it's only you and me, that's all I meant."

His lips trembled, and he didn't let his eyes move down to take in the extra mounding caused by Lenore's intentionally exaggeratedly good posture.

"Maybe," she said, "it was that wine with dinner? Maybe I—"

"Lenore! You're saying that when you're drinking, you feel like showing off your body?"

"No, that's not what I meant! The wine doesn't do anything that—"

"Even worse! You can be perfectly sober, and still, you . . . you . . ."

"Amos."

He looked at his feet and sighed loudly and sarcastically.

"Amos!"

He looked up.

"I just don't know what this is about. You're beautiful, Lenore. You never need to show anything off."

"Amos, don't be upset. Maybe that was just a bad choice of words. Maybe just showing would be—"

"Showing is unnecessary. Lenore, you . . . I don't know."

He started backing himself toward the door.

"I don't . . . I just . . ."

"Amos."

"I, um, I'll be right back. There's a, um, book that I want to remember to, uh, take to class tomorrow."

"Amos."

"I'll be back in a minute. I'll be right back."

The shaky, quick closing of the door led to a soft boom, and Lenore lay in bed staring at it.

But for only a moment. She shook her head and groaned as she got her nightgown in order, then jumped out of bed and rushed to the door.

"Oh, God," she said, frowning as she turned and leaned her back into it.

Her agitated breaths, which she kept as quiet as possible, gave her breasts a steady motion as she waited there, listening.

But she heard nothing beyond the door—no footsteps, no mumbling, not even her name being spoken.

"Dammit. I just wanted to . . . show you."

She looked down at her chest still animated by her quick, deep breaths.

"Dammit, to show . . . someone."

* * *

Amos let go of the bedroom door's knob, huffed out a shallow breath, and looked down the hallway toward the kitchen. He started to take a step and had just begun to lean himself in that direction, but he straightened up and closed his eyes as he tipped back into the door—slowly and quietly, not making a sound.

Squinting at the opposite wall, which carried only traces of light from the kitchen, he said, too softly even to hear himself, "Why?"

One purposefully slow, deep breath got drawn in quietly, then he scoffed without any sound and turned to place his hand again on the doorknob.

But he froze himself there, holding the knob and staring at the dark slab that he'd just closed, leaving Lenore on the other side.

Only seconds later, he crunched up his shoulders, and a shiver worked its way down from there, and he let go of the doorknob.

Looking down at his feet and shaking his head, he ambled toward the kitchen, not making any effort to silence his steps.

Before sitting at the table, he got a hand around the neck of the wine bottle and gave the pair of washed glasses a look.

And he left both of them there as he and the bottle sat to keep each other company.

* * *

She held her breath at the sound of Amos walking away from the door, down the hall and toward the kitchen. After he'd made some progress, she let herself breathe again, but she kept her head turning, giving an ear a chance to monitor the sounds until she heard a chair scrape, something solid clunk on the table, and a male voice groan.

She let a few more seconds pass, then said, "What the hell. Why can't you . . ."

She kept listening, and there were no sounds of footsteps returning. There wasn't even a sound of a bottle clinking on the rim of a glass.

Turning herself enough to look down at the doorknob, she snarled silently, reached for it with one hand to hold it still, then flipped the locking mechanism with her other hand.

With her back against the locked door, she tapped the mounded-up hair at the back of her head into it, her actions slow and gentle and not making a sound.

"Dammit, Amos. You'll know that I tried. I tried with you."

She checked the knob, tried to turn it, and confirmed that it was secure, then she walked back to the bed and its glowing lamps on each nightstand.

The covers were still bunched up where she'd left them, and she got herself in on her side of the bed, lay back against the pillows, and pulled the covers up to her chin. Only a second or two later, she quickly pulled down the nightgown's slender straps, then pulled them farther and bared her breasts.

"I tried."

She scoffed at the ceiling and folded down the covers. Her hands were already in place, and she smirked quickly when she began to rub her palms slowly all over her breasts, tipping them each way, sometimes squeezing them and pushing them together.

"God, I say dumb things, though. Maybe it's on purpose?"

She kept rubbing, and the locked-in frown softened into a calm look, then the beginning of a smile.

"Soft. I sure am soft."

She tipped her head back, eyes closed, and let out a deep sigh.

"So soft and I should be . . ."

With a groan mixed with a very quiet laugh, she gave her breasts a harder squeeze and held it. Then, she let them go, spun herself over, and raised up on her hands and knees.

She looked underneath long enough to tuck the nightie farther back, leaving her breasts unencumbered and hanging down below her.

"Maybe . . . like this?"

With one hand supporting her, she felt around underneath, bouncing her breasts, pressing them up and letting them go, sometimes just dragging her palms across, barely touching only the parts nearest to the sheet.

"So soft . . ."

She left her breasts alone just long enough to reach farther back, to the long garment's hemline that was still most of the way down her thighs, almost at her knees.

Pulling it from one side worked well enough, and she watched herself in the mirror as the cloth moved higher and higher, up along the backs of her thighs, and she hesitated before finishing.

"So soft . . . all over."

With a low moan, she dragged the plain fabric higher, uncovering her bare bottom, and she didn't let it go until it rested on her lower back and hung down on both sides.

"Hmm . . . maybe like this. Kind of a nice profile view. Hmm."

She watched in the mirror as she gave her breasts a few more rubs and squeezes, then tipped her head up enough to look straight ahead.

"Just a soft object."

She let out another low moan as she tipped her head up farther, enough that she could look higher, and she waited there on her hands and knees and baring the parts of her that a proper woman, a future wife of a professor, a respected local business owner, should never expose.

And certainly not share.

With however many.

"No," she said, holding herself still and looking up. "I promise all of you I won't say no. Not to . . . anything."

She waited, grinning at her own comments, then turned her head as if listening.

"What's that? It doesn't matter if I say no?"

She faked a frightened look and said, without much breath and with even less conviction, "No! Oh, please, no!"

Still looking scared, she kept her eyes up, opened her mouth, and arched her back even more. Then, she leaned her hips back just a bit farther.

"Uh-huh. They'd like me just like this. Every soft part of me is just . . . ready."

She held that until her scared expression morphed into a modest grin, then a smile, then she laid herself down and rolled over.

"Oh, God. Amos, you don't know what you're . . ."

She groaned and shifted her nightgown all around, tugging it down and restoring the straps over her shoulders, then sat up and looked at the door.

Her puffed up cheeks let the breath trickle out, then she rolled herself up onto her feet, hurried to the door, and quietly unlocked it.

She'd taken a few steps toward the bed before she tiptoed back and switched off the light, then scoffed in the quiet darkness.

Chapter 19 – A Promise to Not Say No

Amos stretched as well as he could without causing the thin fleece blanket covering him to fall to the floor. And when his feet collided with the arm of the couch, he quit trying and opened his eyes.

The day's beginning sunlight was creeping in well enough through the living room's large window. And it was enough for him to see his wristwatch, even as he gasped out a lengthy yawn, then he snapped his eyes toward the wall clock.

"Oh, shit."

He rolled off and stood, then bent to retrieve the blanket that he'd just dumped, which he folded quickly and laid neatly on the back of the couch. While raking his fingers through his hair and rubbing his face, he walked far enough to look down the hall, then scoffed at the sight of the bedroom door still closed.

Treading carefully and quietly, he got to the door, checked the knob with a couple of light twists and found it unlocked, then turned it all the way and pushed in the door.

The bedroom had less light than the living room, but it was enough that he saw the shape of Lenore under the blankets, on her side of the bed. He left the door open and crept closer, close enough to stand beside her.

She was lying facedown, and the blankets were pulled up high enough to leave only an unruly mound of hair fighting the tyranny of clips and bands. But several wisps and small clumps had managed to escape the hive and venture out to be seen.

He leaned over, careful to not bump the bed, and saw her cheek and closed eyes, both adorned with random strands of her blond hair, some moving with her slow, easy breaths.

Straightening back up, he kept his breaths quiet and tipped his head, still staring at the sight of her shifting her hips one way, then the other under the blanket.

She repeated the cycle a few times, then let out a breath that had the distinct sound of her saying, "Hmm . . ."

Leaning out over her again, he watched her lick her lips a few times, sigh, then resume her sleep, motionless except for the softest of breaths.

Shaking his head while taking silent backwards steps, his outstretched hand made contact with the dresser, and he turned his eyes there enough to locate one of Lenore's drawers.

Dividing his time between easing out the drawer and watching for signs of Lenore waking, he got it open, then reached down for her cheerleader skirt beneath the tight uniform t-shirt and other articles.

With a hand on it, he fixed his sights on Lenore as he slipped the skirt around, then up and out into the open air.

She hadn't stirred, not at all, and he raised it up to hold it with two hands, just high enough to still permit a view of his sleeping fiancé.

Even as he watched her tip her head around, then begin to roll toward him, he raised the skirt closer to his face and began to inhale. And that breath stayed in his lungs as she opened her eyes, which were focused directly at him.

"Amos? What are you doing?"

*   *   *

"Sorry. Did I wake you? I was trying to stay—"

"Amos, that's fine. I'm just wondering what you're doing with my skirt?"

He lowered it, watched it descend until his arms were down all the way, then turned his attention back to Lenore.

112

"Well, I, uh, was going to do some laundry later, and this—"

"You were sniffing it? Why, to see if it was clean, I suppose?"

He tossed it onto the dresser without looking.

"Uh, sure. Not just that. You know, when doing laundry, it's good to—"

"Oh, you're checking other clothes too. I see."

"Well, yes, because—"

Looking at the open drawer, she said, "Looks pretty neat, still. You've checked other things too?"

"Uh, no, not yet. This was the first. Maybe I'm just thinking about it more because we talked about it the other day."

"We did. In case you're wondering, since you've already noticed, I do wash it occasionally. I just toss it in with everything else when it's my turn for laundry day."

Leaning against the dresser with his arms crossed, he said, "Why? Why bother?"

"Oh, I don't know. Like I said before: I read somewhere that garments last longer if you do that, that's all."

"Well, I guess it doesn't need it this time. Good that it's clean in case you ever want to try it on. I can't imagine why, but at least it's—"

She'd been sitting up, keeping the blankets high, and yawning before speaking, then said, "I do model it sometimes. I never feel like I need any kind of reason either."

"It still fits the same?"

"Yes, I'm happy to say that it does. Still looks as good as ever."

"Sure, why not? Alone, at home, in the bedroom is a good place to try it on again."

He laughed and added, "Maybe not so much out in public, though. It looks really short."

"It is really short, Amos. That's the whole point."

"What's the whole point?"

"To, you know, show off my—a cheerleader's legs. It's supposed to be provocative."

"Ah, college days, huh? At that age, it's not surprising that—"

"My legs still look good, Amos. I haven't changed. I like how they look when I model that skirt. It brings back fun memories."

"Memories from times gone by are good. Uh, how fun?"

"Just cheerleading. At the games. You know. Crowds going crazy."

"That, uh, was fun, I'd bet. It's probably so much more satisfying to accomplish your goals at work, though, right? I mean, running a successful business is, one might say, kind of fun too."

"Oh, sure. Just not the same kind of fun."

"Well, no. How could it be?"

"I'll tell you how: if I wore that outfit to work one day. Yeah, I could schedule a costume day at the office. How about that? Good idea. Thanks for thinking of—"

"No, you wouldn't. Lenore, that sounds fun, but you know that would be quite unprofessional."

"I kind of like the idea of scheduling a day for me to wear that."

"I don't believe that would help at all with your professional goals, Lenore."

She scoffed and said, "You're right. I won't be scheduling any days at the office for a costume like that."

"Exactly. Um, I fell asleep on the couch. I was out until just now. Did you sleep okay?"

"Yeah, good enough."

She glanced at the clock and said, "Oh, shit. It's late. And you're not ready either."

He took a few quick steps toward the door and grabbed the clothes hanging on the hook.

"I'll just go get dressed and leave you to some privacy."

"You don't have to—"

Clutching the clothes that he'd worn the day before, he was already passing through the doorway when he said, "No, it's fine. I'd better get going."

She stared at the closed door, then looked to the skirt that he'd left on the dresser top.

"Nope. No need to wear that to the office."

She swung her legs out from under the blankets and sat on the edge of the bed.

"And these legs still do look good. Good enough for that short skirt."

She stood and slowly tugged up at the hem of her nightgown, not stopping until she could see the entire length of her legs, then she looked toward the closed door.

"Or . . . no skirt. Hmm, no skirt for a party favor sounds about right. What do you think about that, Amos? I mean, if I'm tarnishing my image anyway, I'll tarnish it my way: with . . . no skirt at all."

* * *

After waiting and listening for a response to her question to Amos that was barely loud enough for her to hear herself, Lenore scoffed at the closed bedroom door.

After giving the clock on her nightstand a quick glance, she said, "Oh, shit," then hurried to unbind her long hair, tossing all of the clips and other fasteners onto the dresser.

She gave it all a fluff, then brushed it back on both sides before slipping the nightgown straps down over her shoulders, then wiggling the whole thing down to her ankles.

It got nudged to one side, then she looked at her reflection, a view of her totally naked with her hair down.

Grinning, she said, "Naked . . ."

Both hands rose up to hold her breasts.

". . . except for an engagement ring."

She gave them gentle squeezes, shook her head to play her hair out to one side, then the other, then said, "And just like that, I'd be wearing all I need for—"

A few sharp knocks on the door preceded Amos calling out, "I'm ready. Are you close? Clock's ticking."

"Just a second!"

She looked down at the doorknob, saw that it wasn't turning, then scoffed at seeing that it was unlocked too.

With eyes back to the mirror, she turned to one side, still holding her breasts, enough to get a good sight of nothing but bare skin from her back, then over the tight curves of what a small cheerleader's skirt would cover, then down the backs of her thighs.

"Yeah," she said softly, "they'll insist that I lose the skirt so it doesn't get in anyone's way when—"

Through the closed door, Amos spoke loudly, saying, "Maybe I should just walk into town?"

She barely gave the door a glance and said, "No, I'll be out in a second or two. Hang on."

Turning back toward the mirror, she rested her forearms on the dresser, then stepped back, then leaned forward. She freed up one hand to feel around underneath, where she gave each breast a bounce, pressing each one up and letting it go again.

Then, she rested her arm again up with the other and looked into her eyes.

"Maybe even . . . like this? Just . . . bent over?"

She shook her head and grinned, then said, "Could I? Would I?"

The grin faded, and she opened and kept open her mouth. Her breaths were picking up their pace, and she looked from her eyes to her open, waiting mouth, then back to—"

The door got a solid rapping, and Amos said, "It's getting kind of late. I'd better just get walking."

She scoffed, then puckered up, offering a kiss to her reflection.

"Okay, Amos. I'm just, uh, feeling kind of distracted today."

She gave her reflection another kiss while listening to him.

"Don't take too long. You have a business to run."

"Yes. Business to take care of. See you later, then."

"Okay. Bye. We really should get another car someday."

"Yes, we can't keep putting that off. Bye."

The sound of footsteps faded, then the front door closed with a soft thump.

"Hmm."

She tipped herself up just enough to use both hands to gather up her hair, then left it all fluffed straight up with her right hand gripping it tight near her scalp.

Still upright enough to see her breasts, she moved her left hand there, then looked into her eyes.

And she gave her hair a modest pull, tipping her head back, and she gasped loudly, like someone alone in a house would be able to do, as it forced her mouth to open wide.

"No!" she whispered. "I said no! I'm too proper! Not that!"

She gave her hair another, sharper tug and groaned as the force of it jiggled her breasts around.

"Oh," she said, trying to garble her words, "I sure didn't stop you, did I? You even made me . . . after you . . . hmm."

She watched her lips pucker and squeeze together a few times, then open again.

"Oh, another one now? Again?"

Keeping a tight, uncompromising hold, strong enough to keep her head locked back, she said, "Hmm, I did make a promise to not say no."

She turned her eyes to the sparkling ring on a hand that couldn't possibly cover the breast that it was squeezing, then she looked back into her eyes.

"Uh-uh. Not to anything."

Chapter 20 – Every Single Thing They Want

"Your lecture was decent enough today," Emilio said as he handed a cup of coffee to Amos, who was already seated with impeccable posture at their usual picnic table.

"Decent, huh? That's why you didn't inject any philosophy?"

"No, that just gets boring after a while."

"What about the book?"

"I'll get around to it. I think I need to let some thoughts germinate, pollinate, or whatever they do."

Amos sipped, then said, "Yes, something like that. We all have things, I think, that ought to be left alone to germinate."

Emilio turned with a frown, then said, "Like your next lesson plan? Yeah, heavy stuff."

He scoffed and went back to monitoring the park visitors while holding the coffee close, ready for another drink.

"Yes. That. Other things, too, though."

Emilio laughed and said, "If you were a case history come to life, we might be talking about slow cars, fast cars, boring cars, shiny—"

"Who ever said boring?"

"Didn't you?"

"No. I think I said sitting still. Calm. Not too fast to attract all kinds of attention."

"Oh, right. That was it."

He gave it a few seconds, then added, "Which translates to boring."

"You're wrong. There's nothing wrong with—I mean, in the literature that I've studied, no one was griping about anything being boring. Just calm, stable, predictable. One might even say respectable. Proper."

"Yeah, one might at that. So, about the Frat Chat. I had an actual chat with Brock, and he's kind of a greedy son of a bitch with details. I did twist a name out of him, though."

"Oh, for the entertainment, you mean?"

"Yep. Laura."

"Laura, huh? A student here?"

"I really don't know. Could be. Probably is, yeah."

They watched a football fly in from the left, hit in the grass, then bounce off to the right. Both heads, each with a steaming cup close and ready, turned to follow its path.

Amos broke the silence.

"She's probably not an example of a slow, calm, respectable car."

"In her day-to-day life, she might be that exactly. Who knows?"

"But on Saturday?"

"Shit, she's anything but respectable. At least, if all of Brock's hints about it are true."

"What kinds of hints?"

"Just that anything goes."

"Anything?"

"Yep. She's not respectable at all. I hear she does anything they want."

"They being . . ."

"Whoever wants in on the action."

"So, no one would refer to her as a calm, modest, respectable kind of—"

"She's a slut. Yeah, you're right."

"Emilio, I wasn't about to say that."

"Sure you were. You were thinking it, at least."

"Not with such a derogatory term, I assure you. And I thought your mind was trying to solve some issues about, what was it, divinity?"

"Oh, that. That's nothing compared to the thought of a slut named Laura."

"You don't even know what she looks like, though."

"I already know she's perfect. I'll think so Saturday anyway."

"You will? How can you be so certain?"

"I don't know, professor. Maybe because she's being such a slut."

"That's a rather offensive term, you know."

"Hey. It's accurate."

"If anything, I was thinking that the young lady could probably find a better way to spend her—"

"No, professor. Sir. The way I hear it, she's as happy as can be being a slut for anyone and everyone."

"Everyone being—"

"A lot. Yeah. However many."

Emilio gave him a second, then turned to look as Amos only kept staring out over the lawn area.

Grinning, he said, "Plus one?"

Amos smiled for a few seconds, then shook his head.

"Doubtful, Emilio. In fact, I can assure you that I'm focused entirely on the chat aspect of this so-called Frat Chat."

* * *

Lenore stretched up to wipe the higher scribbling from the impromptu morning meeting off of the whiteboard in her office. Reaching way up and balancing on heels higher than she usually wore to work, the sweeping motions got her hips moving from side to side as the notes and diagrams gradually departed and left a clean slate.

"Let me guess. Amos is out of town."

She suspended the housekeeping and turned to look toward the open door.

"Shirley? What are you talking about now?"

The associate, one of her longest employees, smiled as she looked her up and down, then rested with a focus just on her eyes.

"Just guessing by the way you're dressed today."

Lenore grinned, looked down at herself, then back at Shirley.

"Nonsense. He doesn't decide what I wear. I just felt like digging deeper into the closet today."

"Uh-huh."

She looked at her footwear, then back up.

"You never wear heels like those. What's the occasion?"

"Shirley, you're being silly. Same story: just recycling some older stuff. What do you need?"

"Nothing special. We're phoning in an order for some sandwiches again. You want your usual?"

"Yeah, that would be nice. Oh, ask them to throw in some hot sauce for a change too."

"Sure. Living kind of wild today, huh?"

"With hot sauce? Please, I could do better than that."

Lenore scoffed and shook her head, and Shirley only shrugged.

"That's as exciting as my life will ever get. Alright, I'll put in the order."

"Thanks. Can you close the door, too, Shirley?"

"Sure," she said as she hesitated in the doorway. "I bet you're getting home before Amos, too, right?"

"Shirley, just stop. You're being ridiculous."

Shirley waited, grinning, with her eyebrows held up high.

"Yeah. Fine. He won't get home until after me."

"Huh," she said, smiling as she left and pulled closed the door.

Lenore stared that way for only a second, then tapped a few times on her phone.

"Good," said Laura, "glad you called. You saved me from bugging you for a change."

"Laura, you're never bugging me. I just, um, I don't know if—"

"Oh, no. Don't you dare, Lenore."

"You don't even know what I was going to say."

"You're not backing out on your promise?"

"I promised? I, um, was just, uh—"

"No. The answer is no, you're not backing out. Try to tell me you haven't been thinking about it like all the time."

"I won't lie. Yeah, I'm sometimes kind of, I don't know, obsessed with thoughts of it."

"You mean fantasies of it?"

"Yeah. Alright, yeah."

"Believe me, Lenore, it's more intense and fun than you can imagine."

"Oh, I don't know. My imagination is kind of going crazy."

"And lucky Amos is there to take advantage of all that?"

"God, no. No, it's kind of ruining whatever was between us."

"Which wasn't much. Oh, sorry, that sounded kind of—"

"No, it's alright. It was never anything exciting. He's just never been so much, uh, you know."

"That's a real shame. You deserve to cut loose and have somebody cut loose with you. Tell me about some of these fantasies of yours."

"What? Right now?"

"Oh, you're at work. That's right. Okay, pick just one, then. Then, get your sweet ass back to work."

Lenore laughed and said, "Hmm, that's a nice compliment. I don't hear things like that often."

"Huh. Probably never. You'd better be ready for all you'll hear at your Frat Chat debut."

"Like what?"

"I'll tell you if you tell me at least one of your fantasies. Come on. Let's have it."

"Well, I can tell you that they're getting more, uh, bad. The last one, just this morning, oh my gosh."

"Go on."

"Alright, well? Amos slept on the couch, and he was—"

"Things really are going downhill, huh?"

"Kind of. Yeah. So, he wasn't in the room. He just came in to get clothes for work, then he left to get ready."

"Okay. So, you're alone in the room. Were you naked?"

"It didn't take long. Yeah, and I let my hair down, then I—"

"Shit, you never let that mane loose. Okay, you're naked, your hair is wild . . . what else?"

"I leaned against the dresser, and I kind of, uh, was sticking—"

"Sticking your ass out? Giving an invitation to the line of—"

"Laura, a line?"

"It's a big night. Better be ready for it."

"Oh my God. Um, so I played with my breasts while they were hanging there, then I—"

"Yeah. They'll love those. They really are magnificent."

"Oh, uh, thanks. Oh, then I got a grip on my hair, like it was someone else, and I pulled my head back, and that caused my mouth to open."

"Oh, I know what that's all about. You know someone will grab that beautiful hair of yours, and your sexy mouth sure will open, and what happens then?"

"Um . . ."

"Huh. I think you know. That's what you were imagining?"

"Mm-hmm. And I was even more bad because I was talking, too low for Amos to hear, but like I was talking to, uh . . ."

"Them?"

"Yeah. I was saying no, that I didn't want to. But Laura, they wouldn't take no for an answer."

Laura laughed and said, "They won't. Even if you say that, which you won't, they'll know you're just playing. No, they'll know you want it."

"I kind of thought so. Then, I gave in and said yes. I told them that I couldn't say no."

"You can't."

"Uh-uh. I told them I couldn't say no to anything."

"Shit, you're ready. Oh, one more thing: don't forget your cheerleader uniform. They like that."

"You were serious? I don't know about that."

"Tell me you don't want that. Go on, give that a try."

"It's just that, um . . ."

"I know you. And you know you. You're a hot, sexy cheerleader still, and you want to make them kind of crazy."

"And that'll do it?"

"Sure. Until."

"Until what?"

"Until you take it off. Poof. Gone."

"Oh my."

"Or they take it off of you. One way or another, you're going to be some sweet entertainment in nothing but your birthday suit."

"And I can't—"

"No. You can't say no. Not to—"

"Anything. So, you mean, even if they want me to—"

"Uh-huh. And you'll do it. All naked and smiling and doing every single thing they want."

"Oh my gosh."

* * *

"So, you've seriously given up on the divinity concept? Hot and cold? Roller coasters?"

"I don't know about giving up on it," said Emilio. "Postponing it maybe."

"Until after—"

"The Frat Chat. No, I'm still kind of thinking about it. What did I say about it before? Where were we with that?"

Amos pried the lid off of his cup and swirled it around a few times.

"Good. I think I have enough to last through whatever chapter is on your mind. You were, I think, saying something about crossing from cold to hot being a pleasure, of sorts. I think that's where you left it with the divine theorizing."

"Oh yeah, now I remember. Yeah. Because there's something special about feeling the cold, having it kind of overwhelm you, then, right then, feeling the warmth. That's what was cooking in my head."

"Germinating?"

"Yep. That too."

"At the risk of diverting your attention from Saturday evening's—"

"Slut."

Amos coughed and said, "Entertainment. Go ahead and get the ideas sprouting in your brain. Are we still with the passing from cold to warm being divine somehow? A car standing still, then racing down a hill? Divine?"

"Alright. Let me forgot about that . . ."

"I'm not saying it," said Amos. "That's your word."

"I'll keep it. You can say it, though, right?"

"Well, I can speak quite effortlessly, so probably. Sure."

"Go ahead, then."

"Why?"

"I really just make this shit up as I go, professor. And the shit percolating and brewing in my brain is saying that I should hear you say the word."

"Even though—"

"Even though you're far too decent to ever attach that to anyone in particular."

He coughed, then added, "No matter how slutty she likes to be."

"That's quite a lead-up you're offering."

"Hey, here to help."

"Fine. Slut."

"There, was that so difficult?"

"No, it's just a word."

"Exactly. Say it again, just to be sure you got it."

Amos laughed and paused his coffee close and said, "Slut," then took a swig.

"I won't ask you to admit it, but I'd bet you like saying it."

"Divinity, Emilio. Back to that?"

"Sure. So, my latest thought is that it's not really about passing from one thing to another. Oh, no. Nope. It's more about being both at the same time."

"Hot and cold?"

"Yeah, as one example. Like that hot tub on a mountain."

"And why exactly is that divine?"

"Alright, I'm just making shit up, remember?"

"That's probably how some of the most profound ideas come into existence."

"That's beautiful. Neither one of us believes it, though."

"I sure don't."

"I knew it. Dammit. Alright, let's see: it's divine because you're feeling both hot and cold at the same time."

"I'm not following."

"Me neither. Alright, maybe it's like this: if you focus on the cold, you want the heat. But you already have the heat, so you focus on that, then—"

"Then, you want the cold? You just kind of bounce around between the two?"

"Told you. Just all stewing around up there."

"Well, no, you might be onto something, Emilio. Work with me here. You're feeling something like a need for warmth, but you already have it. So, you're also feeling a need for the cold because you're warm, but you already have that too."

"Yeah. And it kind of blows your mind."

"It does?"

"It's all I got."

"Maybe it's more about our senses."

"Now, you're onto something, professor. Yeah, it scrambles up our senses."

"Even if that's what's happening, how is that divine?"

"Uh, I don't know. Oh! Maybe because it jams a wrench in our brains, shuts down all the thoughts about it."

"Which leaves us just . . ."

"Feeling it," said Emilio. "Shit, overloaded with just the feelings."

"Divine?"

"Huh. Who knows?"

Amos tipped back his cup, then tapped on it and set it on his leg.

"Perfect timing. The germinating and the coffee were depleted simultaneously."

"Huh. That's kind of profound too."

He watched as Amos crumpled up the cup and tossed it into the grass.

They both stared at it.

"You're littering, professor?"

"No, I'm getting divine. There's grass, then there's litter in the grass too. See?"

"No, I don't see. You don't really care about either of those. You're not invested."

"Oh. Like I would be freezing to death or—"

"Boiling in oil."

"Where did that come from?"

"Who knows? Oh, forget that divinity nonsense for a minute. There's one other detail from Brock that I forgot to mention."

"About the—"

"Sweet but misguided young lady?"

"That's funny, Emilio. Yeah. Her."

"Well, I try. Alright, she usually wears a special, let's say, costume."

"What kind?"

"She dresses herself up like a cheerleader."

Emilio grinned and waited, and the seconds crawled past in silence, so he turned to look. Amos was staring away, his face blank.

"Sure, not your thing. It's a frat house, remember? So, it's kind of an appropriate little twist to the whole sordid extravaganza."

Amos kept staring, and Emilio waved a hand past his eyes, causing him to snap his head toward him.

"Yeah, it's not for everyone. I guess that's her thing, though."

"No, uh, I don't have anything against that. It's quite a common, um, one might say—"

"Fantasy?"

"Uh, sure. I was just going to say 'costume.'"

"Sure you were. Uh-huh. I've heard that she's an absolute knockout in it too. I mean, short skirt and legs like crazy. Stacked too. Just the typical fantasy cheerleader."

"But not cheering, just being—"

"A slut. Yeah, professor. A completely compliant and cooperative slut."

"Oh my gosh."

* * *

"You what? Laura!"

Lenore was seated at her desk, bags and wrappers and emptied hot sauce packets still scattered around, and she held her phone to her ear.

"I set it up. You figured I would, right?"

"I wasn't sure. I didn't tell you for sure."

"Oh, come on. You know you want to."

"Well, I guess, sort of, but that doesn't mean—"

"Look, Lenore, it's just too late. I already squared it away with Brock."

"Who's Brock?"

"He's my one and only contact at the frat house. A senior, I suppose. Big guy. Probably football. I don't know—we don't chat all that much."

"You don't? At the Frat Chat?"

"That did sound kind of funny. Anyway, I told him there would be a substitute Saturday, and he right away starting bitching and moaning."

"Well, yeah, so maybe we should—"

"No, no, no. I assured him that the sub could be my twin, and no one would even know the difference."

"Oh, I don't believe you sometimes."

"Well, it's true, Lenore. We do look a lot alike. Almost identical. We even sound a lot alike. God, that gives me an idea!"

"Oh, what now?"

"Some other Saturday, we could both do the Frat Chat! Can you imagine that? Those guys would be losing their—"

"Laura, just stop. No. And I don't know about Saturday. I was going to have that drink with you, then think about it."

"It's too late for that. I went ahead and made other plans. I need to get out of town for something, and I couldn't do that without you."

"Without me—"

"Taking my place, yeah. You're a real sweetheart."

"That's what sweethearts do? Really?"

"Okay, maybe only this Saturday. We can figure out that tag-team deal another time."

"Oh, tag-team. Oh my gosh."

"Yeah. Exactly. So, I'll see you at the wine bar. Remember what you need to bring?"

"Yeah, Laura."

"Tell me. It's too important to get it wrong."

"My, um, cheerleader uniform."

"Right. Let's go through it all."

"Seriously?"

"Well, yeah. It's important."

"Alright. Well, the skirt."

"It's short?"

"Yeah, of course."

"How short? You're going to show those legs of yours?"

"Oh my God, it's short. Yeah. Nothing but legs."

"Okay, good. And the shirt? What kind of shirt?"

"It's a, um, long-sleeved t-shirt. Just plain, though. I don't have the original."

"Tight?"

Lenore was grinning when she said, "Yeah, it's tight. Really tight."

"Good. And I shouldn't even have to say it, but you—"

"I won't wear a bra. No."

"Good girl. And some kind of sneakers? Barely visible little white socks?"

"Yeah, all of that."

"White sneakers, right? Really, squeaky clean?"

"Yeah, sure. That matters?"

"Oh, yeah. That's a real big deal. You want those to look just as sweet and innocent as can be."

"That's silly. With all that would be going on, if I were to, um, really—"

"It's not silly. The contrast, Lenore. Sweet and innocent and at the same time, the total opposite. You get it?"

"You've given this some thought, Laura."

"Well, I figured it out after the first few times. It really does make them crazy."

"First few times, huh?"

"Yep. Oh, shit, I almost forgot something really important."

"Don't bother. I'll say it. No, Laura, I won't be wearing any, um . . ."

"Panties! No, you sure won't. You're going to fill in perfectly, Lenore. And from what you've described and what you'll be wearing, you'll look good enough to—"

"Don't say it, Laura!"

Only Laura's laughter came through the phone.

"I got to go. You're terrible."

"I know," said Laura. "And we'll be twins in this way too."

"I still might not go through with this."

"Uh-huh. I hear you, Lenore. I hear you."

Chapter 21 – You Won't See Me

In the quiet house, Lenore was fussing with things on the countertop beside a stove that kept a couple of covered pots engaged and motivated. She paused at the sound of the front door opening, then closing, then Amos's footsteps on his way toward her.

She resumed her work and waited until he'd said, "Lenore, I'm home. Hey, that all smells good."

Looking over her shoulder, she said, "It kind of does. No credit to me. The food gets all the credit."

He dragged a chair out from the table, saying, "Well, one might say that you deserve most of the credit. And you look beautiful, of course, but comfortable too."

She paused long enough to look down at her baggy jeans, the worn sneakers at the bottom, and nearly every button of her loose long-sleeved shirt fastened tight.

"Better than work clothes."

"The office attire is uncomfortable?"

"Uh, I guess I wouldn't say that. It's just good to, uh, get out of that."

"I always like your hair up like that too."

"I'm kind of used to it. It's convenient, and no one wants it getting tangled up in everything."

He laughed and said, "Like dinner, yeah."

"Yep."

"Steamy things."

She turned and said, "Huh?"

He pointed and said, "Like dinner. Steam. It's all cooking. You're really cooking things up."

"Oh, it is kind of steaming, isn't it?"

She switched off the burners, then turned enough to say, "With your late Fridays, you almost missed dinner. You ready?"

"Yes, I'm famished. How about, um, maybe we could—"

"Wine. Yes, I concur."

"One might say that wine is truly something anyone can concur about."

"Uh-huh. Let's finish off that bottle already."

"Perfect. I don't believe wine is a wise choice when one is thirsty, but I—"

"You should still quench your thirst with wine. Yep. Just relax, I'll get it."

"Wonderful. I know it's not the best compliment, but you handle, um, humdrum domestic things with such—"

"You're right," she said, budgeting a sharp laugh. "That's not much of a compliment."

"Sorry. But I'm starving and thirsting to death and—hey, how come there's no word similar to 'starve' but meaning to waste away from thirst?"

She stopped and squinted at him before leaving the bottle on the table and returning to the counter.

"Maybe you should invent one."

"You might be right. I'll run that by that philosopher fellow, Emilio. See what he thinks."

"Smart plan. That task requires the best minds we can throw at it."

She turned and grinned when he said, "Your sarcasm is well received and well deserved. Bravo."

"You're welcome. Always happy to lend some sarcasm to the conversation."

He held up the bottle, saw that it was only about half-full, then set it back down.

"Well, unless you have another bottle open somewhere, your mirth isn't from this bottle—the level is where it was last time. You have a secret bottle somewhere?"

"A secret?" she said, stopping midway to the table with a full plate in each hand. "No, I, uh, don't have any—"

"I'm only joking. You'd never have to hide a bottle from me. Oh, unless you're worried I might drink it before you had a chance."

She set down the plates, then took her seat.

"You seem to have some spare mirth of your own. Too much caffeine at the park?"

"Yes! Yes, that could be it. Seems like a safe enough venture—to chug some extra coffee like that. No real risk there. No, it's just coffee."

He held his fork as he looked up at her in the silent room.

"Yeah," she said. "Coffee is just so, uh, commonplace. So, why not?"

"Exactly. Here, let me."

He took the bottle, pried out the cork, then made quick work of pouring generously into both glasses.

Lenore held hers up and scoffed lightly, then said, "Not like we're saving it for anything, huh?"

He raised his and clinked it into hers, then said, "Only for a general, non-specific supply of mirth that seems to be in adequate supply this evening."

"Yeah. Uh, that," she said and took a sip.

Then, she kept going until half of it was gone.

"I accept your suggestion," he said, then did the same with his.

He hiccuped lightly, giggled, then said, "I, uh, think I'll postpone my turn at the laundry after all. I thought I'd feel more like getting to it."

She scoffed and said, "Until you started drinking?"

He pointed and said, "You've figured me out. Perhaps tomorrow, then."

"Are we out of wine?"

"You're funny, Lenore. No, we have tons of it. This food looks fantastic."

"It kind of does. I helped."

"Yes, you did. And it requires a remarkable woman to take on so much at once, all alone, just by herself."

She coughed and hurried another sip.

"You okay?"

"Yeah, just, uh, got a little something, I think, uh—"

"Stuck in your throat. Yes, that is sometimes unavoidable. Lenore, have another drink. Don't choke."

She swallowed most of what her glass still held, then blinked her eyes a few times.

"That ought to do it. Just make sure you've swallowed it all before committing yourself to even more. No choking allowed."

"Good advice," she said. "That's, um, good."

"The secret, I believe, is to pace one's self. Really, Lenore, you've had plenty of practice swallowing. These minor missteps are likely easily avoided."

"Uh, yeah. Yep. You're right."

He focused on his plate and said, "Maybe we should just eat?"

"That's good advice too. Okay."

She started choking again and managed to say, "I'll just get a fresh bottle before—"

"Before your swallowing is challenged any further. Yes."

She stared at him for a second, then got up and aimed herself toward the wine rack across the room.

And he stayed quiet and watched the sway of her hips and the swinging of a few tight tresses hanging down that must have worked themselves loose sometime throughout the day. But his eyes quickly dropped back down to the energetic action of her hips.

With a hand nearly touching one of the bottles in the rack, Lenore stopped, then turned to look back, and she saw Amos staring and not at her eyes.

"What?"

* * *

Amos quickly turned his eyes to his empty wine glass, which he was tipping around on the table.

"Nothing," he said. "Just you getting more wine."

Standing with the bottle in one hand, Lenore said, "Oh, I don't think that's all, Amos. Were you checking out my butt?"

He looked up, eyes big, and said, "Lenore, I, uh, might have noticed it, but I was mostly just watching the complete you, all of you, as you—"

"Nice try," she said, scoffing as she returned and set down the bottle. "Instead of all that stammering, maybe get to opening this."

"I can surely do that."

She sat and resumed eating, watching him make quick work of the uncorking, then more rapid pouring too. He held his up, and she got a grip on her glass but it remained on the table.

"There's nothing wrong with that, you know," she said.

"Drinking wine? Well, one might say that there are a lot of things right with it. For one thing, it—"

"No," she said while shaking her head and grinning at him. "My butt. Looking at it."

"I, um, will remind myself of that permission for the next instance of—"

"Cheers," she said and rushed her glass up to clink against his. "Let's enjoy our wine. Dinner, too, as long as I don't choke on it."

"Yes, please don't. So, in full disclosure, I did have a very brief, passing curiosity on whether you and your friend, Laura, still appear somewhat similar after, oh, a few years have passed since college."

Lenore was finishing a long sip of wine while listening, and she hiccuped as she set down the glass.

"Huh," she said, then hiccuped again and giggled. "So, you're—"

"Perhaps that's enough wine for you," he said, grinning with his glass in his hand.

"Oh, more for you, then, right? Not a chance. I was saying that looking at my butt shouldn't lead to curiosity and questions about someone else."

"Well, no, Lenore. One might say that that could be interpreted as a slight, even if it wasn't intended that way at all."

"Apology accepted."

He pointed, smiling, and said, "Keep drinking. This is fun."

"Yep. Kind of what the wine's all about. So, to answer your curiosity about my butt, yes, Laura and I are still quite similar in appearance."

"Well, then, Laura must also possess a calm, classic beauty."

Lenore scoffed and reached for her wine.

"I'm not so sure she'd want to be described that way."

"Oh? Why not?"

"Well, she was always a bit on the wild side. She's not exactly what you'd call calm and classic."

"Oh, that's a shame. Still, though, if she looks—"

"It's not really a shame, Amos. She's just always been out for fun, that's all."

"Oh, Lenore, I'm sure you didn't mean it, but that sounded like she still is. By now, I'm sure she's become quite settled in a dignified, productive life that—"

Lenore snorted out the wine that she'd been sipping and caught some of it in an upturned hand.

"Careful," he said. "One might say you're plainly trying to ingest more than a reasonable share."

She froze and stared at him for a second.

"Huh. Well, it's good. To, um, ingest. Laura would do the same."

"Uh . . . sure. What is your friend up to these days? Did she go on to become an esteemed member of the business community, like you?"

"Does it sound like that, Amos?"

"Well, obviously, one can imbibe a fair share of wine, at one's dinner table, and still be that. Like you, Lenore."

She managed to restrain most of her head shaking as she stared across the table at him, then she coughed and spoke.

"Yeah. So, uh, where are you and your park buddy, the philosopher, planning on having that beer?"

"Oh, well, he hasn't said yet. I believe the plan is that we'll select the location when I meet him at the park."

"Good plan. There are lots of bars all around that area."

"Yes. There, uh, certainly are."

"Which one would you pick? If he leaves it up to you?"

"It wouldn't be an easy task to narrow down the selections. They're all acceptable for just a, uh, simple get-together. Like that."

"Yep. I was just wondering if maybe I could drop by after that drink with Laura. It might be nice to meet Emilio—I've been hearing about him, and he sounds interesting."

"Oh, uh, I'm not sure he'd want that."

"He's anti-social like that?"

"Well, no, he just, um, I think he intends for this just to be a guys' evening out."

"Oh, okay. He doesn't like women too much. I get it. He's probably—"

"No, I don't think he is. Probably not. It's just that we're planning a guys' night out, and we just—"

"Hey, forget it, Amos. Go have your fun. I'll be having plenty of fun of my own."

"You will?"

"Uh, yeah. With Laura, remember?"

"Yes, I remember. A glass of wine with a friend. That does sound like plenty of—"

"It will be. Believe me."

"Well, good. You should definitely try to have a fun evening."

"I plan to. You too."

"You're absolutely right. I should try to have at least as much enjoyment as you believe you have in store."

"Fine. You can be sure I won't crash your little party."

"Fine. Rest assured, Lenore, that you won't see me at yours."
"Fine."

Chapter 22 – Free Is the Going Price

Lenore closed the bedroom door by leaning her back into it. After it latched, she hiccuped, giggled once, then walked toward her dresser. She slid out the top drawer, frowned at the garments stacked neatly, then lifted out her nightgown, which she laid off to one side.

Scoffing, then saying, "Oh, why the hell not?" she stooped down and got her hands on the bottom drawer.

But she only held onto it and looked back over her shoulder. With a smile, she twisted her hips one way, then the other, then fell forward onto her knees.

Holding the dresser top with both hands, she arched her back, jutted her hips back, then gyrated them from side to side.

"Hmm. Laura would be proud," she said, giggling again.

She finished her opening of the bottom drawer and took out the tight t-shirt, then stood with it. Still holding it with one hand, she watched in the mirror as she unbuttoned her plain, shapeless shirt, flapped it open, then shimmied out of it and let it fall.

Without further thought, she quickly opened the bra, removed it, and tossed it over a shoulder onto the bed.

A few seconds later, she'd slipped the tight shirt down over her neat mound of hair. It took some dedicated pulling down on the hem, each tug moving her breasts around as she got it straightened out.

But then, she pulled it down even farther, stretching it tight. She didn't make her eyes look elsewhere as they fixed on each breast in turn, noticing details that no one would be able to ignore.

"Like that. Tight," she said.

She said, "Oh, you want," then hiccuped and finished with, "more, huh?"

She unbuckled her belt, pried open the top button, and zipped down the zipper of her unremarkable jeans, then held the waistband on each side.

"Oh, I have to get undressed?"

She began what could be a slow dance, keeping her hips shifting to the left, then the right as she worked the pants down, but she stopped at the first sight of her panties.

"Oh, the panties too? Hmm, I think I know why . . ."

She got a better grip, one that included the panties, and resumed the slow, rhythmic disrobing, and she didn't fight the increasing force of her breaths as her eyes scanned across her breasts, which were boasting even more detail against the tight, thin cloth, and she gave an occasional glance at the skin of her belly, so seldom exposed like that.

"So soft," she said. "Yes, I'm so soft, and I'm only . . . only to be used for—"

The doorknob turned quickly, snapping to its full rotation, and the door swung in as she turned her head, eyes wide, and looked that way.

*　*　*

"Oh, Amos, it's you."

He froze in place, squinting but looking only into her eyes, and said, "Well, Lenore, who exactly were you expecting?"

She giggled, hiccuped, and said, "All the neighbors, of course."

"You're funny when you drink."

"Uh, yep."

"I thought you'd be ready for bed. If you need another minute, I could—"

"You could wait right there. Uh-huh."

She turned to face him, and his eyes dropped to the sight of her breasts straining against the thin cloth, threatening to puncture it in two places without the bra's protective layering.

140

"But I, um, you—"

"Don't be silly," she said.

She let go of the pants, which were well down past her hips and making clear that she'd been stripping herself of her underwear too. With both hands pinching the shirt's bottom hem, she started lifting it up across her belly.

"Lenore! I can give you a minute, I mean, if you—"

"Nonsense. It'll just take a second for me to strip all of this off and—"

"I don't mind, really," he said, already backing through the doorway. "Privacy is a, um, good thing. And I, uh, always try to respect—"

Lenore was giggling and still holding her shirt, which was close up under her breasts, when Amos's phone chimed loudly in his pocket.

"Oh, it's the neighbors," she said and giggled again. "They want me to open the curtains better."

He shook his head at her but didn't smile as he got the phone out and checked.

"It's that, I mean, a student. Remember? The philosopher? He wants me to call. It must be an emergency of some variety. I'll be right back. Right back!"

Lenore watched the door close with a decisive thump.

"Huh."

*　*　*

"Emilio, what's the emergency?"

Amos had gone as far as through the front door and stood on the porch with the door closed completely.

"I lied to you, professor. I feel bad about it and just had to confess."

"What? Right now?"

"Oh, is it late there? I thought you'd be up grading papers, reading about roller coasters, or something else thrilling like that."

"No, I'm about to go to bed. What is it?"

"I lied about the Frat Chats. Professor, I know all about them. I've been to them a few times just not recently."

"So, why did you feel a need to lie about that?"

"Besides just messing with you?"

"Yes. Besides that."

"Alright, I just thought if I seemed more like an outsider to the event, you'd be more likely to agree to go."

It took a few seconds before Amos responded.

"That's actually quite astute. Yes, it had that effect. Why is it so important that I go and have a beer with you there?"

"Well, it's more than just about a beer or three. You know that."

"I'm trying not to think about the rest of it."

"That's interesting."

"What?"

"That you have to try to not think about it. Hmm. Nice."

"No, that's not what I meant. Oh, come on, Emilio. Really, why does it matter what I think about it?"

Emilio's voice lost its hint of imminent laughter.

"Because I see you sitting in a nice, safe roller coaster car, and man, it's not going anywhere."

"I resent that. I believe I'm on my way to a full professorship someday here at the university."

"Uh-huh."

"And I'm making all kinds of valuable career contacts. And Emilio, I'm teaching subjects that I like, and I—"

"Haven't said a thing about being engaged."

"Huh?"

"Have you? Did I miss it?"

"I was, um, getting to that."

"Right. Could take a while, though, in a safe, tame car that doesn't go too fast, just kind of sits there, never gets going with any—"

"Emilio, it's late. We can pick this up some other time."

"Yeah, sounds good. At the Frat Chat. Don't be late!"

"Or else, what?"

"The beer will be warm. What else? You worried that the you know what will be gone by the time you get there?"

Amos listened to the laughter, then said, "You're getting back to a chapter with that single letter that denotes abject failure."

"Yeah, I'm kind of always heading for that. See you tomorrow."

"Uh, sure. Okay. Goodnight."

* * *

Lenore had just begun a serious smirk toward the door after Amos closed it, then her phone chimed too.

Facing the mirror, she shifted around to get her pants up, then her shirt down, but she didn't zip or buckle before taking out her phone.

She read the text and said aloud, "Laura, you're a pest. I sure can back out if I want. Maybe I don't want to be ravaged, treated like just a sex object."

She giggled and added, "Like you, Laura. That's you."

She typed for a while, then hit send before leaving her phone on the dresser.

"So, maybe I was thinking about it. That's not a big deal. That doesn't mean I'm going to—"

The vibration rattled the device around after the brief tone had already quit. She picked it up and read it, then scoffed.

"I'm thinking all kinds of stuff. That's what."

She kept the phone in her hand as she cupped both breasts and looked again at the size of them and how the ring still sparkled from even the dim bedside lighting.

"Oh, Laura . . ."

She wiggled her jeans down, farther than before, then grinned at being so close to revealing more than she should. With a quick giggle, she pushed down on the waistband a bit more.

"Oh, Lenore. Shame on you."

Looking in the mirror, she used her non-phone hand to twist around her tight t-shirt, lifting the hem, and she kept fussing with it, hiccuping once, until she'd managed to leave it so high up that the material covered only the very tops of her breasts. The hem was pulled tight across her, and it squeezed itself in and stayed in place.

"Oh my goodness."

She switched her phone to selfie mode, lined it up to not get a portrait along with all of the other facets of herself and her fantasizing—from her entirely exposed breasts down to bunched up jeans and panties partway down her thighs, plus a sparkling ring on a hand that was posed provocatively low on her bare belly, aimed like it was about to go even lower—then snapped the photo.

Looking at it, she said, "Oh, I really shouldn't."

She hesitated with her finger ready to send it, glanced back at the door, which was still closed, then scoffed loudly and sent it to Laura with a typed message saying simply, "For sale."

"Oh, I shouldn't have done that."

She read the quick reply and laughed.

"Yeah. You're right, Laura. Free is the going price for all of that. All of . . . me."

She put the phone down, then let one hand caress her belly, low, and the other, her right hand, kept busy with her breasts, which were still exposed.

"I mean, if I go."

She added her right hand to the one resting low on her belly, then studied the sight of the unique setting sparkling as her fingertips explored.

"If I go. Oh, that's so bad with that ring. Hmm."

* * *

The bedroom door swung into a room darkened except for a faint glow plugged in on the far wall. Amos stopped and listened, then closed the door quietly.

144

Slow, quiet steps got him near the bed, and he quickly and stealthily stripped down to his boxers before peeling back the thick layer of covers, then sitting, easing himself down and not shaking the mattress around.

"Oh," Lenore said, then added a yawn loud enough to hear, "you're back. Everything okay?"

"Sure. Yes. He was, uh, confused about the assignment for the weekend. We straightened it out."

"Well, good. Oh, that wine's catching up with me. I'm so tired now that I'm lying down."

He lay beside her and when his shoulder bumped her back, which was turned toward him, he shifted himself over and lost contact.

"Yes, me too. We sure did finish that second bottle, too, didn't we?"

"Mm-hmm. It's kind of nice."

"The wine?"

"Yeah. That and, uh, just letting go. Just enjoying it."

"We certainly did that. And the weekend hasn't even started. Imagine that."

"I plan to. I have only enough energy left to imagine things. Goodnight, Amos."

"Goodnight, Lenore. You, uh, did look fantastic. Before."

"Oh, thanks. That shirt really is thin and tight. This is comfortable, though. How I'm dressed for sleeping."

"Yes, that's quite important. One might say that comfort is paramount for a good night's sleep, while other outfits would never do."

"No, not for sleep. How true."

Chapter 23 – Who Says I'm an Angel?

With quick flicks at the sleeve of her robe, Lenore chased off bits of lint but not a single hair from the bound up knot of it on her head. Some of the lint floated long enough to drift back onto the kitchen table, and she finished with a sweep of it all onto the floor.

The coffee mug was sending a tentative wisp of steam up toward the overhead light, which she'd left off. And having tidied up her usual comfortable at-home attire, she closed her eyes, one hand on the cup, and leaned back in her seat.

Even as slow, dragging footsteps drew near, coming from the direction of their bedroom, she left her eyes closed and lifted the coffee for a drink. But sensing the heat, she only blew on it instead.

"Oh," Amos said, "you got the coffee going already. I could have done that."

She opened her eyes long enough only to size up his appearance— a long robe, thinner than hers, hair a jumbled mess, one hand rubbing at his eyes, but quite good posture— then let them drift shut again.

"Yeah. You could have."

She gave the silence a second, then added, "But I was up so, what the heck."

"Well, thanks."

She cracked her eyes open again, just enough to see his back as he poured himself a cup, then rubbed her eyes and leaned forward over the table.

A chair got pulled out, and she stopped fussing with her eyes long enough to look across at him, over two cups of coffee that almost perfectly flanked the empty wine bottle from the night before.

"It's good. Hot is good."

"Mm-hmm. Get it while it's hot."

"One would have to agree with that," he said, and she watched him tip the cup back, grimace at the heat of it, but drink some anyway.

"One would," she said. "While it's . . . yep."

He set the cup down with a clunk, yawned, then said, "Did you do as you were instructed?"

Her eyes woke up quickly.

"What? What do you—"

"About dreaming? Did you have any good dreams?"

"Oh," she said, laughing weakly. "Uh, yeah. A few."

"What about, if one might dare to ask?"

She scoffed at the genuine curiosity that his face displayed.

"Well, running through the jungle. Naked, of course."

She smirked at his lips fumbling around silently.

"A jungle? What kind? Where was this jungle that—"

"Amos, it's a joke. I was joking. Have some more caffeine."

He did—a long drink with more grimacing.

"That's funny. That would be a funny thing to dream. Uh, any real dreams?"

She stretched out the arm holding the mug, held it there while grinding her eyes shut a few times, then blew out a deep sigh as she set the drink down.

"Well, I don't remember much. Just, um, lots of people."

"Oh, that's interesting. Like, at a stadium? The opera?"

"Uh, I don't think so. A smaller place. I think just a room."

"Go on. What happened?"

"That's about all I remember. Just that there was something new and fun going on. How about you? Dreams?"

"Yes. I had a very good one. I was at a formal event in honor of becoming a full professor."

"Oh, that's nice. You'd like that."

"Yes. And you were beside me, dressed quite fashionably, and I remember distinctly being so pleased to have you there and looking so sophisticated."

"Huh. You'd like that too."

"I certainly would. And even awake, here at the table, after that dream has vaporized somewhere, I—"

"Dreams vaporize?"

"Well, Lenore, not the dreams we feel. Those persist, I'm sure. No, just those fleeting images that invade our sleep. But as I was saying, the dream was only like a repeat of the truth: I'd be so thrilled to have you beside me and being so fashionable and sophisticated."

"I could sure do that. Let me guess: my hair was up, right?"

"Well, yes. It's the picture of sophistication, I'd say. The way you wear it all the time. I like it."

"It, uh, sure keeps it out of the way of things."

"Yes. Like tipping your coffee to take a drink. Imagine if your hair was wild and getting in the way? Oh, that would never do."

"Nope. Can't have that. Got to, uh, keep that out of the way."

"Exactly."

Both heads turned at the sound of four slices of toast popping up. Lenore stood and looked down on Amos rubbing his eyes again.

"Butter? Jelly?"

"Both, please."

"Yep. Me too. Maybe it'll soak up the last traces of wine still swishing around in there."

"You didn't have any problem swallowing that."

Her eyes got big, but she was facing away from him, toward the toast, and she got them back to normal before turning.

"No, uh, not that."

Yawning, rubbing his eyes again, he said, "Some things are just too satisfying, I'd guess. And I didn't notice you spilling even a drop."

She spun back around, stared at the wall, then she scoffed silently as a grin took hold.

She heard him chuckle and add, "No, don't ever spill any of it."

"Nope. I don't intend to."

"You sound very sure of yourself," he said, laughing absentmindedly.

Still looking away, she said softly, mostly for herself, "Might be part of the job."

"What's that, Lenore?"

She turned with all of the breakfast items on a tray and said, "Nothing, Amos. Hungry?"

*　*　*

Still yawning while drying the plates and silverware from breakfast, Lenore turned just her head when Amos called to her from the doorway.

"I can't put it off forever, and it's my turn."

He stood there with a laundry basket in his hands, full of all kinds of things that the crumpled bath towels piled on top covered well.

"Laundry day."

"Yeah," she said, "good of you to take care of it. If you wait a sec, I'll give you this towel too."

She waved it around in one hand while the other held a plate.

"Sure," he said and set the basket on the floor near the door. "More coffee sounds good anyway."

He plopped down in his usual chair and squinted at the coffee left over from breakfast having gotten cold.

"Oh, wait," she said. "Hang on."

With the towel over her shoulder, she brought the coffee pot over to him and began refilling. He leaned way back, closed his eyes, and sipped the steaming drink as well as he could without burning himself.

When he'd set the cup down but still hadn't opened his eyes, he said, "The more I think about it, that laundry can sit right there. My head, Lenore. Wine is better in the moment than in the moments after."

"Aw, you got some hangover going there, don't you?"

"Well, yes. Not you?"

"No, I have some. A little. The breakfast helped."

"Yes. Me too. You know what? That laundry can wait until tomorrow. I'll get to it in the morning. I swear it."

She laughed and said, "Swearing your allegiance to that isn't necessary, Amos. Whenever it gets done. It doesn't matter."

She finished up, wiped her hands with the towel, then tossed it across the room.

"Nice shot," he said, grinning at her throw landing it fairly neatly on top of the other items.

"Mm, that coffee's good. Hey, you can thank me if you want, but I even made an extra effort and got your cheerleader things mixed in there too. It's like you said with the—"

"What?" she said, glaring at him. "My uniform is mixed in with wet towels and other dirty things?"

"Well, um, I was just—"

"Amos, you're not supposed to mess with that."

She hurried the few steps over to the basket, leaned over, and began digging around, dumping most of the items onto the floor.

"But it's like you said, right? Better to wash it often and keep it in good shape?"

"No, Amos, I don't want the skirt and especially the shirt sitting around in a laundry basket!"

"Well, Lenore, one might say that tomorrow will be here sooner than your next cheerleading opportunity."

Holding the skirt and shirt together, sniffing both of them, she continued to glare at him, and he lost his grin.

"It's not about that. Of course, I'm not, um, cheerleading anytime soon."

"What, then? I swear, I'll get to it tomorrow. Just dump it back in there and—"

"Oh, I don't think so, Amos. This is just too, I mean, it's kind of a, um, matter of principal. You shouldn't take such liberties."

"Well, gee. Sorry. I didn't know it would elicit such a violent reaction."

"Oh, you think this is violent?"

"Uh, that was a bad choice of words. No, of course not. Not that you couldn't be violent, I mean. You just, uh, don't seem to be what one might call an overly physical type. You tend to—"

"Stop babbling, Amos. You have no idea what you're talking about."

"I don't?"

"No. Not even a little. I was a cheerleader, right? Isn't that physical? I'm still in good shape, right?"

"You're in incredible shape. Angelic, one might say, if one were to—"

"Who says I'm an angel? Maybe I don't always want to be an angel."

"Well, why ever not? Isn't that something like the pinnacle of womanhood?"

She squinted at him and shook her head.

"No," she said, "I'm talking about more, you know, athletic things."

"So, um, cartwheels and jumping and stuff? Like that?"

She blew out a breath to chase aside a few strands of hair that had shaken loose from her clump.

"Yes, Amos. Yeah, exactly like that. Maybe I'll go try some later."

He snickered and said, "Yeah, out in the yard. Hey, that's a good idea."

"It's one idea. Sure."

She scoffed as she turned toward the counter, where she folded the cheer uniform articles neatly.

"Is that basket in the way there? Maybe I should—"

"Maybe you should have your coffee on the porch? That's an excellent idea."

She turned and gave him a smile.

"Go on. Run along. I'll put on a fresh pot and get you a refill as soon as possible."

"I, uh, suppose I could. Sure. It's a nice day."

"Yes. It's going to be a wonderful day."

Chapter 24 – You'll Be Using Them Too

The front door had just closed with a quick shove from Lenore, and Amos lifted the freshly-filled mug up toward the front yard and street.

"To you, neighbors. No peeking at Lenore, either."

He blew on it, then took a healthy drink.

"Not dressed like that anyway. That skimpy little shirt she has but will never really want to wear."

After kicking out his legs, he slumped back into the thickly padded porch chair, sighed, then sat himself up straight.

"No, but at my ceremony, becoming a full professor, when she's dressed like royalty, so appropriate for my esteemed role in this delightful college community, that's when you can all—"

The phone in his pants pocket sent out a tone.

"Huh."

He took it out, saw a text from Emilio, and said, "Again? Now, what?"

After touching it several times, he sent his reply, then let a deep sigh leak out. It took a few seconds of sipping his coffee and watching for neighbors peeking his way before he rose up and opened the door.

"Lenore?"

From somewhere down the hall, he heard her say, "What, Amos?"

"It's Emilio again. The—"

"Philosopher. Yeah."

"Him. Yes. Anyway, I don't think he fully grasps the scope of the assignment that I thought I'd worked out in sufficient detail for all of them to—"

"Just go, Amos. You won't be missing much. You taking the car?"

"It would be much quicker, yes. You won't need it in the next little while?"

"Nope. In fact, I might even take a nap."

"Okay. I really did believe that I was completely clear, even in the written hand-outs that I passed around when—"

"Amos, just go. Close the door and go."

"Yes. Yes, that's what I'll do. I'll be back soon."

He listened for a moment, but Lenore seemed to have said her piece and was done.

"Huh."

He reached inside for the car keys on the table near the door, then shook with a silent laugh as he closed the door just as silently.

"Like I'm sneaking away? No, why would I have to sneak?"

He jumped over the few steps to the walkway and began the short walk through manicured plant beds, mulched to perfection, toward the car parked in the driveway.

* * *

Lenore listened from around the corner for a minute, didn't hear the front door close, then looked around and saw that it was shut. Waiting for it, she heard a car door slam and an engine start.

"Go have your innocent coffee in the park."

She stepped lightly back to where she'd left her uniform on the counter and picked it all up.

"That didn't just happen. No way."

She scoffed and spun the clothes around to inspect them better.

"Today? He was going to leave them in the basket today until tomorrow?"

Groaning, she snatched up her coffee cup and walked toward the bedroom.

"Oh, maybe it's only because we talked about it. That must be it."

After taking two steps into the room, she backed up and closed the door. A second later, after holding still then grinning, she switched the lock lever into place.

"Hmm. That's becoming a habit."

At the foot of the bed, she laid the skirt out neatly, smoothing it down and leaving the pleats, alternating university colors, neat and showing no signs of having been so carelessly crumpled up with all of the other laundry.

The shirt took more effort. She held it by the shoulders and snapped it a few times, held it up to herself while looking down at it, then laid it in place relative to the skirt. A few presses and wipes with both hands smoothed that out, too, and she stepped back, hands on her hips, and scanned over the ensemble.

Then, she glanced at the alarm clock on her nightstand.

"Oh my God."

She scoffed and laughed softly, then said, "Eight hours. Eight hours until I . . . until I'm . . . hmm."

A few steps got her to her dresser, where she pulled out a drawer, sifted through stacks of socks, then pulled out a pair of white ones that would barely be seen when worn with the sneakers.

Which she went to the closet for, and she set those, with the socks, on the floor beneath the bottom hem of the skirt up on the blanket.

"Innocent? Laura said something about the contrast?"

She snorted out a short laugh, then stooped down and turned both shoes to point more toward the sides, and she stuffed a sock in each.

From the side, again with hands on hips, she viewed the arrangement.

"It's like I'm lying there. Flat on my back. It's almost—"

Giggling, she stooped down again and moved the shoes apart. Then, farther yet before resuming her study from a few steps away.

"Huh. Not so innocent like that."

She stared for a few seconds, then giggled and reached for the shirt, which she threw over her shoulder like a towel in the kitchen. A few steps away again, she looked down on only a skirt and two shoes on the floor, spread far apart, where those items would be if she were lying on her back, shirtless, with her legs—

"Oh my God. That's even less innocent and not at all like an angel and—"

She slapped her pants pocket when the phone stashed in there called out for her attention.

"Laura. Hi."

"Well, hello there, twin girlie girl."

"Checking up on me, huh?"

"Well, who else would do it? So, can you talk? Is that former—"

"He's not former anything. Not—"

"Not yet. Yeah."

Lenore sighed and said, "I sure am thinking like maybe that's inevitable, though."

"It's not like me to put pressure on you, Lenore, not for anything, but—"

"Oh, except for the Frat Chat?"

"Well, there's that. Yeah. Be ready and at the wine bar by 6:00. Not even for an hour, though, then you're there and ready by 7:00."

"How could I possibly ever be ready for that? Laura, that's—"

"You're right. But it'll be a rush when things get going, and you see just how many—"

"How many what? Oh, don't tell me."

"You know how many 'whats' I'm talking about. Oh, Lenore, there could be a lot. In fact, you should plan on it."

"Oh my God. You're serious? It's really not just a couple of guys that won me at poker or something?"

"That's an interesting fantasy. Yep, you're getting into the spirit of things alright. Yes, Lenore, more than just a couple."

"So, what? It's just one after another after—"

She stopped at Laura laughing loudly enough that it became snorting.

"What?"

"Okay, try this instead: two after another two after—"

"Two . . . at once? That really—"

"Hey, you just told me you were fantasizing about that. Remember? On your hands and knees, looking up, mouth open, sticking your ass back. Remember that?"

"I, uh, was just sort of thinking—"

"Uh-uh. You were practicing. We both know exactly what for."

"They'll really expect that?"

"Plan on it."

"Oh my God," she said and leaned over, one hand on the bed to support herself.

"And Lenore?"

"Yeah?"

"Don't even think of saying no to anything."

"Because I'm just—"

"Like a party favor, yeah. All soft and sexy and not saying no to anything."

"Soft . . . and sexy?"

"Yep. Soft and sexy, and make yourself as pretty as can be. Hey, do your nails."

"I hardly ever do my nails."

"That's my point. Give the whole look a boost. Ooh, Lenore, red. Bright red nails."

Lenore scoffed, but Laura didn't see her smile.

"I can do that. Easy enough. Get prettied up like a party favor, huh?"

"Naked too. Well, maybe. Half-undressed is always nice too. You'll figure it out as you go."

"So, what were you saying? More than two of them. Alright, I get it. But then, another two? Four altogether? That's already a lot—I've only had one at a time forever."

"Lenore, think. Four? Come on. You've seen those frat houses, right? How many do you think will show up for a sexy party favor up in that room?"

"Um . . ."

"A lot. Yeah."

"God, they'd just be using me."

"All a matter of perspective. I'd say, you'll be using them too."

"How? Laura, what are you talking about?"

"Think about it, Lenore. They might think they're using you, but you, what you are, really leaves them no choice. And you'll take part of them away, for yourself, and they'll never get it back. You'll leave them with just a memory—a hunger—that they'll never outlive."

"You think so?"

"I know so. Even if they don't know it, you'll be using them with a genuine superpower."

"Superpower? Laura, you're—"

"They're really the ones that can't say no. Think about it."

"But—"

"None of them can say no. Even if they think they'd say no, uh-uh. They'll change their minds real quick. Superpower."

"Oh my gosh . . ."

Chapter 25 – Like a Superpower

"Don't even mention my finances. I took out another student loan."

Amos accepted the hot coffee, and Emilio took a seat, too, at their usual picnic table in the town square park.

"Just since yesterday. That's a pretty efficient loan system."

"As long as you get your coffee, don't ask too many questions."

"Right. Like a crime operation."

"Speaking of which . . ."

"Uh-oh. Now, what?"

"Nothing, really. I'm just building up the drama."

"Like you do in class. Blurting out things like, what was it, 'divinity?'"

"Hey, it starts with a thought about wanting to blurt something out. Like, to stop that lecturing professor in his tracks. Then, I scrounge around for something to say."

"And that's what you found."

"Yeah. It's like knowing you want to throw something, and the first thing you see is a rock down by your boots."

Amos scoffed, gave him a glance, saw that he wasn't about to notice, then scoffed again and looked away.

"And you saw 'divinity' written down there by your boots."

"Something like that. You got the basics of the process. Hot and cold, same time. That's the template."

"I'll write my own chapter about it in my own book when I—"

"Hey, after tonight, yeah. Speaking of which . . ."

"Oh boy," said Amos. "What about tonight?"

"Nothing big. I just don't want you to freak out and make a scene."

"About what? I'm just having a beer, some good conversation, and—"

"Chat. Let's call it a chat."

"Oh. That's right. So, why would I freak out and—"

"Um, just in case a cop shows up."

"Hey, wait a minute. Cops?"

"Only if someone gets too loud. Usually, that doesn't happen."

With his voice rising, Amos said, "Usually? So, you mean that—"

"It only happened that one time. In recent history."

"So, what happened? People got arrested, he called for backup, they—"

Emilio was laughing too hard for Amos to continue.

"What?"

"Professor, no, that cop saw what was going on and took a shot himself."

"With the, um, Laura? With her, you mean?"

"Yeah. Wouldn't you?"

"Well, no, I'm not planning to—"

"Look, he probably said the same thing, then he saw her. Let me tell you, that changes an attitude real quick."

"No one got arrested, then?"

"Shit, no. The biggest problem was convincing him that the party was a one-time thing. Otherwise, he'd be—"

"Back for—"

"Sniffing around for more. Damn right."

"That's not exactly how I was going to phrase it, but yes."

"So, that all worked out fine. Everyone was happy."

"Even Laura?"

"Maybe mostly her, professor. I think she liked that she flipped him onto the plan—kind of won him over. She probably liked having that kind of control over him. Like a superpower."

"But you don't, you don't think that later today, when—"

"Shit, he might show up. The thing is, we have to keep everyone from screaming their heads off."

"They would?"

"You might."

"Emilio, I already told you that I—"

"Superpower, professor. Remember? Don't ever underestimate the superpowers of an available and willing beauty doing her thing."

"Oh my gosh . . ."

Chapter 26 – Tell Me I'm Pretty

"Pretty, huh?" Lenore said, then held her left hand out for an inspection of her fingernails.

"Hmm," she said to the empty room.

She squirmed into the couch cushions, then pulled her legs up and crossed them. After letting out a satisfied sigh, then pausing long enough to hear the wall clock ticking, she gave it a glance.

"Oh, God. Getting close."

The clock received a length of uninterrupted staring as she waved her left hand around to dry the fresh acrylic. Leaving the clock to its business, she blew on the nails a few times, then turned them around under the light, viewing them from different angles.

She'd just gotten her left hand on the polish bottle beside her, on the end table, when she heard an engine shut down, then a car door shut.

Not paying attention, she let go of the bottle and resumed waving her hand while keeping her eyes on the door.

Which opened a few seconds later.

"Oh, Lenore. There you are."

"Here I am. Yep."

"You, uh . . . what's that?" he said with the keys still in his hand, then he clinked them onto the table before looking her way again.

"Nail polish? Even college professors must have heard of it."

He kept his sometimes squinting eyes on the sight of her left hand, which was moving but not enough to disguise the color she'd applied.

"It, uh, looks nice. That's different."

She held the hand out for inspection and said, "Not really. I shine them up once in a while."

"Red, though? Bright red? I've never seen that before."

"It was, um, on sale not long ago, so I picked it up and stored it away until I felt like using it."

"Which is today."

She held his gaze, then pointed at him.

"Brilliant. Yes, today is certainly today."

He laughed and said, "That did sound pretty unintelligent. No, I just mean—oh, it's for later."

"Later? No, I wasn't even—"

"A nice, relaxing glass of wine with a friend. That kind of later."

"Oh, yeah. Uh-huh. I sort of thought it might be fun. Not like it's important, though. It's just more about—"

"Fun. Yes, we all need just a little from time to time."

"Uh, yep. A little."

She kicked one leg out, then the other, held them up, and rotated her feet in and out before letting them drop to the floor.

With the back of her left hand again out and level with her eyes, she said, "Hmm."

"They look nice," he said.

"Nice? Yeah."

"Pretty is what I mean," he said. "You look quite pretty."

"Oh, well, thanks. I do like when you tell me I'm pretty."

"Well, you are. Oh, and that ring, Lenore. I'm so pleased that you wear that all the time, even when doing up those nails."

"I thought about taking it off, just in case—"

"No need. Just be careful. I like that you keep it on all the time."

"All the time. Yeah."

"Even when doing things like that."

"Like this or . . . whatever. No matter what."

"There's no reason to ever take it off. Somehow, with the nails red like that, it's quite a striking effect. It adds some special emphasis, I think."

She gave her hand a few shakes, turning it a few times. Then, she held it up close to her face, back of the hand toward Amos, and gazed at him.

"Oh, that looks quite good. It looks good when modeled near your eyes, which are kind of, uh, big."

"Big? Huh. I guess. I like that you notice that. I like the ring," she said while lowering her hand. "And I like the nails too."

"You seem like you do. You seem quite pleased with that color."

"I guess I am. Yeah, it'll do just fine."

"For . . ."

She dropped her hand and said, "For a drink with that friend of mine. She'll love the nails and probably the ring too."

"Of course."

"She'll probably want the ring for herself. Maybe I'll give it to her."

"You wouldn't."

"Not even just to borrow? It probably fits her the same too. And her nails are sometimes red, too, so—"

"You'd better not. You promised you'd always wear it, remember?"

"Hmm. I did promise, didn't I?"

"Yes, you most certainly did."

"Well, enough of that. It'll be nice to see her and have a drink too. Wine is good. You like wine."

He tipped his head back and laughed, then said, "Yes, and I still feel it."

"You like beer too. Are you happy to be getting out for some?"

"For some, uh, beer?"

She stared for a second, then shook her head and said, "Well, yeah. Nothing wrong with a drink or two."

"No. Not a thing. Your hangover seems like it's gone."

"It does? I mean, yeah, it kind of is. You can tell?"

"Yes," he said. "You just seem happier."

"Yeah, well, I can do without a hangover. How about you?"

"I'm feeling better. I think another cup of coffee did it."

"From that Emilio character. He's buying your time with coffee. He's using you."

"Uh, sure. That's one way to look at it. I don't mind. He's kind of interesting."

"You don't mind being used?"

"It's more of a trade, I'd say. Good for both of us."

"Yep—good for everyone involved."

"Everyone, as in just him and me. Sure."

"Yep. Um, you planning to watch me paint my other nails? Isn't that kind of like watching paint dry?"

"Sure, why not? Unless you don't want me watching."

She held his gaze, while he held up his eyebrows, then she laughed and looked to her left for the bottle.

"I don't mind being watched."

He nodded a few times, not smiling, then said, "Yes, I suspect that's quite true."

She squinted first, then said, "I, uh, don't know what you—"

Pointing, he said, "From when you used to be a cheerleader. Center of attention?"

"Oh," she said, then laughed softly. "Yeah, but that was a while ago."

"Yes, of course. All in the past."

She jabbed the bottle toward him and said "You can watch me paint, though."

"You don't mind?"

"Nope. Center of attention, professor."

* * *

He watched in silence, politely not moving much at all, as Lenore painted the nails on her right hand. She'd just finished the final brush stroke, kept the applicator close, and turned her eyes up to meet Amos's.

"Hey, that kid's alright? That coffee pusher in the park?"

"The philosopher. I guess he's okay. He sure disrupts class, though."

"How so?"

"He just adds odd comments, things that make everyone curious what the heck he's talking about. Like just in the last lecture, out of nowhere, he yelled out the word 'divinity.'"

"Divinity? Why?"

"Truly, the entire class, myself included, wanted to know. So, the question was put to him. He tries to elaborate on—"

"Wait, Amos. You just gave up the floor to him?"

"Uh, not for long. And not the actual podium. But yes."

"He sounds like he enjoys being the, uh, center of attention."

"I suppose that's true. He does seem to revel in it. That seems a little alien to me."

Lenore snickered and said, "He seems like a tiny little alien to you? The ship dropped him off for classes?"

"Funny, Lenore. My, but your hangover seems to have evaporated. Good for you. You're quite cheery this fine Saturday."

"I'm just, uh, kind of happy that my nails turned out nice. You never know with an operation like that. But never mind that. You're saying you don't care much for being the center of attention? You, who stands in front of a giant class, all eyes on you while you're doing your thing?"

"Oh, I could see how you might think that. But really, I'm focused kind of mostly on the subject matter. I hardly think about how much attention is focused on me."

"Spoken like a dedicated professor."

"Thank you. I do try."

"Yes, you sure do."

"How about you? I can't imagine you wanting oodles of attention on your every little move."

"Oodles?"

"Well, a lot. I see you as more of a behind-the-scenes, management type. Like at your office. You're probably never surrounded by people, all focused intently on you."

"Uh, that doesn't really happen in my office."

She held up her right hand, inspected the fresh polish, and said, "But I probably wouldn't mind as much as you think."

"What? Being the center of attention?"

"Mm-hmm. It could be quite flattering. A compliment."

"I suppose. Well, you will be. I'm sure your friend will compliment your fancy nail polish."

"Yeah, she probably will. But she's just one person. This whole conversation is about more, I think."

"Oh, yes, a crowd. All clamoring for something from you. Not taking no for an—"

"What? What are you talking about, Amos?"

"Uh, like an autograph? What else?"

She coughed while her eyes darted around, then she said, "Oh, I was thinking like what brand of nail polish I use. You know, stuff like that. So, forget that. What's going on with that Emilio fellow that's got him all riled up?"

"Who said he's riled up? He just, uh, he . . ."

"Go on, Amos. What?"

He coughed and stared back at Lenore before saying, "He, um, just found out that he caught something."

"He went fishing? Or he set a trap and—"

"No, like a sexually transmitted something."

"Oh my God," she said, and her quick shake all over got her hand to tip over the nail polish bottle.

"Oh, good that it's closed," he said while pointing toward it.

"Yeah, Amos," she said as she set it upright.

"It's not like Emilio got arrested or anything. No, nothing like that. He, to the best of my knowledge, would never put himself in a situation where—"

"He's in trouble with the police?"

"No, he certainly isn't. I was just letting the thought processes examine the many possible undesirable circumstances that could befall a, um, someone. That's all. His health condition is his only concern, I believe."

"That's terrible enough. I guess that really is a, uh, possibility, though, right?"

"Well, sure. Promiscuity does present some retaliatory results if—"

"Oh, Amos, it's just natural, right? Not some kind of retaliation."

"Yes, of course. I just kind of threw that word in there. Anyway, that's one reason why anyone and everyone should always be cautious. I'm always thinking of the need to be—"

"Always? Why?"

"I'm just saying, Lenore, that some dire situations are easily avoided if one were to commit oneself to remaining responsible at all times, regardless of—"

"Hey, easy, Amos. What's with the lecture?"

"Oh, no, I was, uh, just thinking out loud. Sorry. One might say that I tend to bring the lecturing aspect of my university work home with me at times. It's not ideal. But I do believe that one might say that—"

"Yeah, I think I understand. Look, uh, now that my nails are dry, I was planning to call and check on our meet-up time."

"Oh, a wise action to take. Yes, I'm sure your being punctual is valued immensely."

"Yeah. Uh-huh. So I've been told."

"She told you that?"

"No, I just mean in general. Not her. Not about this. Just . . . in general."

"Huh," he said and rubbed his chin while giving her a look. "Well, perhaps I'll leave you to your call or text, then, and dash out to the yard for a second."

"Okay, good. Thanks. Maybe take your time. You could, uh, call that character and follow up. Make sure he's got a plan to fix that."

"Fix? Oh, you mean—"

"Yes, whatever he thinks he caught. There are cures, right?"

"Well, I suppose, Lenore. But like a prudent individual might say, prevention—or rather, avoidance—is the surest form of—"

"I really do need to call her."

He rose up quickly and said, "I'll be off, then. And then, later, we'll both be off. Different activities, though, of course."

She squinted up at him staring at her nails.

"One with plain nails, the other with nails that will warrant extra attention and likely compliments."

"Well said. Thanks."

"I'm off," he said and clunked the front door closed behind him.

"Oh my."

Chapter 27 – Record Number, Actually

Lenore gave Amos a few seconds, then got up from the couch and crept close enough to the living room window to see where he'd gone. She blew out a noisy sigh at seeing him pacing the sidewalk near the street and holding his phone up to his ear.

She hurried back to the couch and sat, then groaned and climbed up enough to sit up on the back with her bare feet on the seat cushions, which gave her a clear view of Amos.

With her eyes on him and the phone to her ear, Lenore listened to Laura's ringback tone and said, "Come on. Pick up."

"Hi, Lenore. It's your big day!"

"Hi, Laura. Hey, uh, about that. I was just thinking that—"

"Stop. No thinking allowed. Your brain will only get in the way."

"No, Laura, I have to think about it. I don't do anything without my brain, even if I—"

Laughing, Laura said, "They won't be wanting much to do with your brain, cheerleader girl."

"Laura. You don't—"

"Unless you're using it to say sexy stuff."

"But my brain will always—"

"Want me to list the parts they'll want most? First would be—"

"Laura, stop."

"Sure, let's not call out parts by name. How about what they'll want to be doing? What they'll want is to be grabbing you and squeezing you and . . . should I say what else?"

Managing her own brief laugh, Lenore said, "Oh, go on. What else?"

"Hmm. Licking you?"

"Well, they'd probably—"

"Mm, tasting you too. Lots of tasting going on. When's the last time you felt like a tasty treat, Lenore?"

"Laura, stop. That's enough for—"

"Wait. Just one more."

"Just one, huh?"

"Yep. It's an important one, though."

"Fine."

"I'm almost embarrassed to say it. But I will anyway, and I'll just imagine that I can see you blushing. They'll also want bad to be . . . penetrating their sweet party favor."

"Laura . . ."

Laura gave it a few seconds, then said, "I don't hear you complaining."

Lenore covered her grin with her free hand, and a few more silent seconds clicked past on the wall.

"Well, that's because I'm not so sure about any of that. I was just talking with Amos, and he—"

"You told him? Good for you. He should just respect that a girl's got to—"

"What? No! Laura! No, he just mentioned something about a student getting a disease, one of those kinds."

"Oh, yeah, I can see why you'd be thinking about that."

"Well, good. So, I can't take that chance. I mean, even if I, uh, wanted to."

"If you wanted the squeezing and rubbing and tasting and—"

"Laura!"

"—and penetrations. Plural. Way more than plural."

"You're too much sometimes."

"Huh. They always think I'm just the right amount. Oh, I should have told you. Sorry. Brock is pre-med, besides football, and he runs a very professional Frat Chat. Everyone involved, everyone that will be squeezing you and rubbing you and—"

"Laura."

"Oh, sorry. The thing is, he makes sure everyone gets tested. He's got a partner who has access to the clinic and if some stud doesn't pass the test, he's out. He won't get his hands on you or anything in you or—"

"Laura, you're making me crazy."

"Hey, it's a crazy night."

"They make you get tested, too, right?"

"Shit, no one's ever mentioned that. Horny young guys, Lenore. You really think they give any thought to nonsense like that?"

"I don't suppose so."

"So, what do you think? You should be done with all that pointless worrying. You'll be fine."

"Are you sure?"

"Yes, I trust Brock. He really is a good guy. He just knows that all of his friends have, well, appetites. Like big appetites. Him too. So, what the hell, right? Frat Chat."

"Oh God. Frat Chat."

"So, you're in?"

"God. Yeah, Laura."

"Good! Now that you're sure, I can tell you the latest news. I just got a text from Brock. He says—"

"It's canceled? The Frat Chat is—"

"What? No. He only said that they have a, uh, large number of tests going on. For the Frat Chat."

"God. Large?"

"Yeah, Lenore, lucky you. Record number, actually."

"Oh God. For tonight?"

"Yes, and I'm damn flattered," Laura said, adding a satisfied scoff.

"You? Why?"

"Well, Lenore, they think it's me, remember?"

"Oh, yeah, they don't know that—"

"No, they don't. And the rubbing and licking they're going to do, all the squeezing and all the—well, you say it."

"Laura, I don't know if I should—"

"Say it, Lenore."

"Fine. Dammit, Laura. All the—"

"And imagine it while you're saying it."

Lenore giggled and said, "All the . . . penetrating."

"Yes, there will be a lot of that. Oh my goodness, yeah."

"And it won't be with you. It'll all be—"

"For you, my hot twin girl. Driving them crazy. Center of attention."

"Center of—"

"You, uh, might want to plan on a late night."

"Oh my."

* * *

"Yeah, I'm still in the park, professor. I got money to burn from that fresh loan, so I'm guzzling all the coffee that bum can sell me."

Amos laughed and said, "A simple hello would have sufficed."

"One might say that it would."

"Hmm. Mocking one's professor isn't a—"

"Hey, easy. Sorry. You sound all worked up. What's the deal? Can't wait to get your turn at that—go on, you say it."

"I'm not saying it, and that's not it."

"What, then? Damn, I can almost see you shaking."

"Because, because the slow roller coaster car, it can't be too shiny, right?"

"Who says it—"

"And when someone, like in the literature—I'm still talking about the literature—when someone has a car that they're happy with, and it's calm and rational and just shiny enough to—"

"Shiny enough for who?"

"Well, for the individual in the, uh, case study. That person. He might be seen as believing—"

"Wait a second, professor. Doesn't the car have any say in it?"

"What? No, of course not. That's part of why that particular individual insists—"

"No, back up. What if the car, the one in the literature, of course, wants to be shined up? It might even want to make a run for that hill, right?"

"Well, no, it can't. It shouldn't. Not ever."

"It just might be itching for some kind of thrill ride, right?"

"No! No, it can't!"

"That just seems kind of harsh. I mean, come on. Cars have feelings too."

Amos listened to Emilio laughing until he grimaced and said, "The only feelings that car should have are to be the car that that particular individual wants. That's all, Emilio."

"Huh. I still say that's a bit harsh. So, a total paint job, pinstriping, the whole deal . . . that's out?"

"Yes! Very much out. And I can anticipate your next rebuttal, Emilio. Oh, I surely can. 'Oh, professor, what about just some really sexy pinstripes? Not the whole paint job, just . . . a few simple flourishes?'"

"I don't believe I've ever used the word 'flourish' in my entire, stinking life."

"Well, I'm sure it doesn't stink. But you can easily understand the point I'm making. The car is fine. No paint, no pinstripes, no anything. Nothing!"

"Alright, I get your point. But I'm all about the torment, right? So, chew on this, or write up your own case study, or whatever. Would a supposedly modest, barely noticeable 'flourish'—I can't believe the lengths I go to for you—could that tiny upgrade—"

"You buy me coffee too. I appreciate it."

"You're welcome. So, could that miniscule striping prompt said coaster car to crave a plunge down the hill too?"

"Oh, damn you."

It seemed that Emilio knew to wait until Amos had finished shaking his head while glaring up into the trees.

"That, uh, yes. A theoretical flourish could elicit such a motivation. I don't doubt that I could find—"

"A case history about it. Yep. Uh-huh."

The longest sigh of Amos's life got blown into the phone.

"So, tonight, Emilio. I, um, if the offer's good, still, about, um, just taking a look to see the, uh—"

"Slut?"

"Her. Yes. There's really no harm in, uh, just a quick look."

Emilio roared out a laugh, cut it short, then said, "That's what that cop thought."

"Oh. He, uh, liked the sight of—"

"The slut. In action. Yep."

"What if he didn't get impressed and decided to deploy handcuffs for anyone and everyone that was near and far, whether actively engaged, only waiting their turn, or having already consummated the—"

"Hey! Easy, alright? Look, I'll keep you on the straight and narrow law-abiding path. If there's any sign of that guy, we won't wait to see if he goes for the—"

"Slut."

"Good for you, professor. Yep. If there's any sign, we'll sneak you out the back door."

"There's a back door?"

"Yep. Back stairs, too, which are kind of out of the way. The bozo with a badge wouldn't even know where to look."

"So, I could get out of there quick, after I get a really short look— just for future literature write-ups—at the, uh—"

"Oh, just say it. You know you want to."

"At the slut."

"Whatever else she is, at any other time, she's at the Frat Chat because what she really wants most is to be . . ."

"A slut."

"Yep. Class dismissed."

Chapter 28 – Even More Like an Object

Amos dropped down onto his usual seat at the kitchen table, looked at what Lenore had arrayed in the middle, then up at her. Her head was tipped, and she gazed back for a second, then tipped it the other way.

"You're waiting for me to ask?" he said.

"Mm-hmm."

"Okay. I see sandwich stuff. That's what that all is, right?"

"Yep. Perfect for a late lunch."

"Um. So, all indications are that I have the, uh, honor of assembling however many sandwiches are needed by—"

"One is enough for me."

"Are you absolutely sure about that?"

She squinted with her head fully upright, then laughed and said, "I don't eat that much for lunch. You know that. So, yeah, one is all I want—one sandwich."

"I accept this opportunity and will fashion our sandwiches for us. May I ask why you seem to be projecting a, um, reluctance to—"

She'd already begun to lift her left hand, showing him the back of it, and she wiggled the fingers around.

"Oh. You don't want to nick up the fresh paint."

"The what?"

"Um, nail polish. Hey, did you ever think of adding pinstripes to any of them?"

"You must not be too hungry if you're asking peculiar questions like that."

"No, actually, I am kind of hungry. I'm just, uh, thinking about paint jobs. Stuff like that."

"Hmm."

"I'll just, um . . ."

He got into the bread and everything else, then began neat and balanced crafting of two identical sandwiches under Lenore's careful watch.

"More mustard for me," she said, then gave him a modest grin when he looked up from his work. "More is sometimes better."

"Uh, yes. Sure."

He dipped the knife in for a large glob, then began smearing it around on a slice of bread. He looked up before he finished.

"You're staring at it like you're starving, Lenore. Give me a second. Some tasty things, like this, are made to be spread around generously."

"Yeah, um, all around."

"What?"

"Just . . . I guess I am kind of hungry," she said.

"Not hungry enough to—"

"Risk my paint job. No."

"Funny. Paint job."

"Your words, Amos."

"Uh, yes. Uh-huh. Here you go."

He nudged her plate toward her a small amount at a time until it was close enough for her to pick up the sandwich. But she picked up a fork instead.

"Wait," he said. "You're not serious."

"I am. Watch."

She cut down on a corner of the sandwich, freeing a small bite, then slid the fork under and held it up.

"Small," he said, pointing. "So you don't—"

"Choke. You're right. It deserves some care, don't you think?"

"To not choke? Well, sure."

"I don't imagine the sight of me choking would be too appealing."

"Uh, no. Nope."

He picked up his sandwich but only held it up as he watched her feed herself the bite, then chew it slowly and deliberately.

"Oh, I know what's going on," he said.

"You do? You know?"

"Yes. Slow and careful, chewing well until you're very sure that you're ready to—"

She swallowed it, then said, "Swallow it."

He squinted at her and said, "I don't believe we've ever entertained a conversation such as this over lunch."

"So, perhaps today's a good day to start."

"Okay, sure. Um, I guess the guiding principle here, then, one might say, is that a meal can be reduced to a series of careful swallows, each one—"

She hacked once with a hand over her mouth, and she stared at him with eyes wide.

"Not again," he said while shaking his head.

She frowned as she forced the food down, then followed it with a drink of water.

"Perhaps I wasn't careful enough."

He glanced at her sandwich, the majority of it still untouched.

Laughing once, he said, "You'd better take the lesson to heart before you expire yourself. There are still countless more swallows to go."

"Yes, well, that's one way to describe a time like this."

"A time like this?"

"You know—lunch," she said. "Lunchtime."

"Oh. Yes. I'm going to go ahead and eat and hope for the best."

"Which would be?"

Her hand with the fork fell slowly and rested on the table when Amos snickered and said, "The best would be that you're able to remain very careful for the countless, necessary swallowing ahead of you, all while . . ."

She stared at a face smiling back at her with eyebrows perched up high.

"... you're careful to keep your fingernails looking as flawless when you're finally through the drama as when you began."

She kept staring as she tried to silence two more modest chokes, then she chugged some more water.

"Uh, it's just lunch."

"Well, yes," he said. "Of course."

"It's just a lot of thought going into a simple lunch."

"Professors. We just like to talk. And watch. Watching, too, because—"

"Watching me eat?"

"Yes. Exactly."

She cut another bite with her fork.

"When we're done, I just thought of something else I need to ask Laura."

"Like what?"

"Uh, just girl stuff. You can run off and talk to Emilio about guy stuff."

* * *

Seated up high on the couch back again, Lenore pressed her bare feet into the cushions and wiggled her toes around while she watched Amos through the front window.

"Clock's ticking," was how Laura answered her call.

"Yes, I know, but it doesn't matter. I'd like that drink with you, Laura, but there's no way for the rest. There's just no way."

"Lenore, slow down. What changed? You were all in just a minute ago. Center of attention, remember?"

"I know. I did say that. But I just had lunch with Amos and dammit, it was almost like he suspected something."

"What makes you say that? Guys never figure things out."

"Mostly because he talked a lot about me swallowing—about being careful when swallowing a lot. He just kept going on about—"

"Lucky guess. He doesn't know anything."

"Wait a second. So, you're saying that his so-called lucky guesses were right? Laura!"

"Well, what do you think, twin girlie? You must know that'll be the most attractive option every time one of them—"

"Laura!"

"Shit, they'll want to watch that, too, because—"

"Hey! I shouldn't even do that once, and you're saying that—"

"Oh, Lenore. You might want to, um, oh, I'd better not say it."

"Oh, go on. What?"

"Maybe you'd better skip the appetizers when we meet, which is really soon, like just a couple of—"

"Don't eat? To get ready for—"

"Well, just being practical. So, your ex-fiancé is right about—"

"He's not my ex anything. Not yet."

"Yet. Yeah. Well, he's right about the swallowing. Oh, come on, Lenore. I'd bet some part of you would love to do that."

"I've never said that, and I don't think—"

"Have you ever fantasized about something so bad like that?"

"You mean—"

"Uh-huh. Like you're starving for it?"

"Uh, maybe. Alright. I told you I was up on my bed, on my hands and knees, and I was thinking of . . . that."

"Good. We're finally getting somewhere. So, in this fantasy, you finished one, then . . . what?"

Lenore giggled and cut it short.

"Then, right away, there was, um, another."

"And you did what you had to—I mean, what you wanted to do?"

"Well, it was just a fantasy, so it didn't count."

"But you did it?"

"Yeah. Oh, I sure did, Laura."

"And the next one too?"

"Well, of course," she said, giggling.

"And did you get the feeling you wanted to stop?"

"Mm. Uh-uh."

"How did you imagine that was? You liked it?"

"It was just a fantasy and yeah, I liked it. It felt so, I don't know, wild."

"It sure is a wild scene. So, you're on board. We're just talking numbers now."

"You never did say. What is that number, you think?"

"There's no way for either of us to know. The best you can do is get yourself prepared. You have to see yourself as, well, I guess the word is 'insatiable.'"

"That's quite a word."

"In your fantasy, was that the right word for you?"

"Um, yeah. I sure was. But it was just—"

"Oh, Lenore, you're going to feel that way anyway once you get going."

"I will?"

"Mm-hmm. Right to the very last . . ."

"Uh, drop?"

"Shame on you. I was going to say very last Frat Chat guy. Your answer's better, though."

"Laura, even if I can do all that, so many times, what about catching something? I'm still worried about that."

"Don't be. Really, Brock is a thorough kind of guy. That's not even an issue. All you need to do is be prepared."

"How prepared?"

"I think it's mostly in how you see yourself."

"Okay. Like, how?"

"Alright, just hold up a second. Close your eyes. They're closed?"

"Yeah."

"Alright. Now, just think of that fantasy you just told me about, and think about how you're going to offer that to however many horny studs show up."

"Okay. I'm, um, imagining it."

"You're doing all of them."

"Mm-hmm. I am."

"And there's a lot of them, Lenore."

"Mm-hmm. So many."

"So, when you're there, right from the very second you start, what are you?"

"Oh, you mean . . ."

"Uh-huh. That's exactly what I mean. You're a what?"

"I don't know if I can—"

"Stop, Lenore. Keep your eyes closed, and get back to that fantasy. I mean, be there. Feel it. You feeling it? All of it?"

"Mm-hmm."

"Okay, right at the beginning, one of them asks you what you are. What's your answer, the truth they want to hear from you?"

"I'm a . . . slut?"

"Yep, that's the word. Now, try again, and say it how you'll say it to them."

Lenore hesitated, kept her eyes closed, and didn't fight the smile that appeared.

"I'm . . . a slut."

"Again. Like you mean it."

"Hmm. I'm a slut."

"You are so ready, you sexy slut."

"Oh my God, I'm going to be a—"

"A slut at the Frat Chat. Oh, yeah."

* * *

"Guess where I'm at?" Emilio said into his phone.

"At the park. Drinking coffee on student loan money. Look, Emilio, I can't do it. I just can't."

"I don't accept that, but I will listen to your reasoning."

"That's incredibly charitable of you," Amos said, scoffing. "I can't risk it. I'm a professor, and I have a reputation to uphold. If I were to get arrested? I'd be throwing away my entire career."

"Just to watch a slut in action."

"Yes. And that doesn't sound like a fair trade."

"Not at this moment, no. I'll ask you again when you're there, watching her—"

"No! The answer simply has to be no."

"I urge you to reconsider. Bear in mind your vision of a perfect cheerleader giving herself so freely and indiscriminately. That's not something you want to miss."

"I'm bearing it in mind, and the answer is still—"

"It'll be better than your imagination. We're talking a live performance, here, professor. Really, just knowing that you have the option of joining in on what you're seeing will probably give you a stroke."

"Well, that's convincing. I hope I'm not quite that ancient."

"Okay, forget the stroke part of it. The rest of it, though, makes sense. You can't even argue the point."

"I can, and I shall. I must insist that—"

"Yeah, I know. All you want to see is a parked car without any pinstripes. That's not going to make it for you, and you know it."

"I see that as a completely rational choice. Especially when considering my chosen career and how easily it could be derailed by the allure of—"

"A slut?" Emilio said, laughing.

"Yes. That."

"Don't make me do it, professor. I feel it happening."

"What? Now, you're having a stroke?"

"Not on your life. If anyone's having one, it'll be you when your eyes bug out of your skull. No, I meant that I just might have to lose some respect for you."

"Over this? That's not warranted."

"Still. It's happening. It's all just slipping away."

"Because I won't risk my career for the sight, the actual live witnessing, in just a few hours, of a—"

"Slut in action. Oh, yeah."

The silence dragged on, then Emilio laughed.

"A sexy slut, professor."

*   *   *

"I might be ready, Laura," Lenore said into her phone while still sitting high on the couch, "but the answer still has to be no."

"It doesn't have to be. And it can't be. No, Lenore, if you care about me at all, if our friendship means anything, you have to do it. You have to do what you already said you would."

"I take it back. You just go and handle it and tomorrow, you can tease me with all the details."

"Uh-uh. Not that simple. Remember, I already told Brock that I was sending a replacement tonight."

"You shouldn't have."

"Well, I did. That's you, by the way. He's nice enough, but I'm not about to stiff him like that—no pun intended."

Lenore giggled, and said, "Uh, that's an appropriate pun."

"They're young. It's the right word."

"Oh my gosh."

"And I made other plans that I can't ditch. It's too late. I can't be there and dammit, someone has to be. You. You have to be."

"If he's such a great guy, he'll understand."

"Sure, he'll understand, but he'll still give me some grief."

"Would he?"

"Hell, yeah. He knows enough about me to cause me some serious problems. Oh, Lenore, you just have to go through with it."

"Laura, no. Then, he'll find some way to give me grief, won't he?"

"No, here's the thing: he's got to run out of town for the night, so he won't even be there. He'll never see you."

"How would I even know where to go? I don't even know—"

"I'll give you good instructions at dinner when you're not eating. Because you're saving your appetite for—"

"Don't say it!"

"I won't. You can brag about it next time we talk."

"Brag?"

"Uh-huh. Try to keep count. Anyway, there's a back entrance to the frat house. You park far enough away, then sneak right in there. I'll give you directions up to your room."

"Oh, my room."

"Sounds kind of nice, huh?"

"Oh, Laura, this is crazy."

"You're just being a . . . what?"

"I'm not saying it again."

"We'll see. Anyway, you see how anonymous this will all be for you? Really, could you cook up a better plan to live an experience like you've always wanted?"

"I'm always wanted it?"

"You have from the very second I first mentioned it to you."

"Oh, Laura . . ."

"Tell me I'm wrong."

"Hmm . . ."

*　*　*

"She might be a sexy, you know, but at least my career is mine. It's not just something I'm watching for a few thrills on a Saturday night."

"You'll keep your career. I told you about the police scanner, right?"

"No, you did not."

"Well, now you know. We're tuned in. We're staking ourselves out. If the cops get a call, we'll know, and I'll scoot your professor ass right out the back door."

"The back door."

"Yeah, really sneaky. Get you back to your squeaky clean life like nothing happened."

"Nothing will happen. Even if I—look, I just can't take the chance."

More silence dragged on as Amos paced the sidewalk in front of the house.

"Hey," Emilio said after a while, "you know that girl, Lindsey, right? In the front row?"

"Oh, don't tell me she's really the one that—"

"What? No. Don't be silly. I think she's some kind of prude or something."

"Because you couldn't score with her?"

"Sure, that's part of it. Not the point. I'm just saying that I know other girls that aren't so nice."

"So?"

"So, I give one a call, and she files a report with the university."

"A report about what?"

"About the sexual abuse you've been throwing her way. Oh, you should be ashamed of—"

"I haven't done anything! What are you talking about?"

"I'm talking about a lie being as damning as a truth. Get it?"

"You wouldn't."

"Well, I wouldn't want to."

"Why are you doing this? Why is my going to the frat whatever so—"

"Frat Chat."

"Whatever. Why does it matter so much to you that you'd blackmail me like that?"

"Can we just say that I believe your participation will further your philosophical perspectives on life?"

"No."

"Alright. Sure. So, I'm just tired of getting failing grades."

"You could just do passing work."

"I could. Sure. I like this plan better."

* * *

"You're not just messing with me, are you, Laura?"

186

"No, seriously, Lenore, I could have some horrible problems from Brock. Besides, he's a good guy, and I don't want to let him down. Please, tell me you'll do it."

Lenore gazed out at Amos pacing along, sometimes looking up and waving around his free hand, then she scoffed and allowed a smile.

"Fine."

"Really?"

"You're not leaving me much choice, Laura."

"No, I'm not. I'm sorry about that. But you'll thank me later."

"I can't believe I'm going through with this. Especially with you making up stuff."

"No, really, Brock is the kind of—"

"Not that. You talked about me sneaking in and said it was perfectly anonymous. Well, how can it be?"

"Oh, that reminds me: I always wear a blindfold."

"What? So, that means—"

"You'll have to wear one too. Uh-huh."

"Laura! This is getting crazier all the time. So, I won't have any idea who's—"

"No idea at all. It's more exciting than you can imagine."

"I doubt that. It's just creepy. There's no way—"

"Won't you feel even more like an object? Hmm?"

"Well, yeah. That would sure do it. But Laura, it's just—"

"You've fantasized about doing this. You told me about one time. Were there others?"

After an exasperated sigh, Lenore said, "Uh, yeah. A few."

"And in those fantasies, what did you think of yourself?"

"I don't know what you mean."

"Come on. I know you. You were probably saying things, right?"

"Maybe."

"Like you were talking to your, uh, admirers?"

"Sometimes. Yeah."

"Tell me. What did you say?"

"Laura, really, we should—"

"Remember what you just said a second ago, as if you were telling them what you are?"

"What I am?"

"You know what I mean. Come on. What else?"

"Fine. I said I was an object. Just an object."

"That's a good start. What else?"

"Um, something to be used. Something soft that's meant only to be used."

"I'd say you got this deal figured out."

"No, I was just—"

"Listen. Close your eyes again. And that's what you'll see: nothing. Keep them closed, and say those things again."

"Laura, I can't—"

"Try it. Humor me."

"Oh, fine."

She took a deep breath, gave Amos another quick look, then closed her eyes.

"I'm just an object."

"Good, and they'll have a nice view of what you're offering too."

"If I—"

"Shh. Keep going."

"Tell me I'm just an object," Lenore said, eyes closed and sitting high on the couch. "Something that's meant to be used."

Laura didn't prompt her, and a few silent seconds passed.

"I'm so soft all over. Something soft that's only, *only* for . . . sex."

Laura whispered, "One more line, Lenore. Tell them what they already know—they really want to hear it from your lips. Mm-hmm, your lips."

Lenore sighed, eyes still closed, and slid down the back of the couch, stretched her legs straight out, then smiled when she moved them apart.

"I'm a slut."

She shifted both legs as far to each side as she could.

"Really, I'm *nothing* but a total slut."

After a few seconds of Lenore listening only to Laura's deep breaths, she heard her say, almost whispering, "Damn. Just like that, Lenore. I love that bit about 'nothing but' and 'total.' I didn't make you say any of that."

"Oh my God. No, you, um, sure didn't."

"So, maybe you really are? You're, um, really nothing but?"

Lenore still hadn't opened her eyes, and the silence dragged on.

"Lenore?"

"Hmm . . ."

"Lenore. You're really going to say those things, right? That's part of the deal."

"You're serious?"

"Oh, yeah, I talk like that a lot. I really get into it. I should get an award. You have to do the same, or word will get back to Brock that something wasn't right."

"Ooh, he'll be ticked off that we switched."

"Yeah. Don't let that happen. Lenore, you know what to say. So, say it. Say it all. Say it all as sexy as you can. Can you do that?"

"I can't just make myself say anything like that, Laura. I'm not an actor."

"Here's what'll happen: if you have to, just pretend at first. I guarantee you that once things get going, you'll mean every word of it."

"I will?"

"Uh-huh. You'll be surprised at all you're saying when you're feeling so much attention. So much attention, Lenore."

"Oh my . . ."

* * *

"Alright, fine, Emilio. I'll go to the party. And you won't get that friend to lie about me?"

"I swear, I won't. Alright, glad you're going."

"Yes, I'm sure. Fun time."

"Your eyeballs will sure think so."

"Not if I just sit around and chat."

"Professor, you'd be the only one. No one sits around chatting at a Frat Chat."

"Wonderful."

"Just park in front, come up to—"

"Oh, no. No way. I'll walk. I might even wear a disguise."

"Smart. That's why you're in front of the class and I'm snoring in the back row."

"Or screaming things like 'divinity.'"

"I do have my moments. I'm going to figure that out, you know. The whole divinity theory."

"Hot and cold. Sure. Well, whatever you scribble down will probably now get the highest possible grade."

"You're alright, professor. I'll keep the coffee flowing, and you and I, together, will figure out just what the hell could be divine about hot and cold."

"At the same time."

"Damn hot tub on a mountain. Yeah, we'll do it. Hey, meet me right here at our table, alright? We'll hang out, then cruise on over."

"Alright. I can hang and cruise with the best of them."

"Damn, professor. Yeah, I'm sure you can."

* * *

When the doorknob cranked and the door began swinging in, Lenore popped open her eyes and tried to get her legs back together before Amos could see.

She wasn't quick enough.

"Stretching?"

"Yeah. I think I was sitting funny or something. Whatever, that helped. How's that coffee guy?"

"He's good."

While walking toward the couch, he continued.

190

"He's still talking about his philosophical ideas. I don't know if he's making sense or not, but at least he's trying."

He plopped backwards with enough space for another to sit between them.

After a few seconds of quiet, he said, "Your friend is okay?"

"Yeah, she's always okay. We were just making sure about our plans for, uh, you know, later."

He sighed and stared out the window.

"Sounds good. I hope you have a good time."

"I think I kind of have to."

"Huh?"

"I, uh, just mean that I can't be unenthusiastic with, you know, spending time with a friend. That's not the kind of woman I want to be."

"Well," he said as he slumped down and kicked his legs up onto the coffee table, "you'd never be that rude. Besides, you're already almost a perfect woman."

"Almost, huh?"

"As perfect as a real woman can be. How about that?"

"Sounds like a pretty high bar. It could be that I'm not all that close."

"One might say that you're as close as—"

"As I want to be. Yeah. Who wants to be an angel?"

"It's a fair question. One might think that a lot would."

"Sure. So, uh, we'll have to leave soon. Alright if I take the car? We really should get another one."

"Soon. Yes. Go ahead. I'll walk into town to meet Emilio."

A half minute of silence played out with only a few sweeping clock hand clicks to divide it.

"Okay," she said. "About the car."

A long, quiet moment brought more clock sounds.

"Right," he said, his voice slow. "Walking is . . . good."

"Uh . . . yep."

Her sigh seemed to consume a lot of time and only marginally competed with the ticking from the wall.

"So, uh, you need to get ready?"

"No," he said, "I'm good."

The clock's steady cadence tried its best to add something to the room.

"Yep," she said. "Uh, I'll get ready after you leave, then."

More clicking.

"Alright. I'm going."

He stayed seated. The clock measured out the seconds.

He finally got up and stretched and said, "Alright. I'm off. Have a good time."

"You too, Amos. I'll see you soon."

He pointed, winked, said, "Soon," and pulled in the door.

Then, he was gone.

"Oh my gosh . . ."

Chapter 29 – You Just Tell Me for Sure

Lenore drove slowly along the narrow alley behind the row of frat houses, and she nodded quietly at the sight of certain specific posters in the windows, as described by Laura, in the Frat Chat house.

Between the tall buildings, light was scarce, and her large sunglasses, the same ones that she'd used when walking around out front with Amos, made it all look like night.

She parked where Laura had suggested—close enough for only a brief hike but far enough for the car to not be noticed. Turning the engine off and removing the key, then clutching it in a tight grip on her thigh, she looked around at the relative scarcity of figures walking about. Only the two that she'd passed while driving in had continued past her, paying her no attention.

"Last chance, Lenore," she said, almost holding her jaw too tight to force the words out.

She looked each way again, then sighed and tipped down her glasses while leaning, looking up at a single, dark window on the third floor of the Frat Chat building.

"You're really doing this? You're seriously going up there?"

The glasses got a push back in place, and she pulled her generous hood farther forward. Staring straight out through the windshield, barely noticing the old bricks and weathered wood siding of that building, whichever one it was, she scoffed again and shook her head.

"I did tell Laura I would."

She grinned, then tipped her head back briefly with a short laugh.

"Oh, I sure told her some things. Like, I'm an object. Something . . ."

She looked out the driver's side window again and let her eyes focus again on that third-floor window.

"... soft. Something soft that's ... oh my gosh ... maybe I really want to be only for sex."

With both hands, she tugged at the sunglasses, pulled them out of the thick bunch of her hair, and set them on her lap, which was covered completely by her overly long raincoat.

With a hand on each cheek, she half-laughed as she said, "Hmm, that's not all you said. Say the rest."

Looking up at the window again, she said, "Say it while you're looking up there. They might be up there. Thinking about you and very ... ready. Say it to them."

After installing the glasses again, and keeping her eyes focused up high on the Frat Chat building, she said, almost whispering, "I'm ..."

She looked down at her hands in her lap and laughed.

"I can't. I just ..."

Again looking up high, at a window that might be letting bits of light in on a crowd that's waiting just for her, desperate to have her there, she said, "I'm a slut. I'm here because I love being ... nothing but a slut."

Letting a serious expression shift into a grin, she added, "I probably shouldn't have used the words 'nothing but,' though. Because, of course, I'm other things too."

The grin faded, then vanished altogether.

"But being a slut is what ... I love most."

Her smile reappeared after a few seconds.

"Fun to say anyway. Oh, Laura, I still don't know ..."

* * *

"No coffee this time, professor."

Amos didn't smile as he closed the distance to their picnic table in the park. Emilio was already seated, and he held out toward Amos a brown paper bag wrapped around something.

"What's that?" he said while sitting with his back straight.

"Courage, my friend. Also goes by the name whiskey."

"Huh. Why not?"

He accepted the hidden bottle and took a short drink.

"Ooh, that's strong. Good, though."

"Yep."

"I can't believe you threatened me with a false accusation. I thought we were getting to be pretty good friends. One might say that we were even moving beyond the typical professor-student arrangement."

"Professor, I'd never really be that much of an asshole. I was just talking shit."

"What? You forced me into coming here, meeting you so—"

"Yeah, that's it exactly. It was only to get you here, in the park, and to take at least one taste of the whiskey. That's it, I swear."

"That's bad enough."

"Uh, yeah. I admit that. I'm an upstanding guy only maybe ninety-nine percent of the time."

"Huh. Sure. So, I'm free to go back home and not be concerned about your threats?"

"You're absolutely free to go. And I swear, I'd never do that to you or anyone."

Amos didn't get up. He just leaned back against the table, matching Emilio's pose, and they both looked out over the fading light about to abandon the park to darkness.

"And I shall go," said Amos. "Yes. But I do want just a sip more of the whiskey."

"Can't blame you for that. Here."

Amos tipped it back, swallowed, then hiccuped.

"So, you won't try to stop me from leaving?"

"Nope. But you can appreciate that I do want to remind you of what you'd be missing if you crawl back home."

"No one said anything about crawling."

"Bad choice of words. You won't exactly be skipping, though, if you remember exactly what you're passing up."

"Yes, I can appreciate that you might try to sell the idea."

"Sell. That woman at the Frat Chat, she's not selling anything. No, she's giving it away. All for free."

"To anyone."

"Yeah. And everyone. Because she's a . . ."

Amos scoffed and said, "Give me that bottle," then took another drink.

"That's a fill-in-the-blank pop quiz, you know."

"And I know the answer, Emilio."

Emilio chuckled and said, "And you're about to fail the class. Even though you'd only be going for the talk—the chat—what exactly is that woman upstairs?"

"No harm in saying it," said Amos. "She's a slut."

"Well, there's a lesson here: a few sips of whiskey help pass pop quizzes. I'll make a note to help me get through my third freshman year."

"Funny. Give me that bottle."

He handed it to Amos and said, "So?"

"So, what?"

"So, let's go hang out. Chat, one might say."

"Mocking me again."

"Blame it on the whiskey."

Emilio stood and continued, saying, "Ready?"

Amos looked up at him while handing back the bottle. A few seconds passed.

"Fine. There's no reason I can't go and spend some time chatting."

"Yeah. Now, you're talking. Chatting, I mean."

Amos scoffed and stood, and they both laughed as they began the short walk toward Frat Row.

* * *

Alone in the alleyway, Lenore groaned as she swung open the car door and looked down for an unsoiled patch of dirty alley asphalt, then she stepped her clean white sneaker there. Standing, she tugged down on her long jacket, checked that the bottom hem was smooth all around and hardly even showing her ankles, then she pulled the hood forward as far as she could.

Before closing the door, she looked both ways, then leaned her backside into it to latch it. After a quick glance up high, at a small third-floor window in a distant building, she scoffed and began a normal walk toward the back door that she'd seen while driving in.

She heard the basketball bouncing and looked up from her careful steps. Two young men were approaching, walking casually in her direction as one of them dribbled the ball. Their low conversation was sometimes peppered with laughter from one or the other or both.

As they drew near, she reached up, pretended that her glasses needed some adjustment, and sighed when they'd passed. But she still heard the ball striking the pavement and some of their talk until they'd gone too far.

"Who was that?"

"Who knows, and who cares? Looked homeless."

"Yeah, pretty shabby. Hey, before the game, let's . . ."

Still walking, Lenore didn't turn to look back at them but kept her eyes focused, through the dark lenses, on the shady alcove that harbored a back entrance to a building about to host what they all called the Frat Chat.

Her sneakers didn't make a sound as she got close enough to get a hand on the doorknob, and she scoffed down at seeing her ring. She quickly switched hands and used the ring hand to take out her phone. After a few taps, she held it up, hand on a doorknob and eyes scanning the alley in both directions.

"Come on," she said, her voice shaking. "Pick up. Please."

"Hey, Lenore."

"Oh, thank goodness. Laura, I don't—"

"Don't have a minute to waste. Uh-huh. Are you there? Are you in the room? Tell me you're ready to go."

"I'm, uh, close. But Laura, I don't know if I can do this!"

"Sure you can. Like we talked about, you don't really have to do anything. Just—"

"Let them use me. I know. That's what I—"

"No, no, no. You're forgetting something. You're using them, too, remember?"

"I remember you saying that. I just don't know if—"

"Lenore, just stop. Hold up. We have a minute to talk about this. Just take a breath, alright?"

Lenore let out a deep breath and said, "Okay."

"First, you should—oh, I almost forgot. Don't drink anything anyone offers you. They put something in it that'll make you go really crazy."

"Oh boy. Some kind of drug?"

"I suppose. That first time for me, damn. I was so out of control."

"Well, okay, Laura. As long as I don't get too thirsty, I'll—"

"No, Lenore, promise me. Don't drink anything."

"Fine. I'll remember."

"Good. Now, you need to think about those fantasies you had. You liked them, right?"

"Well, yeah, but I was just at home. They weren't real."

"I know. Yeah. Think about them, though."

Lenore closed her eyes and breathed as naturally as she could.

"Are you thinking about them?"

"Yeah. Sure, Laura."

"Just for fun, and it doesn't mean anything, just tell me some of the things you were saying."

"What, like I was imagining saying to, um, them? Tell it to them again?"

"Yeah, those things. Come on. Just for fun. I think you had fun telling me all that, didn't you?"

Lenore giggled and said, "I, uh, yeah, I did."

"So, go on. I'm listening. Oh, yeah, pretend I'm them. You're up in the room and saying it to them. Go on."

She cleared her throat, looked each way along the narrow roadway between tall buildings, then closed her eyes again.

"I'm just an object. I'm something . . ."

"Go on. Keep going."

"I'm something soft that's only . . . for . . ."

"Come on. Only for what?"

"I'm only for sex."

"How does it feel to say that? Just be honest."

"It feels . . . exciting. Like some kind of weird relief to say it. But Laura, I still don't—"

"Uh-uh. Try saying one more thing. Whether they actually ask you or not. Go on."

"You're terrible, Laura."

"Yep. Still, though, what else?"

"Even if I say it, that doesn't mean I'm going in there."

"Fine. Just say it. Oh, Lenore, you know you love saying it."

She scoffed and said, "I, uh, yeah. It's a fun thing to say."

"Say it, then."

"Okay. I'm—"

"Remember, you're up there in the room, and you're saying it to them. Forget I'm here."

"I'm . . . a slut. I love being nothing but a slut."

"Nothing?"

"Nothing."

"Mm-hmm," said Laura. "That sounded damn honest to me, Lenore."

"It's not. It was just for fun."

"While you're dressed like a cheerleader for the Frat Chat?"

"Laura, I don't think I can do it."

"Well, Lenore, you have to because—"

"I really don't think I can. Laura, can't you just do it yourself?"

"Didn't you say, sexy cheerleader, that your engagement is just about trashed anyway?"

"Yeah, and it might be. Why can't he just see that I'm not only someone's fiancé, a respectable business owner . . . all that? If he could see even a little that I—"

"That you're a slut?"

"Uh, maybe not that extreme. Oh God, Laura, there's no way to fix this with him. I'd rather fix it somehow than lose him."

"Shit, I'd say you've already lost him."

"Maybe just from wanting to go out and meet you. That alone might be too much for him."

"That's all it takes?"

"I don't know, Laura. He could tell that I was excited about it—even doing my nails and teasing him about loaning you my ring. I think I've already ruined it all."

"Well, he's a fool, then. You seriously want me to lead the cheers tonight at the Frat Chat?"

"Could you?"

A car cruised by, and no one looked her way. A basketball bounced in the distance. Voices, laughter, sounds of traffic ventured weakly into the dim area between the uneven lines of buildings.

"Oh, dammit, Lenore. Yeah, I probably could. You just tell me for sure that you don't want to do it. You tell me right now."

Lenore switched hands for the phone, then held out her ring finger for a look. Taking another moment before answering, she stepped back far enough to gaze up at the third-floor window.

"Oh, Laura, I think . . ."

Chapter 30 – Tonight, She's Just a What?

"It looks familiar," Amos said as he and Emilio approached the frat house. "I just saw this the other day. I was out walking with—"

"They kind of all look the same, you know. I wasn't kidding, though—I've been to the Chats before. This is the right house."

They stood at the bottom of ten wide concrete steps leading up to a porch, just as wide and deep, and a thick wooden door back out of the daylight.

"Behind that door . . ."

Amos finished for him, saying, "There's a whole lot of chatting going on."

"Actually, you're correct."

He pointed up, and Amos tipped his head back to see.

"Behind that little window, though."

"Uh, yes. You did say the third floor."

"Yes, sir. Oops, I almost made reference to your occupation, but I'm going to try to stop that. Third floor. She's probably already waiting up there."

He looked at his watch, then resumed his study of the window.

"This is an operation, though, and no one's going in there until the official start time."

"But she's . . . she's already in the room, you think?"

"Yeah. Bet on it. Uh-huh, she's ready to go."

Amos stared up for a few seconds, then looked down again.

"So, this isn't just some practical joke. This really happens?"

"Well, shit, yeah. It's a wild time too."

"Hey, Emilio," a young man said as he ran past them, then up the steps.

"Hey."

Another ran past them, saying, "Almost time. Get out of the way, Emilio, or get run down."

"Hey, Jake, there's plenty enough, uh, chatting for everyone."

The two rushed inside and let the door swing shut behind them.

"That's kind of a rule.. No direct reference to anything but—"

"Chatting. Got it."

"Especially when you're inside. Except when you're on the third floor. Up there, I mean, good luck trying to not say something about it. It's overpowering."

"Makes sense, Emilio. Sure."

"Out here, too, is alright. Look up again, and tell me what's waiting in that room."

"You're relentless with that."

"Yeah, it's fun. So, upstairs. She could be anything imaginable all during the week, right?"

"Uh, sure. She could be anything."

"She might be just sweet and innocent, and no one in her life has any idea."

"That could be. Sure."

"But not here. Not tonight. Tonight, she's just a . . . what?"

"Oh, I give up. She's a slut. Tonight, she's just a slut."

"By golly, you're ready to go inside."

He elbowed Amos and started a jog up the steps, and Amos followed, just not as quickly.

* * *

Inside, even while the front door was still swinging shut, Amos snapped his eyes around and said, "Oh my goodness."

There were small groups of men scattered all around, and a few were standing and talking, sometimes laughing, partway up the staircase.

"See the papers?"

"Huh?"

Amos looked around and saw that many of the frat guys were holding small bits of paper.

"No. Don't tell me."

"Alright, I won't. You tell me, then."

"Take a number. Wait in line?"

"Told you—it's an operation. Look."

Amos looked down as Emilio raised his hand, showing him two small pieces of paper like all the others.

"You and . . ."

"Me and you. Yeah. I mean, if you change your mind."

Amos leaned around, trying to read them.

Emilio laughed and said, "Three and four. I pulled some strings, but I couldn't get one and two. Sorry."

"It doesn't matter because I'm only—"

"Chatting. I know. No pressure. Just, our numbers are here. Ready. Much like upstairs, that, uh . . ."

Amos, looking toward the top of the stairs, where a small landing hosted a few more with papers in hand, said, "That special guest. She's, uh, probably—"

"Probably more eager to get going than any of us. Yeah. Oh, by 'us,' I don't mean you, of course."

"Of course."

While Emilio smirked and shook his head, Amos glanced around the large common area, then pointed.

"That couch. I'm going to stake a claim to—"

"Sure. Maybe later. Let's just run up and scope out where it's all going to happen."

"Oh, I don't know. I think I'd rather just—"

Emilio got a firm grip on Amos's arm and laughed while maneuvering him toward the stairs.

"It's just upstairs. No big deal. Come on."

Amos didn't resist, and they began the walk up two flights, mostly single file to get past the others standing around, laughing and talking excitedly.

At the top of the second flight of stairs, Emilio pointed without ceremony to the large grouping of young men farther down the hall. All were talking softly amongst themselves, and none of them were laughing.

One broke from the group and stepped near the only door, which was closed. He looked at his watch, then gestured for another frat guy to join him, and he did.

"Uh, that's the room, I guess."

"No need to guess," Emilio said, scoffing loudly. "Yep. She's in there. Those lucky two dudes get the first go at her."

"This really isn't some kind of joke."

"Bet your ass, this isn't a joke."

He pointed in their direction, but lower, and said, "Two seats are open. Want to just hang out up here for a while?"

"I, um, I should probably just—"

"Come on. Just for a minute or two. That's a lot of steps to climb back down."

Amos laughed and said, "Yes, blame it on the steps. Alright. Just for a minute."

"Good call. Come on."

They took a few steps closer to the two men outside the closed door, then both plopped down in aged, upholstered chairs across the hall from the room and only a few steps away.

Chapter 31 – She's Bought and Sold

Amos and Emilio both stared intently at the closed door and young men numbers one and two.

Emilio didn't look behind him at Amos when Amos said, "How come those two? Why are they first?"

"It was an auction this time, and they were the highest bidders. Brock cooked up a little fundraiser idea. Pretty cool, huh?"

"They bid the highest?"

"Yeah. Probably trust fund brats. Bastards get all the best stuff."

"So, that woman in there, she's kind of being sold?"

"I guess you could put it that way. Yeah."

"She's volunteering to be sold for sex?"

Emilio turned enough to squint at Amos.

"You raise a good point, my anonymous friend. No. I think the answer to that is 'no.' I don't think she knows she's bought and sold like a fine piece of meat."

"This is incredible . . ."

"It's really something, isn't it?"

Emilio gave him a grin, then turned his attention back to the closed door.

"Hey, that kind of, uh, makes her even cheaper, doesn't it? Shouldn't someone have told her?"

Emilio turned back to him and held his eyebrows up high.

"You're an ethical sort. Yes, she should be made aware that her sex services are being parceled out by order of a bidding process."

"She'll probably stomp right out of here. No way would she—"

Laughing, Emilio said, "You really don't get it. You're not capable of thinking like a slut. If anything, she'll get off on that. She'll feel like even more of a sex object."

"Just incredible."

"Yeah, but you do make a good point. You can tell her."

"What? How would I? I'm not—"

"No, relax. I just mean if you decide to go in there. If, is what I'm saying."

Both looked toward the door when one of the lucky auction bidders swung the door in slowly, and all of them in the dim hallway on the third floor paused their talk to listen to the sultry instrumental blues flowing into the hallway.

The first two up to bat froze in their tracks, neither one yet in the room but both motionless and staring inside. Seconds passed as the music played, then one hit the other with an elbow, and they walked inside.

As the door closed slowly, the rest of them in the hallway stayed quiet, eyes locked on it. And the relative darkness inside the room seemed to suck at the dim hallway light as the music faded and got snuffed out completely.

* * *

Nearly a minute passed by without anyone outside the room saying anything—not even Emilio. Amos only stared past him at the closed door.

"They, uh . . . how long before—"

Emilio turned his head back toward Amos but not his eyes.

"No strict time limit for anyone. It's strongly urged to get down to business, though. You can't hold back a herd of horny frat boys forever, you know."

"Yes, a herd," Amos mumbled. "More on the stairs too."

"Uh-huh. All over the house. We got ourselves a record turnout. Oh, I get it. It's capitalism. They all feel some pride at paying a reasonable price for a worthwhile product."

"Product?"

"Sure. Service maybe? Both?"

Amos let out a nervous laugh.

"Yes, both. A slut is a product and a service."

Emilio gave him only a brief glance and a quick grin, then quickly set his gaze on the room again.

"Yeah. Unless you can make a verb out of slut. Maybe I should add a chapter to my book on that."

"Slutting Around on the Third Floor? That's the title?"

"Perfect. I'm stealing that."

The waiting group were getting fidgety, some walking up to the door, then getting called away from it. Most were talking, sometimes laughing, and most eyes didn't drift anywhere else.

A few minutes passed as Amos looked past Emilio, both of them sitting forward on the edges of their seats.

"Hey, I don't think this is for real," Amos said, causing Emilio to turn enough to squint back at him. "Maybe they're just talking in there. You're still messing with me."

Emilio scoffed and began shaking his head, and he kept it up while Amos continued.

"Or . . . or maybe there's no one even in there. This is all a big joke, right?"

"It's a joke?"

"Yes, that's my conclusion. Alright, you've had your laughs. What a fun prank to play on the new guy. That's it, right? I figured it out?"

"You're unbelievable. You raise a good point, though. There's no substitute for just seeing shit the way it really is. Come on."

He stood and waited for Amos, who pushed himself all the way back in his seat and shook his head.

"No, really. Come on. We can't go inside anyway—it's not our turn."

He held up the two stubs of paper.

"Remember these? No, we'll just take a quick look. No harm in that, right?"

"No . . . harm," said Amos. "Sure."

He stood weakly and barely kept up with Emilio's slow, relaxed pace toward the door. Emilio grabbed the doorknob, then paused to grin at Amos.

"Just a peek, alright?"

"Maybe that's not such a good—"

"Aw, come on. Just a quick look. What do you say?"

"I, uh, don't know if—"

"If it's just a big joke on the new guy, you deserve to laugh your ass off. How about it?"

"Uh, okay. Sure."

While grinning at Amos, Emilio held a finger to his lips and turned the door handle very slowly.

* * *

Still holding Amos's gaze, Emilio began to swing in the door. If it had any tendency to squeal or squeak, the low, steady, driving blues beat that ramped up through the widening entryway would have covered it anyway.

Emilio didn't look inside. He only tipped his head toward the opening and the darkness and the music, then shifted to the side just enough for Amos to lean closer and take a look.

But Amos was frozen. He'd become a statue dedicated to a new professor on campus, one that had a blank expression chiseled to mask over whatever emotions it might have had as it spent an eternity in a frat house's dark hallway.

"Look," Emilio said, then bounced his eyebrows. "Just a quick look."

Amos grimaced at him, then scoffed and leaned close enough to peer into the room.

And he immediately rushed a hand up to cover a mouth that had flapped open in what would have been an audible gasp.

The large, dim room contained mostly just an expansive bed in the middle, one with four high posts and a thick wooden headboard. Surrounding the bed were a mismatched collection of upholstered recliners, folding metal chairs, even a ragged loveseat, all facing the bed.

A lone, wide dresser graced the side wall. But there was no mirror above it, and its top surface was empty except for a lumpy plastic bag with part of a jacket sleeve hanging out of it, and next to that was a water bottle.

As the music's steady beat throbbed out past Amos and into the hall, his eyes adjusted to the dimmer light until he saw the object that had been raffled to a pack of horny frat boys.

Her back was toward Amos, and she was on her knees on a pillow, near the bed and not more than a dozen steps from the door. Her striped skirt was short enough to show bare thighs and just the bottom curves of more below its hem.

The skirt's waistband was snuggled around a trim waist covered by a very tight, very thin long-sleeved t-shirt. Higher up, an ornately tied mound of blond hair was piled high, and if it allowed any strands and wisps to fall back down over her back, it was too dark to see them.

Just beneath the well-controlled hair, a wide band of silky white cloth had been worked into a secure knot that rested against the back of her head.

Her hands were in front of her, out of view from the door, but she didn't block the entire view of lucky frat boy number one, who was standing directly in front of her.

He gasped up at the ceiling, then looked to one side, where lucky number two, on the edge of one of the seats, pointed at him and smiled.

And the cheerleader kept up a steady pace, moving her head slowly, carefully, and gently back toward the door—toward Amos—then toward number one, over and over. And she only paused long enough to reach up with her right hand, pull some clips out of her hair, and let it all fall down over her back.

While the standing frat guy got his hands in her hair and started fluffing it around, pulling it out to both sides and holding it there, she returned her hand back to her work.

And her blond hair that wasn't in his hands shifted about lazily with every calm, rhythmic bob of her head.

Amos kept the hand over his mouth as he backed away, then stared at Emilio, who only scoffed with a big grin, bounced his eyebrows, and quietly closed the door.

Chapter 32 – A Choice Woman in Action

Emilio allowed Amos to stare at the closed door for a full minute, then he waved a hand in front of his face.

"Hey, you alright?"

Still fixed on the door, Amos said, "Yes. Oh, shit. It's for real."

"Damn right."

"She was . . . she was—"

"On her knees. Oh, yeah. What a sight that is, right?"

"She, uh, was really dressed like—"

"Like a cheerleader. Yeah. Did you get a look at her ass? I sure did."

"Well, kind of. But she—"

"I know. She still had that skirt hiding most of it. But you could tell, right? Isn't that some fine kind of ass?"

"Wow, yes. It was, um, kind of perfect."

"And she's happy to share that body with everyone. No, actually, I think she needs to. She craves it."

"Huh?"

Amos finally took another step back and held Emilio's gaze.

"Yeah. I think that's it. She's feeling the heart and soul of a true slut. That's what's going on in there. She doesn't really feel that part of herself unless she's giving it all up, over and over."

"And that's what she's going to do to everyone?"

"What? No, man, that's probably just what that particular guy wanted. Nothing wrong with that, right?"

"Uh, no. So, she's going to—"

"Do a hell of a lot more than that. Bet on it, no-named guest at the Frat Chat. That was quite a sight, wasn't it?"

"Uh, it was more than I expected."

"Me too, actually."

"Huh?"

"Shit, another confession. Yes, I've been to the Frat Chat before, but it's been a while, and I was drunk, and I remember so little that this is like my first time."

"So, you're a—"

"Virgin. Yep. You too."

"I'm not a—"

Laughing, Emilio said, "Hey, we're both Frat Chat virgins. That's all I'm saying."

"You're too much. And that might be another chapter in your book."

"Good call. You're keeping that educated brain in gear. Here," he held the wrapped flask up to him. "Calm your nerves."

Amos let out one cackle of a laugh and said, "That might help."

"Worth a shot. Literally."

Amos downed a quick drink and handed it back.

"Seriously, isn't it something to see a choice woman in action like that?"

"Um . . ."

"Think of it, pro—oops, can't be saying that. Sorry. Look. She got herself all dressed up as a cheerleader, just to come here and offer up everything she has."

"Everything?"

"Hey, the night is young. Wasn't that a hot sight, though?"

"Uh, yes, it was."

"You saw her head moving, right? Couldn't you almost feel it yourself?"

"God. Yes."

"Of course, you could. Here."

Amos took another drink.

"You ready for another look?"
Amos didn't hesitate.
"Yes. You got the door?"
"Yep. Here you go."
Nodding at Amos, with neither one of them grinning, Emilio turned the handle very slowly again.

* * *

Amos took a deep breath and shook his head once, then leaned for another look. His mouth again snapped open in a gasp, but he kept it quiet and didn't cover it with his hand. All he did was stare.

The woman still had her back mostly to the door, still stood near the bed, and turned her head toward frat boy number two, to her right, and nodded. Both young men smiled and pointed as they watched her reach for her skirt with both hands, pull the bottom hem up as high as she could, then lean onto the bed with both hands, leaving the skirt not covering her at all.

All of her behind, smooth and shapely, picked up enough of the room's light for a clear view of it. The second man stepped into place behind her, right up against her, and his pants were loose and sagging on his hips.

Long blond hair hung over to the side, and it shook gently with each steady thrust of the standing man's hips.

Amos heard the first man, who was slouched nearby in a chair and totally relaxed, say, "Give it to her good, man."

"Oh, shit, I sure am. Damn, she feels good."

The man kept going, and the blond hair kept bouncing lightly, teasingly, as it fell over the woman's shoulder and toward the bed.

"Ask her if she's a slut," said the seated man, laughing lazily.

"Hey," said the standing man, "are you a slut?"

While Emilio grinned, listening but not seeing, Amos and the other two watched as the blonde nodded.

"You like being such a slut?"

A feminine voice, only slightly louder than the soft music, whispered, "Mm-hmm."

"Of course, you like it. You love it. You are one fine, hot little slut."

"Hey," said the guy in the chair, "since when do sluts wear shirts? Come on, strip that shit off."

The standing man laughed and said, "Come on, slut. Get that dumbass shirt off. You want to show them off, don't you?"

They both laughed at her nodding, then she straightened up, which forced her to arch her back even more to keep the action going. With both hands, she got the bottom hem of it and began peeling it up over her belly.

"Yeah, here we go," said the busy young man behind her, who had slowed from the distraction but hadn't stopped altogether.

"Oh, God, they're big," said the man in the chair. "Oh, shit, those look good from the side."

She kept lifting it, and it pulled her long hair up before it all fell back onto nothing but bare skin. She twirled it a couple of times and let it fall on the bed.

"They bouncing?" said the man behind her, who began putting more force into his work.

"Oh, just like that," said the first man, off to the side. "Oh, that's a sight. Slut's got them bouncing."

Amos watched as the woman's arms moved gently, hands unseen with whatever they were doing in front of herself.

The talkative young man in the chair said, "You like playing with them, too, don't you?"

She nodded and again whispered, "Mm-hmm."

While the blonde was obviously fondling herself and liking it while getting steady attention from behind, the man giving her that determined attention held her very slender waist with both hands.

"Oh, that's good," he said. "Damn, such a tiny little waist too. Yeah, you sure are built for this."

The man in the chair snickered and said, "She had no choice—she was born to be a slut."

Amos backed away quickly, and Emilio shut the door quietly.

215

Chapter 33 – Pure Sex and Lust

"How about that?" said Emilio.

Amos stared at the door and shook his head slowly.

Emilio only grinned, let it go on for half a minute, then grabbed Amos's arm.

"Let's give them a minute. Come on. Back to the chairs."

Sometimes laughing at the sight of Amos almost in shock, he led him back to their seats several steps down the hall, then gave him a gentle shove down into it before sitting himself.

Amos said, "She was on her knees for the first guy . . ."

"Yeah, uh-huh, she sure was."

"And the second guy, he . . . he got her from behind."

"Told you. Girl does it all. How's that for a Frat Chat?"

"I'm in shock."

"Nah. You're just horny."

"I'm . . ."

"Admit it. It's like some primitive ritual. You can't help but get caught up in it. And you haven't seen anything yet."

"Huh? What else is there?"

"Oh, damn, man whose career won't be named. How about both of what you just saw her doing but at the same time?"

"She'll do that?"

"Damn right. All the time. I think that's her favorite."

"Both?"

"Yeah. Same time. She's not seeing it this way—because she's as horny as the rest—but it's more efficient. That keeps it all moving like a factory or something."

"Because there are—"

"So many guys to do. Yeah. Shit, she doesn't even know how many."

Emilio gave his watch a quick glance then looked directly at Amos.

"Any second now, I'd bet. Get ready. We're next."

"What? No, I can't."

"Hey, you saw her legs and ass. I know you did."

"I, uh, did. Yes."

"Nice? Be honest."

"Well, yes. Very nice."

"She took her shirt off. I know you want a better look at them."

"I, uh—"

"Tell me you don't want to see that sexy blond cheerleader without her tight shirt? You had to have seen how tiny her waist is, right?"

"I did. Yes."

"Doesn't that kind of make you crazy?"

"Sure, but I don't—"

"And think of how bad she wants to do that again. Either one. Or both."

"She, uh, might, but I have a reputation to—"

"Hey, she's wearing a blindfold. Did you notice that?"

"I saw something, a cloth, uh, around—"

"Yep. She's blindfolded. She'll never even know who you are."

"She wouldn't?"

"No, and if you really want to stay perfectly safe, make sure you stay behind her. Just in case, you know, somehow that blindfold isn't working."

"Oh, good point. Alright. She really likes it that way?"

"Damn right, she likes it that way. It's some kind of cheap turn-on for her. It's all anonymous—just pure sex and lust."

"But I, uh—"

"Just quit fighting yourself. Come on. You know you want to. You said you're ending that engagement anyway, remember?"

"I am thinking about that. Yes."

"Because your fiancé is . . . what? Becoming something you don't want? Is that right?"

"Uh, yes. I guess."

"So, what you do here doesn't even matter, then. Have some fun, alright?"

"Okay, fine. I'll at least go in there. I'm not making any promises other than that, okay?"

"Sure. I'm good with that. Let's just see how you feel when you're up close and personal, alright?"

"Uh, sure. Okay."

"And remember: I tend to talk a lot at such times."

Amos laughed haltingly and said, "Yes, you did say that."

"Uh-huh. But here's something for real: I have an absolute talent at knowing what people want to hear."

"You do?"

"Always. So, when it sounds like I'm just being a fool, focus on her. She'll be digging it. There won't be any mistaking that."

Chapter 34 – A Ring on Her Left Hand

Amos and Emilio waited at the closed door, with Emilio smiling and Amos almost hyperventilating. Only a minute later, both pairs of eyes watched the door handle turn, then the door swung into the room.

The two guys smiled as they stumbled out and barely noticed Amos and Emilio while bumping them aside.

Emilio tipped his head toward the room, and Amos took a step close enough to look inside.

The blonde's cheerleader skirt had dropped back down and was covering most of what it should. But not all. Just enough of the soft curves leading up into the skirt were still exposed.

With both sneakers on the floor and her legs straight, she leaned forward, supporting herself on the bedcovers with her right hand while the left kept busy out of sight in front of her.

"Hey," Emilio whispered, "don't talk at all. She'll never even know your voice."

"Okay. Smart."

"Yeah. Remember to stay behind her, too, just in case. Let's go."

Their footsteps were barely noticeable over the steady beat from the stereo, and the blonde tipped her head contentedly from side to side with the music, swaying her long hair around, until she heard them approaching.

She gave her hair one decisive twirl, then lifted one knee up on the bed and arched her back, causing her skirt to ride up high enough to prove that she wore nothing beneath it.

While Amos stared from just a few steps from her, Emilio nudged him around and got him behind her, then gestured for him to stay there.

"We're next," Emilio said. "You ready?"

She nodded, causing Emilio to smirk toward Amos.

"Hey, before we get started, tell me what you are."

She hesitated and tipped her head slightly.

"Come on. Don't be shy. You're hot as hell, and you're here for sex, right?"

She nodded.

"So, what does that make you?"

Her whispering, feminine voice blended with the music, standing out just enough to be understood.

"I'm a . . . slut," she said, and Emilio winked at Amos, who gestured for him to keep going.

"Yes, you sure are. You're other things, too, though, right? Besides that?"

She shrugged but didn't answer.

"No? Oh, I get it. You really don't count for much else besides that. Got it. Say it for us before we put that body to good use. Spell it out."

Amos watched her straighten up and shake her hair back, then pull her shoulders back, too, and he leaned out to see the side of one of the large breasts that she was propping out.

Emilio gasped and said, "Damn. You're really something."

"I'm something," she whispered. "Something . . . soft."

"Not just the stunning pair you're sticking out."

"Mm, no. Not just my breasts. Everything."

"Uh-huh. Keep going."

She hesitated, then sighed and continued, her voice becoming more calm and deliberate with every word she whispered.

"I'm something soft all over. Something that's good for sex."

"Yeah, any fool can see that. You good for anything else?"

She laughed just loudly enough to get past the music and shook her head and her blond hair. Amos and Emilio leaned in closer to hear her.

"Uh-uh," she said with a soft giggle. "I'm not good for anything else."

"Nothing else?"

"Uh-uh. See how soft I am? I'm good *only* to be used for sex."

"Used, huh?"

"Mm-hmm. That's all I'm good for: to be used for sex."

Amos's eyes almost fell out when she reached down with both hands, found the bottom edge of her cheerleader skirt in front, and lifted it up high enough to completely uncover her bare bottom, which she shifted to the left then the right.

She repeated, "I'm not good for anything but sex. I'm nothing but a complete slut."

Emilio was fighting hard to not laugh out loud, but Amos was staring at what she'd exposed while it was aimed right at him.

"And you like that, don't you?"

She didn't hesitate.

"Mm-hmm. More than anything, I love being *just* a slut."

"You mean that?"

"Oh, yeah. It feels so good to say it."

"I'd bet. Say it again, then. Shit, give us a whole paragraph."

"Okay."

She hesitated, then took a breath and let it out.

"There's nothing that I love more than being a slut. I love being so soft and being only for sex. That's all I'm good for. *All* I am is something soft to be used for sex."

"Well, shit, it's our lucky day. My buddy and I want you at the same time. You alright with that?"

Emilio scoffed at seeing Amos shaking his head frantically, then grinned and held a finger to his lips.

"Mm-hmm. I can't say no. Soft things made for sex don't ever say no."

"Well, of course. You sure are made for it."

He gestured for Amos to hold her waist, which he did with both hands, helping her hold up her skirt and staring at her skin like he was in a trance.

"Good. Let go of that skirt now and straighten up," he said, and she shifted around in Amos's hands as Emilio stood up on the bed in front of her.

With her hands free, she straightened herself up more.

"Yeah, there's good. You can get started with me, but why don't you get that hair up and out of the way?"

"Okay," she said, took a band from around her wrist, gathered it all up at the very top of her head, and tied a pony tail tight to her scalp.

It all sprouted straight up, then fell back, some of the ends touching her shoulders and back.

"That's nice," Emilio said, and Amos looked up to see her nodding, which got the thick ponytail tipping lightly. "Let's get you started."

Amos leaned around when he heard Emilio unzipping, and he saw enough of the side of the woman's face to watch her tip her head back and open her mouth.

"Yeah, just like that. You want something in there?"

With her mouth still open wide, she said, "Uh-huh."

Staring at her open mouth, Amos rubbed his hands down onto her hips, squeezed her lightly, rubbed up and down her strong thighs on the sides then in the front, too, then shifted them back up to her waist.

Just then, Emilio leaned in and found his target, and the blonde moaned softly.

"Yeah, there you go. Oh, damn, that feels so good. Like you said: this is all you're good for, right?"

"Mm-hmm," she murmured while she nodded.

"I want a good view of those big breasts of yours. Be a good girl and put your hands up behind your head, alright? Just stick them right out for me, okay?"

"Mm . . . mm-hmm."

And when she got her hands up there, and both of her hands were against the back of her head, Amos saw two sets of perfectly painted red fingernails.

And a ring on her left hand, one custom-made and like no other.

He looked down at his hands around the soft skin of her slender waist, then back up at the ring, which shined playfully in the room's dim lighting.

He stared in shock at the ring, even as Emilio continued with her.

"You got some nice breasts there," Emilio said, then he leaned forward enough to hold each of them in a hand. "Oh, they're so big and soft."

"Mm-hmm."

"I think they want a little pinch. Yes, they need to be pinched."

She tried to giggle but ended it quickly and gasped instead.

Emilio said, "Yeah, they like that. Just like that. Your big breasts are just begging for any kind of attention, aren't they?"

Still staring at the ring, Amos also noticed her straight-up ponytail tipping as she nodded.

"Of course. Huh, maybe a few more pinches, since you can't really say no at the moment."

Her hands were still up near Amos's eyes, and she was still holding her shiny red nails and sparkling ring almost close enough for him to kiss.

"Really big, soft breasts and such a tiny waist. Damn, you're a sexy little slut, aren't you?" he said, then stepped back enough to allow her to answer.

"Mm-hmm. It's all I am," she whispered. "It's what I love more than—"

She stopped when Amos dragged his hands free and she heard his footsteps as he backed toward the door.

As he was opening the door, he looked back and saw the blindfolded woman, not clear in the dim light but turned toward him, as Emilio fondled her breasts with both hands.

Then, looking for the door handle, he heard the woman giggling and Emilio saying, "Wait on your hands and knees, slut."

She giggled and said, "I'm just a slut."

"Yep. Nothing else. Stay, slut. Be right back."

And as Amos was hurrying into the hallway, he heard the woman whisper, "I'm not going anywhere. Mm-mm."

Chapter 35 – It's Who She Really Is

By the time Emilio had zipped up, raced into the hallway after Amos, and closed the door behind him, he met Amos's gaze, laughed, and said, "What?"

"Nothing. I, um, just panicked."

"Well, panic or not, we have to get our asses back in there. Come on."

"Wait."

Emilio watched Amos breathing deeply and staring down at the floor for a few seconds, then said, "What?"

Amos looked up and held his gaze.

"That's the chat? That's it?"

"Huh? What are you talking about?"

"The chat. The Frat Chat. Her saying that she's a slut. Is that the chat?"

"Oh, you've really hit on something there. Yeah, I think it is. That's the chat."

"Huh."

Emilio snickered and said, "You should recite it so you never forget it. Go on. Start with a complete sentence, saying what that woman is."

Amos didn't have a trace of a smile or grin. He only coughed to clear his throat.

"That woman in there, dressed like a cheerleader, is a slut."

"Yeah, she is."

"A, uh, total slut."

"Yep."

"And she . . . she—"

"Loves it more than anything else," said Emilio. "Yeah. That's really something, huh?"

"She loves it more than anything," Amos said in a slow monotone. "Anything."

"Yeah, good for us. Damn, what big breasts too. And such a tiny waist."

"Yes, it's, uh, kind of like she said."

"Go on."

"She really does seem to be, uh, made for sex."

"You're getting the chat. Keep going."

"She's just something soft."

"Yeah. You should know—you were feeling her up."

"I was."

"You like that skinny little waist of hers?"

"Yes, it's, um, something. I think she really is made only for sex."

"What about the rest of her life? She must have some kind of life, right?"

"Um, no matter what else she is . . ."

"Good. Keep going."

"No matter what else she is, she's a slut. That's really what she is. What she loves . . ."

"The most. Being a slut. By Jove, I think you've got it. You're got the chat. Unless it's the drugs talking."

"Huh? What drugs?"

"It's just something I heard—that they like to slip her something."

"Something like what?"

"Man, something that makes her say crazy shit like that. She can't help but go wild."

"That's not very ethical."

"That's your only ethics complaint with a Frat Chat? Oh, come on."

"Alright. Fair enough."

"Ready to get back in there?"

"Um . . ."

"Come on. You know you want sex with that slut."

"I, uh . . ."

"She's blindfolded, remember? She'll never, ever know who you are."

"You're sure?"

"Sure as can be. Let's go."

Amos shook quietly as he looked up at the ceiling, and Emilio only watched and grinned at the sight of him. After half a minute, he was still shaking, but he looked at Emilio.

"Okay."

"Because? You should say it. I have to keep you focused."

"Because . . . because I want to have sex with . . . that slut."

Grinning, Emilio said, "Because that woman is . . ."

Amos sighed, then said, "That woman is nothing but a slut."

"That's the damn chat—you got it."

He reached for the door handle, then stopped before turning it.

"Oh, wait."

He got his phone out of his pants pocket.

"What's that for?"

"Brock gave me clear instructions that I have to photograph her."

"What? Why?"

"To prove it was consensual. Think about it. It makes perfect sense. Told you: this is a well-planned operation."

"It does make sense."

"So, don't get alarmed when I snap a pic, alright?"

"Alright. She's, uh, blindfolded anyway."

"Huh?"

"I understand. About the consent and all."

"Good. And you know me: I like off-the-wall drama, right? You've seen that in class, right?"

Amos laughed and said, "Yes. All the time."

"So, don't be surprised when I do more than just take a simple pic like Brock wants. All I know is, I'm going to have fun with it. See what happens. Sound okay to you?"

"Sure. You might as well. In fact, make her say more. Can you do that?"

"More about . . ."

"About what she is. Get her to say a lot about that."

"Easy enough. I can already tell she loves that. She's starving to tell everyone what she is."

"It did seem that way. So, see how far you can, um, push her."

"I might as well. Yeah, I believe I'll make it a damn spectacle."

"A spectacle, huh?"

"Yeah, and you watch—she'll never stop playing along."

"Wow, that would mean she—"

"It would mean that she adores all of it. Everything that's happening. Hey, how do you like that raspy, sexy whisper she's got?"

"I don't know. It's, um, I can understand her, at least."

"Well, I like it. She sounds desperate for sex. You ready? Let's go."

"Wait."

Emilio whined quickly, then said, "What now? Hey, you're trashing that engagement, remember?"

"I, um, probably should."

"Probably?"

"Uh, no, I really should. Dammit, there's no way in hell things can continue like they've been. Not after . . . this."

"Not after the Frat Chat. Exactly. Let's do it. And stay behind her."

"Okay."

"Nice view back there? Fine ass?"

"Yes. She—that slut—has the most incredible ass."

"And think about how she's so eager to share it. With everyone."

"I am. God, I sure am."

Emilio bounced his eyebrows a few times, then turned the handle.

* * *

Emilio was walking right up to the blonde on the bed, who had remained as ordered on her hands and knees.

Amos's steps were slow and careful, and his eyes stayed mostly on the backs of her thighs, which were bare and smooth and led up to the perfect curving out then up of her bottom, where the rest of it stayed teasing behind the skirt.

He looked up when Emilio spun his head back toward him, held a finger to his lips, then waited. Amos nodded, then showed the same gesture.

"We're back," Emilio told her. "Now, where were we?"

"Hmm . . ." she said, then she straightened herself up more and held her mouth open.

"Oh, that's right. How could I forget that?"

He turned enough to smirk toward Amos, then paused at the look on his face. He waved a hand, got Amos to look up, then shrugged and mouthed the word, "What?"

Amos shook his head a few times, then stepped closer behind the woman.

Emilio pointed down toward her, and Amos held her again by her waist with both hands.

"Yeah, hold her still," Emilio said, then he stood up again on the bed, in front of the woman, and reached for his zipper.

Before working on that, he said to her, "Get yourself ready for it. Because it's ready for you."

Amos leaned out to the left and still didn't have a clear view of the woman's face, just part of her cheek caressed by a few wisps of hair and the corner of her lips. But he saw enough to know that she'd stuck out her tongue.

"Yeah," said Emilio. "Time for that tongue."

Still watching her mouth and what Emilio was about to give her, Amos groaned and waved his hand around. Emilio saw it, then squinted at him.

Ignoring Amos's shaking head and still waving hand, Emilio said, "No stopping now. No, it's time."

Amos held her tight and kept leaning, and he gasped at the sight of the woman's lips quickly closing tight around what Emilio had given her.

"Yeah, there you go," Emilio said. "Happy now?"

She nodded, and Emilio winked at Amos, who squeezed the woman's waist more tightly while trying to look around to see her waiting patiently how Emilio had left her.

"Hmm," Emilio said, touching her cheek, "you sure are soft. Warm and wet too. Hey, you should add that to what you are. Try that."

He backed away, and Amos watched her lick her lips before answering.

She giggled first, then whispered, "I'm something soft . . . and warm . . . and wet . . . and good *only* for sex."

"Nothing else?"

"Uh-uh, not me. I'm not good for anything else. Just sex."

"But you must be good for something, anything more than just that, right?"

"It's all I want to be good for. I'm happiest being something *just* for sex."

"Well, good girl. Here's your prize," he said, then leaned back into her.

Amos stared at the sight of the woman's enthusiasm, her lips and sometimes tongue busy, then he stooped down just enough to look at her bare breasts. They were hanging straight down toward the bed, and they swayed gently from everything she was doing. He was about to reach for them with one hand, then he heard Emilio.

"One little thing," he told her, "like every other time."

He got his phone out, tapped it, then pointed it down at her.

"You know we need a quick pic, just to prove it's consensual."

She squirmed around in Amos's hands for a second, but he didn't let her go.

"Come on," Emilio said. "This isn't something new to you."

She relaxed with a muffled sigh and nodded.

"Yeah, that's right. Just hold still. Don't stop what you're doing."

She didn't stop, and Amos stared at the back of her head moving in and out, swaying her blond hair the slightest amount.

Emilio touched gently under her chin, said, "Oh, such nice soft skin," then began coaxing her face up toward the camera. "Just like that. Up a little more. Look up for the camera. There we go."

He laughed and said, "Don't try to talk. We just need,"—with his free hand, he began to pry up on the wide cloth covering her eyes—"to do it right."

She squirmed again in Amos's hands, protesting with a soft groan, but he held her tight and didn't let go of her waist. Her mumbling wasn't able to form any clear words, and Emilio didn't give her a chance to speak.

"Now, now," Emilio said, "just be good and cooperate. Just a quick photo, alright? It's just like every other time. You shouldn't be at all surprised."

She calmed instantly and stopped shifting around in Amos's hands, and he looked up to see Emilio grin at him quickly. Then, he watched as Emilio kept working at the cloth hiding her identity.

"We just need to move this a little," he said. "Hold still. Let's just see what kind of pretty . . ."

He got the bottom edge up above one eye and said, "Oh, hello there."

He uncovered her other eye, and he paused and left the cloth there, the bottom edge of it snug over her eyebrows.

"Oh, what nice eyes you have. They're so big and bright, and they make you look so innocent."

"Mm."

"That's a sight, how you're just looking up at me like that. Big eyes looking up while I watch you servicing me."

"Mm-hmm."

He glanced at Amos and saw his gesture to keep at it.

"You're . . . servicing someone you don't even know?"

"Mm. Mm-hmm."

"Do you like having absolutely no idea who you're servicing? You're just on your hands and knees, servicing some stranger?"

"Mm-hmm."

"Well, that's a sight. With such nice eyes too. Let's just get that off of you altogether now. Can the camera see how pretty you are?"

She nodded.

"Good girl. You don't want to hide who you are, right?"

"Mm . . . uh-uh."

"The camera will make it perfectly clear what you have in your mouth, you know. You're not ashamed of what you're letting everyone put in there, are you?"

"Mm-mm."

"You're sure? It'll be such a clear photo of you, so pretty, such big eyes, and it sure will show that you're servicing someone with your mouth. You're okay with that?"

She shrugged and managed to say, "Mm . . ."

"Good girl."

He looked up again, just long enough to see Amos shaking his head.

"A nice photo of you and what you're doing."

He kept going and worked it all up beyond her forehead and left it up in her hair, bunched up where it rested against the root of her straight-up ponytail.

"Okay, there we go. Just like that. All out of the way now. Such a sweet, pretty face you have."

"Mm . . ."

Her entire face was out in the open and ready for the camera.

"Oh, you're a pretty little thing with such big, innocent eyes. What a nice contrast: big innocent eyes but a mouth that's very full at the moment. Not such an innocent mouth at all. Do you like looking up at me like that while you're servicing me?"

She gave him an exaggerated nod, and Amos scoffed silently at the sight of her tall ponytail swaying around.

"Aw, you're so sweet. That's something: you're so pretty and innocent but such a slut at the same time?"

The woman shrugged, causing Emilio to snicker, then he grabbed and held the base of her ponytail.

"This is how to hold a slut for her special photo. You're so pretty like that."

"Mm."

"With your pretty lips holding on tight too. Feels right for you, doesn't it?"

"Mm-hmm."

Amos's continued gesturing made him smile.

"Bet that's one of the happiest things for you, isn't it, pretty girl?"

Amos saw her back swell a bit, then she let out a sigh and said, "Mm-hmm."

"Of course, it is. That's mostly what your pretty mouth is for. It's so obvious your mouth isn't good for anything else."

Her short giggle ended up being more of a soft snort.

"That *is* funny: even your mouth isn't good for anything else. Just this."

"Uh-uh."

"You even like how I'm taking my time and playing with you, don't you?"

He backed himself out just far enough for her to giggle, then whisper, "Yes, I'm here to be played with."

"We both love that sexy whisper of yours."

"Mm-hmm," she whispered, big eyes still looking up.

"You're fun to play with."

"I want to be a fun thing to play with," she said.

"And you are. I'm going to keep playing with you. Is that okay?"

"Mm-hmm. Play with me. Make me play," she said, then leaned herself to meet him.

Emilio snorted a short laugh and said, "Damn."

Amos watched as Emilio shook her lightly from side to side by her ponytail, saying, "Don't let go! Don't let go!"

"Uh-uh," she said around him, and she didn't let go.

Amos leaned to one side, but she was facing straight forward, and all he could see was her open mouth, which Emilio was using selfishly to help hold her head still.

"Yes, good girl. Just like that for the camera. Look up, pretty girl with big bright eyes."

He smiled down toward her tipped back head, then moved the camera to the side and said, "Just one from here too. Hold still. What a perfect view of you and what you're doing. You look gorgeous like that. Mm, those lips, doing all they're good for. Damn."

She kept still, and Amos held the warm, soft skin of her slender waist while she was being photographed in action, servicing someone she didn't know.

Emilio lowered his phone and said, "There, that wasn't so bad, was it?"

With her blindfold still up and out of the way, she shook her head and said, "Mm-mm," still unable to actually speak.

"Just one more thing," Emilio said. "I have to get a quick video with you talking, making it clear that it's consensual."

She groaned and tried to turn away, but Amos held her waist and Emilio kept one hand on her cheek.

"Oh, come on. It'll be fun. Keep being fun for the camera."

She didn't answer quickly enough.

"Don't you want to say fun things to the camera? You're just such a pretty thing. Come on. You can even keep whispering."

She nodded and when he backed himself away but stayed close enough for the camera to see what she was doing, she kept looking up as he tapped his phone.

"Okay, we're live. And you know that the camera sees you perfectly?"

"Yes," she whispered.

"Anyone that knows you would sure recognize you?"

She only shrugged.

"I'd bet you kind of like that, huh? No secret identity. Just you, whoever you are, telling the camera what you want so bad to admit."

She hesitated for only a second and seemed to be aligning her face better for the video.

"Yes. I want so bad to say it."

"In a live video, with your identity as obvious as can be?"

"Mm-hmm. Yes."

"And you're not just making up what you're saying?"

"Uh-uh. It's all the truth. I want to say it."

"Good. Keep those big innocent eyes on the camera, and tell us what you told us before."

Amos leaned one way, then the other but without letting go of her waist, he couldn't get a good look at her. But he did feel her sigh, and he held himself still, straining to hear her raspy whisper over the music.

"I'm a slut," she told the camera, which easily captured the complete image of her face with no part of the blindfold covering any of it.

"Yes, you are. And you're here for sex, right?"

"Mm-hmm. Yes, I'm here for sex."

"How much sex?"

"Hmm. A lot."

"Because?"

She shook in Amos's hands with her light laughter.

"Because, like I told you, I'm something soft that's only for sex."

"Soft everywhere?"

"Hmm, yes. I'm soft all over."

"Oh, you're more than just soft, right?"

"Mm-hmm," she said softly, then giggled. "I'm—"

"Wait," Emilio said. "Get that pretty mouth busy between each word, and keep those bright eyes looking up for the camera. Can you do that?"

She giggled, said, "Mm-hmm," then took him with her lips, held for two seconds, then quickly backed away only a small distance.

"I'm soft . . ."

Still looking up, she took him again for another two seconds before allowing herself to continue.

"... and warm. Mm, I'm so warm ..."

She tipped her head forward and squeezed with her lips, big eyes still on the camera. She moaned for two more seconds, then backed away only enough to whisper while still mostly offering a kiss, so much of a constant kiss that her lips could barely form the words.

"... and wet. I'm something that's very ..."

She leaned into him as far as she could and held herself there for five seconds before backing away, still too close to easily use her lips.

"... very, very ..."

She giggled while leaning, then couldn't giggle for another five seconds before she let herself back away again.

"... very wet."

"Damn, that was good."

Emilio grinned at Amos's stare and look of disgust, then he looked down again.

"Such a cooperative thing you are. And you're here ..."

"Hmm. To be used for sex."

"Good. God, you're a hot, sexy little slut. Hmm, those big eyes ..."

"Mm-hmm, that's me. I'm nothing but a little slut with big eyes."

"Nothing?"

"Mm-mm. Nothing else at all."

"Yeah, you're a slutty little girl for all the boys to play with. Whatever they want?"

"Mm-hmm," she said with a giggle. "That's all I am: just a slutty little girl. I'm nothing else at all, and I'll do anything."

"For everyone that wants you?"

"Mm-hmm. Yes. All of you."

"Seriously, there are a lot of us."

"Mm ... yes, please. I'm soft and warm and wet and slutty. You should all make me play."

"God. A tiny waist, big perfect breasts, all soft and warm and wet, and big innocent eyes. You're a perfect little slut."

"Mm-hmm. That's all I am. It's all I want to be."

"You're such a perfect little slut that I think I want to keep you. Can I keep you as my own little slut?"

She took him again, still looking up at him, and moaned for five seconds.

Emilio gasped and said, "Oh my God . . ."

She backed herself away just enough to talk, then whispered, "Uh-uh. But you can use me. Everyone can use me for sex."

"Damn . . ."

He grinned over her at Amos, who kept staring at the back of her head, his eyes too big to blink.

Emilio tapped his phone, then jammed it into his pants pocket.

"Perfect. You can be sure all of that is our little secret."

She didn't respond.

"Oh, wait. I think you kind of want everyone to see that, don't you? You wish everyone in your life knew what a slutty little girl you really are?"

She shrugged, then giggled and said, "Um, maybe I do."

"They have no idea what a slut you really are, do they?"

"Uh-uh. No one has any idea."

Then, she turned her eyes lower to what Emilio was still holding ready for her.

"Well, we can't share any of this," Emilio said. "That's just for the records. The people in your life will just have to find out about you some other way."

Amos watched her take a deep breath and let out an equally deep sigh.

"Let's just hide away those big, beautiful, innocent eyes," he said. "Ready to be anonymous again?"

"Mm-hmm. Okay."

"Good girl."

He slid the cloth back in place while maintaining a hold on her ponytail.

"There, those big eyes are all hidden away again. Back to being a secret slut. You're such a pretty thing and still, so much of a slut that you want two at once. Don't you?"

She only said, "Mm . . ." as she shifted off of the bed just enough to stand up against it with her legs completely straight.

"Yeah, offer yourself to him, little slut."

"Okay."

She reached back with one hand to tug at her cheerleader skirt, and she shook her hips around until it fell in a bunch around her ankles.

"Oh, that's nice," Emilio said. "The little slut is all naked now."

"Mm-hmm. All naked. I'm just a naked little slut."

Amos watched as she moved each of her clean white sneakers farther apart, keeping her legs straight as she spread them.

"A naked little slut that's soft and warm and wet," she whispered.

Amos looked up and saw Emilio tip his head toward her.

He looked back down at his hands on the woman's hips, after she'd just bared herself for whoever was standing behind her.

Still holding her, his hands firm on her smooth, warm skin, he leaned again to look. And he saw her held still by a grip on her ponytail, her mouth open, and her lips wet and busy.

Trying to keep his groaning silent, Amos let go of the woman with one hand and worked his own zipper down all the way.

But he hesitated, looking at what she was offering, until Emilio spoke.

"She wants it," he told Amos. "She wants it bad."

Amos still waited, staring at her naked bottom.

"Tell him," Emilio said and used her ponytail to tip her head back enough to talk.

Amos heard her say, "I do want it bad. I'm nothing but a slut. It's all I'm good for."

Amos held her hips and stared down at her shifting them slowly.

"Tell him you don't even know who he is," said Emilio.

"Hmm, I have no idea who you are."

"Tell him you don't care either."

"Mm, you could be anyone. This is what I . . . love most. Just being an object, something to be used for sex."

"You certainly are a gorgeous slut," Emilio said, snickering. "Time for the boys to play with you."

While she was still moaning, Amos lined things up and gave the woman's hips a fast pull, then smiled at the sound of her saying, "Oh, yeah, there it is. Mm-hmm, I'm just a soft thing. Mm, for all the boys to play with. No matter how many want to—"

And Amos didn't bother to look around and see exactly how Emilio had silenced her so abruptly.

But Emilio's smile at the ceiling gave him a hint.

Then, he locked his eyes on the woman's left hand, palm down on the blanket and displaying bright red nails and very nice engagement ring.

* * *

Both staring straight across the hall at the worn wood paneling, Amos and Emilio slouched in their own upholstered seats.

When Emilio passed the brown bagged bottle across, Amos accepted it without looking, took a long drink, then rested it on his leg.

"Damn."

Emilio snickered and said, "Bet you're glad you took a chance on the Frat Chat."

Amos looked over at him and grinned.

"Yeah. I mean, damn."

"I've never seen you so, I don't know, less knotted up."

"I'll take that as a compliment."

"You should," he said and reached out for the bottle, which Amos handed back to him.

"We need to get you back here for the next one."

"Oh, I don't know," Amos said. "I don't think so."

"Well, consider it a standing invitation, then."

"Alright, I will. Thanks."

A minute passed in silence before Amos spoke again.

"Hot and cold."

Emilio paused the bottle midway and looked back at him.

"Huh? Don't even think of getting back to that philosophical bullshit. I'm still in shock by what a damn slut that woman is."

"She sure is a slut. Yeah. Good to know."

"Huh?"

"Just, she's really such a slut."

"Yeah. Unless it was the drugs," Emilio said.

Amos held out the water bottle from the room's dresser, and they both stared at it. The water level was quite high.

"Oh," Emilio said and pointed at it. "Look at that. Maybe she took a sip, though. Maybe—"

Amos kept the bottle out, twisted the cap and broke its seal with a series of sharp snaps, then screwed it back on tight.

"Well, alright, then," said Emilio. "I guess it was my playful charm that made her crazy."

"Dammit," said Amos. "Or all of that—it's who she really is."

"Yeah, that makes more sense. God, what a slut."

Amos said, "Was it her? The same as last time?"

"Oh, that's a good question. I'm not sure."

"Could be, though? That slut in there, she's done this before? A lot of times?"

"Maybe. She was a blonde. I remember that."

"The photos. I want that first one at least. Her looking up at the camera."

"While I kept her busy," Emilio said with an easy laugh.

"Yeah. That one. That's a keeper."

"Sorry. No can do. Brock would flatten my skull."

"Just the one so I can check to be sure that—"

"You're not checking shit. Forget the photo."

"Maybe I, uh, know her. I just want to—"

"No. The answer's still no."

"Dammit."

They both looked over when the door opened, two young men came out, relaxed and smiling, and two more hurried into the room. The relentless blues beat ventured out only until the door slammed with a soft boom.

Emilio chuckled and said, "And two by two . . ."

"Add that to the chat."

"What's that?"

"The Frat Chat story, remember?" said Amos. "She's a slut, she takes them two by two, it's all she's good for . . . that chat."

"Oh, that chat. Sure. Let's add that."

Emilio downed some more whiskey, then passed it over to Amos, who also took another drink. They sat in silence, sometimes watching the door, then, minutes later, the door swung in.

Amos and Emilio watched as the two walked out, and two more stood and walked toward the door. But only one of them went inside, and the other stood there, laughing, and gesturing for another to get up and join them.

Emilio scoffed, and Amos sat forward on his seat, eyes locked onto the young men laughing and talking while the third got up from his seat. He walked over, got slapped on his back, and they joined the first guy in the room and closed the door after them.

Emilio said, "Or three by three. Damn."

"What? The other guy is, what, taking more photos?"

"Oh, no way. No cameras in there. That's allowed just for official business," he said and slapped his pants pocket.

"What, then? Just to watch?"

Emilio shook his head for a few seconds, staring at Amos, then scoffed loudly.

"Uh-uh. Damn, she really is a slut."

"Oh, you don't mean . . ."

"Believe it. Go look."

"No way. They wouldn't be—she wouldn't let—"

Laughing, Emilio said, "Go look. Shit, I want to see it too."

"Huh," Amos said as he stood, waited for Emilio, then led the way to the door.

"Voila," Emilio said as he swung in the door and gave Amos room to lean close and look in on the scene.

"Well, shit," he said. "That's pretty damn . . . athletic."

Emilio looked inside, over Amos's shoulder, and said, "Slutty is the word. That, my friend, is one remarkably athletic slut."

"That third guy isn't just standing around," said Amos. "He's, um, he—"

"He found something to do too. Yep."

Emilio pulled the door closed, and Amos's face was still close to it, staring as if it was still open.

"She's unbelievable. She's—"

"A slut," said Emilio. "No doubt about it."

"Yeah. And she's . . . shit, I don't even know. I can't . . . I can't even—"

"She's just a slut. Yeah. We're back to that chat. Come on."

He led Amos to the chairs, where they both sat and drank more whiskey. He'd just handed the bottle to him, then they both looked as the door opened.

Emilio didn't look down when Amos's hand groped around for the bottle, but he let it go when it got pulled away. He kept staring at three men coming out of the room.

"Hey," Emilio said, slurring his words a little, "you think . . ."

He kept staring as three more laughing, energetic young men rushed into the room and slammed the door.

"She," he said, then coughed, "she must really like . . . when she gets three of—"

He turned just in time to see Amos's eyes studying the scene over a tipped-back bottle, which he then raised high for the last drop.

But his eyes closed, and his arm started to sag, and Emilio had just enough sobriety left to catch the bottle as Amos slumped back into the chair.

Chapter 36 – Same Damn Time

Amos paused with his hand ready on the front door of Lenore's house, which he'd moved into after moving to town to someday marry her.

From there, he looked out at the neat yard, where flowers and plants in all of the beds were reaching out to embrace the first sunlight of the day.

A motion across the street caught his eye, and he looked up and waved in return to a neighbor on his porch.

He turned the knob and walked in, saw the car keys on the small table, then closed the door by leaning his back into it.

Across the living room, Lenore sat quietly on the couch, her sleepy eyes focused on him.

He stayed quiet, too, as he looked her over, not offering any change to his expression as he studied the thick robe pulled close in front, hiding whatever modest nightgown she wore. With her feet up on the coffee table, he saw her worn, fuzzy slippers and just a slice of her ankle where the long pajama pants did their best but couldn't reach down all the way to the bunched up white socks.

He finished with a leaning of his head as he examined her hair, which was all woven and twisted and fastened together without leaving any stray wisps.

She stretched her arms out to the sides and yawned but never took her eyes off of him.

A steady clicking came from the far wall.

"Hello," he said but stayed at the door.

"Hi. You didn't come home."

He took a few steps closer.

"No. Did you check your phone? I sent a text about having too much to drink. Emilio's couch seemed like the prudent idea."

"Prudent is always good—a wise choice."

"Yeah," he said and took a few more steps toward the couch. "Always good to be prudent. In all things."

She laced her fingers together and held her hands in her lap, looking up at him as he walked between the couch and the table and stood over her.

"Did you have a good evening?"

She nodded and said, "Yes. It was good. I, uh, got home, saw you weren't back yet, then did that basket of laundry, took a long, hot shower, then waited up."

"Laundry and a shower. That's always good."

"Uh-huh. Yep."

He made it obvious that he was looking at her hands, then met her gaze.

"Those nails look good."

"Thanks."

"And the ring. I always like seeing that."

"Uh, thanks. I promised, remember?"

"I remember. You look . . ."

She scoffed, didn't smile or break their gaze, and said, "Frumpy."

The clock on the wall sneaked in a few clicks.

"Beautiful."

She tipped her head but kept staring up at him.

"Yeah," he said, then nodded. "And I have two things I have to say to you."

"Amos, wait. I—"

"Shh."

"No, really, whatever you're—"

"No more. Shh."

She got quiet and sat still.

He looked down, lifted the leg nearest her, and wedged it between her shins, then stepped in the other one too. She watched that, then looked up at him.

"Amos, I only—"

"Shh."

With enough room, even with the long robe crowding and blocking, he was able to kneel on the rug up against the couch. She controlled her breathing, but her chest was moving noticeably every time.

He said, "I know . . ."

She stared, her eyes big. The clock did its part.

". . . that I haven't been insistent on setting a wedding date."

"Yes, that's true."

Holding her gaze still, he unknotted the floppy cloth belt, then snapped open her robe. His expression never changed as her breaths quickened more.

Looking down, he reached for the bottom hem of her long, plain nightgown and began lifting it up.

"Amos, what are you—"

"Shh. You're not shy."

"Uh, no, but—"

"Shh."

He took his time, letting the cloth drag along the smooth skin of her thighs until it wouldn't stay any higher on its own.

"Amos, it was just—"

"Shh," he said, then reached around her hips with both hands and pulled her forward, right up to the edge of the couch.

She lay back against the cushions, watching him with her head tipped and keeping her hands resting on the cushions to both sides of her.

While easing down his zipper, he held her gaze and said, "I want you to promise me something."

"I will. What?"

He freed himself, found the spot he wanted, and pulled her hips forward as far as he could. He smiled at the gasp that she tried to hide.

"Amos, what is—"

"Promise me . . ."

"Yes?"

More ticks from the wall.

"Promise me you'll . . . never again . . ."

He pulled her harder, driving himself in deeper.

"What?"

"You'll never again . . ."

All she did was stare, mouth frozen open as two more seconds vied for attention.

". . . *not* meet Laura for . . . a drink."

"What? Me? I . . . meet Laura again?"

He nodded, then said, "As often as you want."

She squinted and began forming a response.

"As often as you . . . need."

She scoffed, shook her head, and said, "Sure. I, uh, can. I can, you know, meet her again. Like on a Saturday again?"

"Uh-huh. Yep."

She stared as the clock counted out two more.

"I haven't pushed for a wedding date because I knew there'd come a day—"

He gave her hips a sharp pull into him.

She kept staring.

"—when I'd feel compelled to . . ."

Lenore didn't wait for the clock.

"To what? What, Amos?"

"To . . . to plead for you to marry me as soon as possible. Lenore, I have to keep you in my life. I love you—let's get married as soon as we can."

She blinked, then wiped at her eyes, and said, "You're saying this while I'm here, all frumpy for you?"

He shifted her in his hands, bouncing her hips forward. While holding her gaze, he took his time and slipped out every pin and unwound every band from her hair, then let it all cascade down.

"Amos, I—"

"Shh . . ."

Still watching her and not changing his unreadable face, he forced her robe down over one shoulder, then the other. She lay still against the couch cushions as he did the same with the thin straps of her nightgown, and he jerked it down with both hands quickly enough to make her large breasts bounce free.

"Amos, the window . . . the neighbors might—"

"Let them see you. And your breasts. Your incredible, perfect breasts."

He yanked her nightgown down roughly, low enough that he could hold her trim waist with both hands with it out of his way.

With a solid hold on her waist, he shook her just enough to get them swaying while he gazed from one to the other, then up into her eyes.

"No need to hide what you are."

"What I . . . am?"

"You're something that's . . ."

He gave her another gentle shake.

"I'm . . . I really am, um, something that's, um . . ."

"Mm, you sure are."

He used his strong hold on her to pull her into him, repeatedly, steadily, like it would never end.

While she was staring into his eyes, he said, "You're not frumpy, no matter what you wear. No, you're gorgeous. You're so incredible . . . I can't even understand it. My mind—I just can't."

"Oh, Amos. Really?"

"Hot and cold. Same time. *Same* damn time."

"What?"

"I could never explain it."

"But Amos, what do you mean, at the same damn—"

"Shh . . ."

Her eyes were stretching open, and her mouth was opening for a gasp when he leaned in for a kiss, and she didn't close her eyes.

And when he broke the kiss, he leaned himself back, took her robe with both hands, and pulled it closed over her breasts and covered them completely. He then made quick work of tying the belt in a secure knot.

"You can be a modest woman," he said.

She nodded and said, "Amos, yes, and—"

"And a business owner, a professor's wife . . . almost an angel."

"Well, sure but maybe not an angel."

He laughed and said, "Not always, no. Tell me what else you are."

Her eyes got wide, and she said, "Amos? You were . . . when I—"

"Yep. You said it before. Say it again . . . for me."

"Uh, Amos, I don't know. God, this is—you were really—"

"Whisper it in my ear, Lenore. Tell me what you love being, maybe more than anything. Right now, while you're so modest in my arms."

He held her tight, their bodies joined and locked together by his strong hold on her hips. Between them, her breasts were soft mounds which he'd hidden away beneath thick layers of cloth.

"Oh, what the hell," she said with her arms up around his neck. "Okay. I, uh, kind of love, maybe more than anything . . ."

He leaned in closer, his rhythm as steady and reliable as the clock on the wall, and held his ear close to her lips.

"What I also love, Amos, is being a—"

She finished with a whisper in his ear.

A quiet few seconds passed, then he pulled her in more forcefully, laughed softly, then turned just enough to kiss her cheek.

She said, "Do you understand me now, Amos?"

He leaned back enough to look into her eyes.

"No, Lenore. I can't. And I can't help but love you."

Enjoy the Story?

Thank you for reading! If you enjoyed the story, please consider telling the entire world on your social media and, best of all, just talking with friends. You'll be helping your fellow readers to meet Amos and Lenore and helping the author greatly too.

For more about Edward Allen Karr and his books, visit:

www.LakesideLetters.com

About the Author

Edward Sechkar is a writer and producer who resides in Ohio, USA. Under the pseudonym of Edward Allen Karr, he has written more than twenty novels across multiple series and genres. The stories range from middle-grade coming of age (A World So Close series) to books that are best enjoyed by mature readers (Risk and the Killers series; Thrills N Kills in the Hills series).

To see all series and books, visit:
www.LakesideLetters.com

What happens next for Amos and Lenore?

The Frat Chat has come and gone, and Laura, Lenore's look-alike best friend, has been invited to be the star attraction at another kind of party, one much more sinister and demanding.

Lenore, still engaged to Amos, is starving for thrills. When Laura suggests that Lenore take her place at what they call the Frat Chat 2, Lenore is hesitant. But her lusty promiscuity in just interviewing for the event leaves her blackmailed by nearly everyone.

Amos was invited to the same party but not for the same reasons. He's poised for a promotion at the university, and he'll be the guest of honor. With everyone wearing masks, he doesn't know that the beauty there for bawdy fun is Lenore, and she doesn't know that the one she'll be offered to for the grand finale is Amos.

And the intense fire that consumes them both leaves them admitting to themselves what dark hungers they have.

Content Advisory: This book is intended for a mature audience.

www.ingramcontent.com/pod-product-compliance
Lightning Source LLC
Chambersburg PA
CBHW061802190726
48289CB00007B/2040